I0647896

The Spirits' Cabin on Lake Eagle Talon

PAUL ARGENTINI

A Novel

SUNBURY
PRESS

Mechanicsburg, Pennsylvania   USA

Published by Sunbury Press, Inc.
50 West Main Street, Suite A
Mechanicsburg, Pennsylvania 17055

SUNBURY
PRESS

www.sunburypress.com

NOTE: This is a work of fiction. Names, characters, places and incidents are the product of the author's imagination or are used fictitiously, and any resemblance to actual persons, living or dead, business establishments, events or locales is entirely coincidental.

For information about special discounts for bulk purchases, please contact Sunbury Press Orders Dept. at (855) 338-8359 or orders@sunburypress.com.

To request one of our authors for speaking engagements or book signings, please contact Sunbury Press Publicity Dept. at publicity@sunburypress.com.

ISBN: 978-1-62006-435-1 (Trade Paperback)
ISBN: 978-1-62006-436-8 (Mobipocket)
ISBN: 978-1-62006-437-5 (ePub)

FIRST SUNBURY PRESS EDITION: June 2014

Product of the United States of America
0 1 1 2 3 5 8 13 21 34 55

Set in Bookman Old Style
Designed by Lawrence Knorr
Cover by Lawrence Knorr
Edited by Allyson Gard

Continue the Enlightenment!

To ordinary people

who perform

extraordinary deeds.

THE ANIMAL LIFE GUIDE

A Life Animal Guide is also called a Spirit Guide as it remains a part of you throughout life and reflects your inner-spiritual self. You may have more than one Life Guide and new ones may come during an expected time. Usually a Life Guidedoes not move away or disappear but remains an integral part of your life.

Today, as in the old days, Native American Indians give special recognition to the power of the animal spirits. We wear their skins and feathers in ceremony and dance. We paint them on our bodies and carry parts of them in our medicine bags. We paint the animals on our homes and wear animal fetishes.

Manataka American Indian Council
Spirit Guides by Takatoka

The longest poem in **Leaves of Grass,**
is a joyous celebration of the human self:

I think I could turn and live with animals, they are so
placid and self-contain'd;
I stand and look at them long and long.
They do not sweat and whine about their condition;
They do not lie awake in the dark and weep for their sins;
They do not make me sick discussing their duty to God;
Not one is dissatisfied—not one is demented with the
mania of owning things;
Not one kneels to another, nor to his kind that lived
thousands of years ago;
Not one is respectable or industrious over the whole earth.
So they show their relations to me, and I accept them;
They bring me tokens of myself—they evince them plainly
in their possession.
I wonder where they get those tokens:
Did I pass that way huge times ago, and negligently drop
them?
Myself moving forward then and now and forever,
Gathering and showing more always and with velocity,
Infinite and omnigenous, and the like of these among
them;
Not too exclusive toward the reachers of my
remembrancers;
Picking out here one that I love, and now go with him on
brotherly terms.

"Song of Myself," Walt Whitman, *1819-1892*

For Joanne Chicco Maehr-Englehardt

Godchild, First Love

Also by this best-selling author:

<u>Fiction</u>
A Matter of Love In Da Bronx
The Fourth Nail – An Historical Novel
Jim – A War-torn Love Story

<u>Non-Fiction</u>
A Treatise – The Art of Casting A Fly
       Vera C. Argentini – Artist

Elements of Style for Screenwriters
     The Essential Manual for Writers of Screenplays
Random House Bestseller

MUSICALS! Directing School and Community Theatre
Robert Boland and Paul Argentini

<u>Full-length plays</u>
The Decisive Point
The Secret of The Sea Island Mansion
The Essence of Being

King's Mate- Off --Off- Off Broadway Showcase

Massachusetts Artists Foundation
   Playwriting Fellowship

<u>One Act Plays</u>
No Gas For Nick – Berkshire Theatre Festival
Pearl Seed – Berkshire Theatre Festival

My Pen Name's Mark Twain
(written and performed in sixth grade)

Theatre Odyssey 2011 Ten-minute Play Festival
   The Ordinance – First Prize Winner
   Sarasota, Florida

One never feels more alive than when one
is terrified to death.
--Joe Caruso

"Worse things can happen to a person besides death."
– Brad McEvily

"Character is man's repository of courage."
-- PMA

The Mahagawany Cabin Warriors, their Spirits Guides, and
Medals:

Joe Caruso – Silver Fox
Silver Star

Richard Thompson - Otter
Naval Cross

Paul Malloy - Dog
Medal of Honor

Peter Malloy - Raven
Distinguished Service Cross

Gerald Malloy – Owl
Silver Star

Brad McEvily - Wolverine
The Bronze Star

Salvatore Caruso - Squirrel
Distinguished Service Cross

Sven Johnson – Puma
Medal of Honor

PROLOGUE

Eagle Talon's nose was seared with the heated blast of the standing sow's roar. The brave's face stung from bits of rotting flesh and the exploding sticky slop, flecks of her phlegm and bone. His jaw clenched. Instantly his heart beat like a war drum. He could reach out and touch the claw of the sow's outstretched paw. Her teeth were bared from lips to throat.

His Shadow Animal Guide gripped Eagle Talon's young heart. Well-steeped in rules of the spirit world Eagle Talon heard the "CAW!" of his Messenger Guide. Its call was of greatheartedness, which he understood immediately. Then, he could feel inside himself the Shadow Animal Guide. He knew it was powerful, arrived at a stressful time, and presented the truth of fearlessness. It was precisely why his Journey Animal Guide admonished him on the path he was to take. He was to be stalwart. This day, any day was a good day to die, he had been taught by the crow, the fox, and the bobcat. Today's sky this chilly day was covered in dull grey and black fish scale clouds, some roiled into long wisps by the insistent pull and blow of the winds.

Eagle Talon was at the ready to propel his lance. It ran up alongside his arm, the point by his forehead, his thumb aimed at the ground. His hand grew bloodless so tightly he held his weapon. To propel it he would hold it gentler to hold its mark. He had found the thick branch on a lightning-felled tree that ran sweet water in the winter. It was longer than he was with his upraised arm. To make it, he patiently, meticulously scraped it straight and true the roundness of two fingers. He fashioned a flat, long chipping stone into a sharp lance head point the length from the tip of his little finger to the tip of his outstretched thumb. He bound it into a slot with rawhide and held it firm with the black residue of fired birch bark. When it was completed, the medicine man gave him two barred owl feathers to draw sacred spirits to the point of the lance.

Late this day his mother, sister, and he had made camp further up on the slope to the lake. After traveling several sunsets, they were close by their tribe's new campsite. They had fallen behind when Yellow Flower, his sister, had taken sick and could not travel.

They made camp, and walked down to the water to refresh them before the evening meal. In the approaching dusk by the thick water reeds, he now knew his mother, sister and he had inadvertently come between the sow and her cubs.

He heard his mother, Yellow Sun, gasp. It told him she was just behind him, and up toward the left. He also knew by his sister's cry that she also was facing the cubs just beyond her mother.

All three knew the danger was serious and imminent.

Eagle Talon also remembered of the lessons by the warriors around the fire pit. A mother bear is never under any circumstances to be killed. It would also mean the death of her cub or cubs, which was against all the teachings. Nothing was taken or killed unnecessarily. Take only as much as was needed. With the sow, the unspoken admonition was escape with your life, if you are able. With no allowances at all, Eagle Talon not only was to escape the bear, but to save his mother and sister as well.

Eagle Talon saw an escape route.

He could push off in an instant to dive into the water. He could out-swim the sow, if she even thought of abandoning her cubs. He would be safe. The problem remained: His mother and sister.

His Spirit Guide, the crow, landed on his shoulder as it did when he stood before the elders circled around the fire. That was when he had passed fourteen summers and was deemed a maturant, one ready to join the elders at fire. First, a spirit guide was to choose him. That could happen only if he passed the ordeal of the fearless. If he refused to participate in the ordeal or did not pass it he would be cast out of the tribe to live as a maverick. Fearlessness was required of every brave to assure the trust in them in every and any situation. It meant instant willingness to take an arrow for a brother. It also meant putting oneself in between a snarling catamount and a fellow brave. It meant fearlessly walking into the face of death. He could learn this only by passing the ordeal, the greatest provocation of cowardliness.

Eagle Talon's ordeal was that he be taken to the base of the nearby mountain by his father and the medicine man. He wore only a loin cloth and was given a flaming brand and a covered basket. In the basket was a mouse he had trapped in preparation of the ordeal. He was to go up the mountain to the cave of the shaking striker snakes.

He was to return to the camp fire before the embers burned down with a shaker snake in the basket or be found dead in the den.

Eagle Talon was told by his father that he should be cleansed before the ordeal so he could be filled with courage.

He found a brook that ran down the mountain. He would lay in it until his skin wrinkled and his man thing looked more like a woman's from the near freezing water. Then, he would hasten to the cave to learn of what he was made.

Standing in front of the cave he called on his spirit guides. He took the mouse out of the basket and held the short, thin rawhide to which it was tied in his left hand with the much burned down brand, which was best. He knelt down and slid onto his belly. He began the task of slithering into the black hole. Progress was so slow and careful he felt he had stopped breathing. By the time he had travelled twice his height, the brand had burned down to a thin glow. The tether to the mouse jerked spastically. Eagle Talon's eyes bugged to see through the blackness. With every bit of ground he scraped over he could hear the strikers sound faintly at first. Sh-Sh-shika-shika. Soon, it sounded as if he had put his head into a hornet's nest. They knew he was there, but he could not see them or tell where they were.

Shika-shika-shika-shika! Faster and faster they bzzzzzzzt!

He stared so hard the intensity caused him pain. His muscles tensed up from his toes into his sand dry throat.

His stomach seemed knotted and filled with stone. Had he stopped breathing altogether?

He knew the snake's skin colors were yellow and black. It was an excellent camouflage here in the reflected ochre light of the flame. The dot of light shone in the wide darting eyes of the mouse.

A SHIKA! sounded so loudly it seemed to be in his ear! Eagle Talon edged his head sideways until he made out the faint coiled diamonds up on a ledge. He gritted his teeth. He grimaced and strained to contract his lower body muscles. If he released water it would be all over. He knew, especially at the point he was, he had to keep complete control over his body and courage or he would not leave the cave alive. The shaking grew louder but the snake on the ledge was out of reach. Going back to the camp without a Shika!-sounder was out of the question. There was no such thing as an excuse. He swallowed hard to fight back the acrid sensation that kept urging itself up from his throat. He repeated the admonition: Return with a snake or be found dead in the den. If he failed or quit he would diminish his father in the eyes of his brothers, but worse, Eagle Talon could not ever say he was a man. He had seen mavericks spotted from afar that were forced to live alone that drew only contempt from tribe and animals.

Eagle Talon pressed himself forward a bit more. He urged his hands to stop shaking. His knee pressed into something soft, scaly. He froze. He tried to swallow but had no spit. He tried not to think of fangs digging into his skin. He closed his eyes and concentrated on seeing through the blackness. Also, he squeezed them tightly to keep out the salty, burning sweat in which his body was now drenched. He opened them slowly avoiding the glow of the brand. The din of the rattles increased so much so they made the light at the point of the brand in his left hand flicker.

The darting, frenetic movements of the mouse told him the little animal was well aware he was surrounded by a death-dealing enemy.

If the boy dared to guess there had to be as many snakes as a basketful of twigs slithering in the depression ahead of him. It seemed the entire floor of the den was becoming alive, moving, twisting. His breath wheezed when he drew it in sharply as he felt a snake crawl over his legs, first one, and then the other. He knew every moment he remained in the den the danger mounted. It was imperative he be bold and daring. He knew if he lost control of himself he might make it out of the cave with no more than a handful of bites. Then, there in the blackness he saw the reflection of the tip of the brand. It was in the eye of a snake no more than a hand's length in front of his face.

It came to him suddenly that the heat of the brand alerted the snake to the movements of the mouse. The snake, tongue flicking, was intent on the furry, little animal. In the slowest of motions, Eagle Talon moved his right hand up past his face and stopped. He had an instantaneous decision to make. Leaving the den without a snake was no longer an option. And, he had run out of time. For certain the end was near. He could be bitten and die, just like that.

His plan was to grab the snake with his right hand just behind its arrow-shaped head as it struck at the mouse. Then, he would drop the brand, and capture the snake's tail with his left hand to keep it from thrashing about and agitating the entire den. Then, it would be a mere wriggle back out of the den. Minimizing the "mere" chore was his sense of not funny humor to bolster the courage he would need to get out of the den alive.

He knew the key was to have his right hand move faster than a flying arrow. That could happen only when his eyes registered the moment and his hand flew out at the same moment without it being told to do so by Eagle Talon. That is what would make it faster than falling water. He had to have his hand leave him without him knowing it had left him. That fast.

ZZzzzztttttttttttttt!

Grasp!

Eagle Talon felt the jaw up against his fingers. He also knew the fangs had pierced the mouse and had also sliced into the fat of his left thumb. Instinctively he jerked the head backwards. He inhaled sharply as the fangs ripped out his flesh with them. He felt his own teeth bite into his lower lip to quell any sound he might make. The brand dropped between his face and the agitated, teeming snakes. He made his wounded left hand trace the snake's body down to the rattles. He pulled his elbows under his body and used them to urge and hasten himself backwards out of the cave. He put his nose to the ground to keep bites away from his face and eyes.

Standing in front of the cave he felt he had to make a victory yell, but he knew better. The sooner he escaped enemy territory, the better off he would be.

He found the basket, coiled the snake in it, and blindly slammed the cover in place.

A short time later, as the last elder arrived and settled in by the dying embers of the fire circle, the heavy-breathing Eagle Talon held out the covered basket.

The first elder waved to him to put it down. He nodded to the youth and said, *"If there is a rattling snake in the basket, prove it is yours by killing it and your fear before us."*

Eagle Talon put down the basket. He cracked the top for a moment, then reached in to pull out the rattling snake holding it by its head. It wrapped itself around his bloody arm. He held it up and walked slowly around the fire circle until every elder saw and nodded. Had the youth acquired the rattling snake by fraudulent means, he would not have been able to do this.

Shika-Shika, Shika-Shika!

The youth stretched the rattling snake between his hands. Without hesitation he bit it behind its head until he felt bones crunch. He handed the dead, wriggling snake to his father, who handed it to the medicine man. The rattling snake was dropped into the dying embers with the intonation of forgiveness for its ritual death in such a worthy cause.

The medicine man then intoned the spirit guides to the young man who proved him a warrior brave. His chant was what everyone knew: The young brave had chased fear out of his life and would know from thereon only bravery. All at the fire circle knew there are some things in life worse than death.

A crow appeared out of the blackness to land on Eagle Talon's shoulder.

"CAW! CAW! CAW! CAW! CAW!" It screeched the help call.

The lad collapsed on the ground. The medicine man covered him with his shield.

Eagle Talon would survive the rattling snake bite. His Spirit Guide would protect him.

And two winters later, the fearless young man would confront a huge raging sow.

Here by the edge of the lake, Eagle Talon knew he could not give the sow the advantage by trying to slink backwards to direct his mother and sister into the water. If ever he learned one thing from the animals it was that they moved faster than splashing water. He understood at this closeness the sow could tear his belly open before he knew it was done.

The alternatives were several. Eagles Talon dismissed them all but one. He could not allow the sow to get by him and expose his mother and sister to her wrath. He needed to consider a superior maneuver.

It was forbidden to kill her. He had to challenge and distract her to give his mother and sister time to get away.

"Mother! Sister! Go into the water and hide quietly!" he shouted as loudly as he could.

He had never before taken on a bear. The reports of encounters usually bordered on the humorous, which were of no help now.

In the fleeting miniscules of seconds he knew what he had to do. He had to antagonize and draw the raging beast away. He knew the danger. She was much too fast. The threat to her cubs was too gross, too imminent. He had to present himself as a danger to her and her cubs. He did not know exactly how to do this, but he knew a misstep could cost him his life.

His guide spirits had spoken, and he had understood. He would devote himself to the ultimate battle. He would do his duty. Perhaps his spirit guide would protect him and move him through the action safely.

He mustered every call of strength in every sinew asking his guide to direct his action. He leaned backwards the slightest bit and planted his feet. His eyes focused on the sow's rheumy, burning retinas. He knew his action was to provoke her, then run, just as dogs would, to antagonize and worry her. Then again, he would provoke her, and escape. The intent was to draw the sow away from his mother and sister. Once far enough away from them, he would maneuver to save his own life.

He picked a spot right in the middle of her waving paw. It would bring instant pain to the sow. If he went for her neck he knew she would swing both paws, one would deflect the lance, the other could tear at his flesh. Besides, he was much too close to her. He needed room between them to allow him to maneuver.

The sow took in four short breaths. She analyzed them in the back of her throat. There was the stink of man, and man's sweat, and the sweet smell of anxious breathing, but something was missing.

There was no smell of fear.

This was an enemy she had never before encountered. This enemy with no fear would take her cubs. Her enemy would not smell fear from her, either. She must make him motionless, dead.

Eagle Talon quick jabbed his lance point into the right paw and launched himself to her right.

Her injured paw flew around at him. Flying blood spattered his face.

Enraged beyond protecting her young, she roared, mouth open wide, teeth fully bared.

The youth leaped in a semi-circle to the bear's right, again to draw her around, away from his mother and sister. The problem was a straight line dash would have kept him further away from her. He didn't see it coming, but two of her left claws caught a bit of the back of his right arm.

"Yaaawwwww!" he screamed. Now anger directed him to use the lance to puncture her side.

He quick-struck, digging the point into her rib cage. He swung around and used the lance to vault. He propelled himself directly away from her but watching all the while.

The sow came down on four paws, the hair on her hump bristling, her eyes searching him out.

He was covered by a chill. She would pursue him until he was dead. She could out-run him, out-climb him, out-kill him because he was bound not to harm her enough to stop her.

He knew of the Promontory. He looked up to find it. It was directly behind him. His scheme now was to halt the sow. He would provoke her with another jab of the lance to make her turn her back to the mount. As she swung to her left, he would fake a run to her left, then reverse himself and dash for the mount. Once at the top, he would fly off the cliff into the water.

He stopped to face her, lance at the ready.

The sow stopped. She took in the air. She searched hard for the scent of fear. There was none. She rose on her haunches.

Eagle Talon charged. The lance point bit into her left paw. He charged to the right.

The sow swung around to cut him off, but he reversed himself and ran as fast as he could in the opposite direction up the narrow path toward the mount. She landed on her paws, now both of them spurting streams of blood, the cuts sending charges of pain to her body. Her roar was so loud it made her eyes even more bloodshot. The sound echoed over the lake and came back as the rumble of approaching death.

She turned and took off after her enemy. She could no longer see him, but she heard his footsteps slapping the ground and could smell his stinking trail. She was intent on only one thing. The enemy with no smell of fear would not escape her.

The sow mauled Eagle Talon severely, then left. For the bear, her enemy was motionless but did not carry the smell of death. She recalled there was no smell of fear and for that she returned. She again attacked him tearing, clawing, biting in many places.

She was about to return to bring out the smell of death when she heard her cubs. She turned to them. The danger was past.

With the full moon his mother and sister found Eagle Talon. They carried him to the campsite.

He floated in and out of consciousness.

Soaked deerskin covered the slits that opened his belly and ran from one side of his chest down to his hip. Blood dripped into his body cavity. One ear hung nearly torn off where the side of his head had been bitten and chewed by the sow. His left shoulder showed teeth marks where she had bitten through and shaken her adversary that had no fear. Flesh from his buttocks hung in a loose slab.

At first light, his mother sent his sister to the tribe's encampment to bring back the medicine man and elders.

Eagle Talon took his last breath in his father's arms.

The Sachem and Medicine Man agreed as did all the other elders there with them.

This is sacred land made so by the bravest of warriors who died keeping the laws of the Mahawaggany. The Spirit Guides were joyous for Eagle Talon. Of such indomitable intrepidity was their spirit world made.

From thenceforth it would be their tribe's springtime encampment on the shore of the sacred Lake Eagle Talon.

The Aphorisim Of The Cabin

A cabin exists for everyone on earth. It may have a different name, be of a particular style, and occupy a variety of spaces.

Real or imagined, it is created for one purpose and no other.

It is a magic place.

It is the safest, most secure place in the world.

It is impenetrable.

It is indestructible.

It is sancro-sanct.

It is more than a refuge; it is a battlement.

From here we contend.

From here we take and give an accounting of ourselves.

From here we make ourselves whole again so we may rejoin the fray.

This is where each of us stands nude, stripped of the world's accretions, and like it or not know of ourselves the truth.

Here alone our spirits make our stand of life,

Where we learn never to know of any timidity and be forever free and fearless.

PMA

CHAPTER 1

<u>1940</u>

The cabin was first a put-up-in-a-hurry forest lean-to before it started to look like a refuge a desperate hiker would seek out on a rainy, lightning-filled night. Joe Caruso wondered if some long-ago design had him decide to build it unknowingly in front of the site of an ancient Indian ceremonial fire pit complete with mystery and portent. Maddy Malloy had no such doubts. She knew the first time she put foot on the cabin's site alongside Lake Eagle Talon, which was hidden in the lush, rolling Bekshire Hills of western Massachusetts. According to her sensations, its beginnings and construction lay in a design and plan arranged eons before. When Joe asked her how she knew that, she told him by the same knowledge that told her they knew each other in another time. They had only to take care they did not let their attraction to one other displease too much the jealous ancients.

"Do you feel it?"

"What?"

"Shhhh! Shhhh! The sensations. Hold my hand. I'm getting goose bumps."

Joe wrinkled his brow, looked around slowly. "Like we're not alone ... ?"

"Yes. Like I feel sometimes when I'm in church. I get lost and this sensation comes over me."

"Like someone is standing right in front of me, nose to nose."

"Like ... another dimension ... ?"

Joe felt the awe engulf him just as it did the first night he spent in the lean-to. He sat cross-legged Indian style in front of the fire. He stared off to the side. The sight made him blink rapidly and open his eyes widely. A rattlesnake was coiled, its rattle clicking. Shika-shika-shika-shika.

Joe surprised himself. He felt not an iota of fear.

He folded his hands in front of him, and felt compelled to welcome the visitor. He could not speak. He simply nodded his head. It was as if the snake was expected.

Joe had no idea how long the snake was there. He had nodded off, then awoke to find it gone. Joe smiled, stretched out, and went to sleep.

"Maddy, do you feel as if we have been transported to another dimension?"

"Whatever it is, it is so weird. Do you still feel it?"

"Yes! Like it's a shroud covering us with magic spirits ..."

"Like we were meant to discover it so we could be guided ..."

"Yes, to acknowledge all its portents and blessings ..."

"Yes!"

"And tells us to follow the word! It says we are to take off all our clothes ..."

"Crazy shit!" she said to Joe and didn't talk to him for the next three days.

CHAPTER 2

It was more than four years earlier when Maddy exclaimed, "Who is he!" the first time she got a good look at Joe Caruso. He was on the ball field snagging a sizzling grounder as shortstop. For her, even though at the time she had never met him, she agreed with her chums that Joe was the most adorable guy in all J. F. Chicco High School in the town of Catamount. He was just at six feet tall and his thick mop of jet black, wavy hair was often the object of envy in the girl's locker room. His face could have been the model for Michaelangelo's *The David*, which Maddy's art teacher taught her to pronounce Da-veed. He was well built, strong, and—especially playing baseball— moved with the litheness of a cougar. He drew attention whenever he entered a room. Maddy made the pronouncement when she was told his name; "Joe Caruso is someone to fantasize about!"

Her eventual nickname for him was "Joker." That came about when she was in seventh grade history class daydreaming. As girls are wont to do, she was checking out how her married name would look, "Mrs. Joe Car ... ." That was as far as she got when the girl in the seat next to her giggled. Maddy stopped writing.

"Whose Joe Car?" her friend asked.

"No joker, I'll tell you that," Maddy said and the name stuck.

Maddy heard the Joker had a tragic reputation—he was a fly-fisherman.

At 14, for him his first meeting with Madeleine Malloy was a pain-in-the-ass. He couldn't be objective at that time but soon after he became a freshman in high school he noticed her smile was a winner and that the sun brought out a harvest of freckles. She had blue eyes and the pinkish gold hair of her northern Italian mother. She wore it long and loose on her shoulders or in a pony-tail. Joe smiled to himself when his friends would say, "Doesn't Maddy remind you of that movie star ... What's her name?" She was tall, leggy, energetic. She turned down cheerleading to play basketball and soccer. She was so healthy, she skipped the folderol of training bras. Despite her baggy sweaters, Joe noticed her figure. As Man had known through all the ages, there was a price to pay for a special woman, and in Maddy's case he didn't mind at all that she loved to fish, too.

"Who is she?" Joe exclaimed to Brad McEvily as they lounged by a bench in the center of town. Joe had picked her out from across the street walking with her mother. Long before Joe and Maddy had spoken to each other, they were both quite aware the other existed, inevitable in a town so small. Although he had seen her a number of times, she was merely an inhabitant, classification: kid; well, okay, girl. On this particular day, Joe zoned in on Maddy as she strolled from one end to the other of the entire block.

"Stay away, man! That's Maddy Malloy!" Brad answered. "That means poison for you so get your eyes off of her! She's Malloy Corporation property. Her old man's the big cheese."

"And my old man and half the town works for him. So what? I've got to meet her," Joe declared.

"Come on, Joe! You go to the wrong church! You know what that means in this town. Railroad tracks run through it," Brad said. "They're still fighting the Pope in Ireland."

Joe knew all about the factions in town, the majority Protestants, the minority Catholics, and the others, smaller, almost non-existent. The country club voted in its members which effectively allowed only a token few who listened to Rome's voice to be heard in the locker room. The civic groups— Rotary, Chamber of Commerce—were as liberal as the fraternal organizations—Masons, Elks—but none as damnably liberal as the veterans groups—VFW, American Legion. There was no open warfare, but there was the pervasive, insidious scend in the political and social stratas. "My dad is his chief salesman and belongs to the same country club. Does that count?" Joe asked.

"Your dad's a great guy, Joe, and they may walk the same greens, but they'll never share the same tea," Brad said mimicking his father's words and tone. "Maddy's parents watch her like a hawk. At her twelfth birthday party? The girls and the boys both had to wear chastity belts." They both guffawed. "Do you know they have the whole house wired so they can tell when someone in it has an orgasm?" They both cracked up at that. He watched Joe intently. "You can't stop looking at her, can you?"

"Me? Looking at who?" Joe said. "What the hell, Brad, she can't bite!"

"No, maybe she doesn't," Brad answered, "but she has twin brothers, about three years older? They attack together, like quintuplets."

Without taking his eyes off of Maddy's provocative walk, Joe declared, "Brad, I must meet her."

"Forget it! Forget it! Forget it! Man," Brad said. "Maybe someday if you're very, very unlucky."

Joe's luck changed while he was walking back from the park some weeks later. He saw a girl a short distance up the hill from him take a bad spill off of her bike. He had seen the pick-up truck sneak up on her out of the dusk and steer as if to hit her, then at the last second, veer away. It was enough to cause her to swerve, lose her balance, and take a surprise flying lesson. No one else was nearby, but it was pure instinct that made him run to her aid. When he got to the scene huffing and puffing, she was unconscious. Then he recognized her. "It's Maddy Malloy!" he said to himself.

"Boy Howdie!" he shouted as he leaped down the bank toward her crumpled figure. He knew she had taken a bad hit because she was pulled right out of her tennis shoes, her feet bare.

As he disentangled her legs from the mangled bike, he said, "Wow! Kid! You really took quite a tumble!"

She didn't answer.

Maddy's front tire had struck the burm and she took off over the guardrail into the gully by the side of the road. She was lying face down, her arms outstretched. He was embarrassed when he caught himself staring at her lace-edged panties. In a quick move, he pulled down her skirt. "Okay! Kid! No blood or broken bones sticking through so you can get up now and walk it off," he commanded with false bravado mimicking his coach's voice and tone.

There was no response.

Joe, unsure of what he was to do, ran to the top of the hillock to look around. Nothing. Nobody.

He went back to her, leaning close to her face. He noticed the clean, straight lines of her profile. He brushed her hair back. Her eyes were closed, her breathing shallow and heavy. "Musta hit her head," Joe said out loud as if to confirm his own thoughts. "Hey! Kid! Snap out of it!"

No answer. Joe had hoped for a groan, at least.

He blinked his eyes rapidly and wiped his sweaty palms on his jeans. He looked around. He knew. If anyone was to help her, it was up to him. There was no traffic. The way she was breathing troubled him. He had an idea she lived about two blocks away. He could leave her and go for help, but he wasn't sure that was the best thing to do. He decided it was important someone was with her when she woke up. A house was a short ways up the hill. There was no alternative. He had to do what he could to get her there ... in a hurry.

With her dead weight in his arms, Joe grunted and groaned to get up to the road. He was surprised something so limp and squeezable could be such a load.

No more than a quarter of the way there, he gasped and sucked hard for air as he fought for his second wind. He noticed the smell of lilacs about her. The house seemed so far away. He became his own coach, always encouraging a stronger next step.

Several times he prayed she would waken as he shifted her body and stopped to physically reach deep for air to keep going. He also pushed psychologically deep to urge himself forward. He was surprised at her softness and found pleasant the faint fragrance about her. With a final exertion, wheezing loudly, he arrived at the house and lugged her up onto the front porch to put her down on the chaise he found there.

Once he put her down, the relief he felt was enormous. He blew loudly. Joe, one hand on his hip, leaned against the porch column shaking his head. He wiped the wet from his forehead. For a moment on the way up he thought certainly someone would come upon them, or, in the worse, would find them on the road both passed out.

He rang the doorbell. Again. And again. No one answered. He put his ear to the door and listened. Not a footstep. He wondered if perhaps he should leave her and go in search of help. Then, Joe had a better idea. He used his elbow to break the porch window. Inside, he told the telephone operator it was a medical emergency and would she send help immediately.

As he hung up, he was assaulted with the scream, "Burglar! Burglar!"

He turned to see backing out of the room a wild-eyed old lady pointing and shaking both hands at him.

"Burglar! Burglar!" she repeated even louder.

Nonplussed, Joe shook his head and waved his hands signing he meant no harm.

All she saw was the blood running down his shirt from the gash he tore in his forearm from the broken glass, and changed her dialogue to, "Murder! Murder!" She turned to run out of the room.

"What the hell!" he exclaimed as he hastened after her intent on putting her at ease.

She would have none of it, and as ancient as she was, she scampered up the stairs inspired by his pursuit.

Yards ahead of him, she made it to the bathroom locking the door behind her.

He rapped the door. "Oh! Ma'am! I'm sorry!" he started just as the doorbell jangled the air in on-and-off impatient spurts. "Lady! Please listen to me! I needed to use your phone and when you didn't answer your doorbell ..." He stopped knocking. "Look! I'm not going to harm you! Someone is at the door, I'll be right back up!"

Pausing in a futile attempt to stem the flow of blood, he held his arm tightly as he tracked down the steps. When he finally found his way back to the front porch, he saw the girl was gone and an ambulance driving away, lights flashing, siren going.

"Was that really Maddy Malloy?" he wondered.

That's when the patrol car pulled up in front and the officer declambored out.

Simultaneously, Joe heard the upstairs window pulled open. Sticking her head through, the old lady screamed, "Murder! Murder! Help! There's a bloody murderer in my house!"

Like magic, a pistol appeared in the police officer's hand as he charged the porch. Spotting Joe, he pointed both the gun and a finger at him, and commanded, "Turn around! Put both hands above your head and lean on the clapboards!"

Joe's eyes shot wide open. With blood spilling all over the place he was about to protest when he spotted the spittle drooling from the officer's mouth. Joe realized the blood had triggered the cop's murder and mayhem alarm because the cop didn't know if the blood was Joe's or someone else's.

"Do it now!" the officer said unnecessarily. "Do you have an accomplice?"

The handcuffs snapped onto Joe's blood-wet wrists cutting off the circulation. Just then, the old lady appeared on the porch. She warned the cop to be careful. He was dealing with some kind of bad-mean killer monster out to rape lonely old ladies who lived alone and unprotected!

CHAPTER 3

DESPITE the somber dark oak paneling, the district courtroom held a festive air induced by the animated chattering from the clots of people gathered about.

The judge was engaged in repeating a lawyer joke to the clerk that ended, "... so the Devil tells God, 'so sue me! Where are you going to get a lawyer?'" The policeman was describing to the bailiff the not-so-smart citizen who tried to dispose of gunpowder he threw into a lit outdoor fireplace which blackened his face and blew off his eyebrows, and the Carusos added their plaudits as they watched the Malloys with quite some reserve praise Joe now that the truth was known. Peter and Paul Malloy were in a heated discussion with Joe's older brother by four years, Salvatore, about whether they should have a world series with Germany invading Poland and saber rattling in the Orient. The old lady who declaimed *sturm und drang* the confrontation at the house sat in the front row and wore a face that looked as though it lost in a curdling contest, a foil to the platonic festivities.

Joe tried to get with the up-beat schmooz-fest wearing a wan smile that couldn't quite make it through the pall of spending the night in jail. He hated himself for being made to feel like a jerk, but was fair enough not to blame Maddy Malloy for his troubles ... at least, not entirely. He missed his shower, toothbrush, but not the repeating reminder of the stale baloney sandwich for breakfast. Then, the final straw, his brother rattled his chain by calling him "jailbird."

Maddy, unconscious until almost midnight, was unable to confirm Joe's story, which would have allowed him to go free hours earlier. His parents, Antonio and Mary,

responded in a controlled panic immediately to his call
from the police station. Because there was no night court
in Catamount, Pop. 7,500, to free him, Joe's parents
settled by wangling an extra blanket from the guard called
in for the duty. They resigned themselves to the fact that
Joe would not bleed to death and that they would be able
to fetch their ex-con son in the morning. It was his first
offense! What could they do to him?

Her parents, Sean and Dorothea, at first fretted when
Maddy failed to show up for dinner then finally settled on
approximating hysteria when they found out she was in
the hospital. At their first frenetic call, the police knew
exactly whom they were calling about. So, her parents
spent the night alternating between holding Maddy's hand
and sleeping on the couch in the waiting room wondering
what kind of a deranged criminal tried to despoil their
precious child. Gerald had considered contacting a certain
element in south Hartford, Connecticut, who would make
his dreams come true for a mere $400.00 and leave the
creep to be fed Pablum the rest of his life.

When morning came, Maddy was sitting up in the
hospital bed in an effervescent, sparkling mood loving the
solicitous attention, totally unable to remember anything
after the bike's handlebars were wrenched out of her grasp.

Joe who? Did what? She would simply die! No way! And
he spent the night where? Crazy.

"Joe Caruso," the judge said, "no question in my mind
you should have been honored as a hero instead of
spending the night in the hoosegow. Instead, as life gets
screwed up at times we find, you are the victim of royal
purple doings. Now that little homily is to tell you and
everyone here to put this behind you, and get on with your
world. And! speaking of the world, let's hope the war in
Europe stops there, and God Bless America!"

To make sure there were no bad feelings—which was a
lousy thing to harbor in a tiny town anyway—as well as to
make sure no one was going to sue anyone else, the judge
ordered the lot of them to shake hands and make amends
as best as they were inclined to do hoping her order would
deteriorate into bear hugs and consoling back patting and
cheek kissing with and without tears as if a needed

wedding had been announced, finally. What she saw were the Malloys with their noses in the air shaking hands from afar with the Carusos. Joe was totally ignored.

"Okay! Enough of this mushball behavior!" the judge said after several long minutes. "Now, Joe, remember this: Faint heart ne'er won fair maid! So go collect your reward. Clear the court and I order you to all go and cheer up Maddy, the darling party of the first part in all of this!"

Joe held up his arm, in true classroom tradition to be called upon, but he didn't wait to be recognized, "Your honor! If it's all the same, I'd like to get home and into the shower!"

The judge rapped the gavel. "Joe Caruso!" she proclaimed. "I don't know where you were raised, but are you aware you saved that young girl's life? That's what the doctor told me. Your presence of mind, et cetera, et cetera, is what kept her on this planet! And now you want to embarrass her by not allowing her the opportunity to thank you properly? Nonsense! That's not what this world is about. You must give a person chance to get out of a corner. It's just plain decent."

"Your Honor!" Joe exclaimed. "I didn't save her life! And this would be too embarrassing ...!"

Mrs. Malloy stepped before the judge. "If young Caruso would care not to come to the hospital room he doesn't have to, really! I'll convey his message to my daughter," she said.

"You'll do not such thing, Mrs. Malloy!" the judge pronounced. "If I were Maddy, I know what I'd like. So, I recess this court and everyone in it to Maddy Malloy's hospital room! Bailiff! Escort this motley crew!" Whack! She struck the gavel again.

"I really think Maddy should be allowed to recuperate!" Mrs. Malloy said. "Mr. Malloy and I certainly appreciate Joe's actions ..."

"Blah! Blah! Blah!" the judge interrupted. "Mrs. Malloy!" the judge said in somber tones, "you just don't understand what Joe did. Your aristocratic air is going to make me puke. To inch democracy forward, I understand Maddy Malloy graduates from eighth grade next June. By any chance, Mr. and Mrs. Malloy, do you have any idea about how to reward young Mr. Caruso and have your daughter understand the art of appreciation?"

The Malloys looked at one another, and simultaneously shrugged, and said, "Money?" The judge shook her head. They looked at the judge and again raised their shoulders.

"I'll give you a hint: Graduation! Escort?" the judge said.

It took a second for their lights to go on, and together they answered, "Yes! Yes! With the proper chaperone it would be fine!"

"That's it then," the judge said smiling broadly. "What a wonderful idea! Joe Caruso is to be her honor guard and escort her to her graduation, and to her graduation parties. All that time, Mr. and Mrs. Malloy, I want you to tell yourselves, 'She would not be alive to enjoy this ceremony if it were not for Joe Caruso! You have a problem with that, Mr. and Mrs. Malloy?"

Mrs. Malloy nodded, then, when the judge started to raise her gavel, she and her husband answered loudly in unison, "No, your Honor."

"Fine! We're adjourned to Maddy's hospital room!" the judge declared.

"Just one moment! Your honor! If it please the court!" The old lady in the first row jumped to her feet waving her purse above her head as if she needed the added attraction to call attention to herself. "I'm not sitting here in court just to press my drawers!"

"What the hell!" The judge rapped her gavel several times. "Kowalchuk? Is that it? Mrs. Kowalchuk?" The old lady, lips drawn as tight as a violin e-string about to snap, nodded. "Mrs. Kowalchuk, we never intended to neglect you. Now just exactly what is it you want?"

"Yes! The Good Samaritan boy I like, too! He did good! He deserves a medal!" she exclaimed. "But my home looks like by a howitzer was hit!"

"Your Honor," Joe said. "I told Mrs. Kowalchuk I would report to her home and reglaze the window, and clean up my mess and whatever else she said if it took every day after school for a week ... and the weekend!"

"Mrs. Kowalchuk, did this young man offer to do this for you?" the judge inquired.

"Yes, your Honor, that's what he told me he would do," Mrs. Kowalchuk replied.

The judge, with her face screwed up, asked: "Then what's all the fuss, Sadie?"

The old lady answered, "I just want it on the record, Rose! Just for the record!"

Her words signaled the party to move to Maddy's room at the hospital.

CHAPTER 4

It seemed, on cue, everyone including a couple of nurses, orderlies, servers, maintenance workers, court personnel, formed a phalanx from the nurses station, to the doorway, right up to Maddy's bedside. They turned in a body to watch Joe make his entrance. The applause rang through the hallways as Joe's face ran the gamut of colors from a deep crimson, to fluorescent orange, to aubergine.

He stared at the doorway until his father shoved a bouquet of flowers in his hands and gently pushed him toward the patient. That brought out more cheers and applause.

Summoning courage, Joe made his way to Maddy's side. Awkwardly, he held out the flowers towards her, and said, "I'm glad you're okay and didn't die because then I'd still be in jail." A chorus of laughter exploded. "You know what I me-me-mean," Joe stammered.

As if it had been rehearsed for centuries, as smooth as ice sliding over wet ice on a summer's day, her arm went around his neck. She said, "My hero!" She pulled him down to plant a long, hot, wet, gooey kiss on his lips—at least, that's what she dreamed she did later on, but really it was standard fare—a peck on his cheek. She surprised herself. Joe had everything to do to override his autonomic nervous system to keep from whizzing in his pants. He'd rather crawl in a rattlesnake den! She did that! In front of everybody! For him she might as well have stripped him nude. He had never known such embarrassment.

The judge stepped forward clapping her hands, and announced, "From what I see, I can save everyone a lot of time and nonsense if I hitched these two right now!"

Mrs. Malloy's mouth dropped two inches; Mr. Malloy's eyes bugged.

Peter, Paul, Gerard, and Salvatore outdid themselves with catcalls as cheers erupted again echoing down and back the long hallways punctuated with explosive clapping.

Zamboni—as the floor nursing supervisor was called—would have none of it reclaiming her kingdom by spreading her arms, figuratively shoveling out the roomful of people and emptied it in twenty-three seconds. She paused as she pulled the door shut to tell Maddy, "The doctor said you are fit to flee, so you are out of here in eleven seconds, or I'm volunteering you and your sweetheart to the romantic job of emptying bedpans!"

When she closed the door, Maddy looked into Joe's eyes and said, "I understand you didn't want to come up to see me. I didn't mean to cause you another hernia."

"It was no strain, really," Joe said as Maddy snickered. "I'm really glad you're okay."

She grabbed his hand, not exactly as if to shake it, "Thank you."

He patted her hand. "You're welcome."

She squeezed his hand, hard. "I wish you weren't such an itch. I could have a thing for you."

"If you weren't such a snot about all of this it would take an act of Congress to change my feelings about you?" he said.

They both shrugged in fatalistic resignation.

As he opened the door to leave, she said, "Like it or not, see you at my graduation in June."

He grimaced, looked down at the floor, looked up at her and said, "Yeah. Like it not."

Two days later Maddy showed up at Joe's front door.

Answering the bell, he said, "I hope you weren't stupid enough to ride your bike over."

Parrying the shot, she answered, "No, I didn't. My mother's waiting out front." She held out a present wrapped with a ribbon on it. "This is to properly tell you, 'Thank you.'"

"You said it once, that's enough," he said. "Sorry you felt you had to do this."

"I didn't 'have to' do anything, I wanted to. I told my mother the judge said I had to do something for you. Besides, I've always wanted to be able to say to someone, especially you, 'Now that you've saved my life ... '"

"Don't you dare finish that," he commanded, "that's a lot of mushy polenta reserved for pre-adolescent daydreams!"

"That's fine," she said, "as long as you understand to what it refers. See you around ... Joker." Her fingers deliberately slid slowly along the back of his hand as she moved away.

"God! I hope not!" he said, he wasn't going to be responsible for anyone's life just because he happened to be around although whether or not he saved it was questionable. Hesitantly, he unwrapped the gift. It was the most intricate enlarged pen and ink drawing of a bass fly he had ever seen.

He looked up to see her getting into the car. He wondered how soon he'd see her again.

She turned, and, in a manner her mother could not see, waved. She wondered how soon she could manage to see him again.

Joe rubbed the back of his hand.

To him a shell had exploded between his ears as he inhaled phosgene gas. To Maddy, girls, maturing faster, had already felt the dynamics inside herself change.

CHAPTER 5

That weekend Joe almost dropped the replacement pane of glass he was carrying when he found Maddy sitting on Mrs. Kowalchuk's front stoop.

"How did you know I was into fly-fishing?" he asked.

"Your mother. Thank you for sending over the fishing lures. How did you know I liked to fish?" she asked.

"Your mother right after she got through laying a trip on me on how I am now your guardian angel in Catamount. Not any of my choosing, I'll tell you that. Your mother is really afraid of the judge," Joe said.

"Not afraid—terrified," Maddy said. "I used the judge as leverage so I could come here to work."

"If you are here to bug me, please bug off," he said tersely stepping past her, "I've got work to do."

"Me, too," she replied.

"What do you mean?" he asked stopping short.

"None of this mess would have happened if it wasn't for me so I'm doing my share of the cleaning," she said, "I'm not one to leave my mess for someone else to clean up."

"No, you're not. I said I'd take care of it," he announced. "Beat it! Go on home before I tell your mother."

"You don't have to be so mean! Besides, my mother dropped me off here because she thought it's what the judge wanted. If my mother knew you were here, too, she'd chain me to a radiator in the attic," Maddy said. "Nude."

"What does she take me for? Some sick psycho?" Joe asked. "One of us should leave!"

"And besides again, Mrs. Kowalchuck wants me to help her do some cleaning inside while you take care of out here. Just kindly notice all that stuff that spilled out of your veins and made a horrible mess isn't blue, so stop being so conceited and stuck up! I promise I won't attack you."

"Maddy ... !" he started authoritatively in a sing-song voice.

"Maddy yourself, Joker. Just try and stop me!" she said as she stood.

As she marched through the front door, he asked, "What's with the 'joker' business?"

Joe had just finished reglazing the window when Mrs. Kowalchuck came onto the porch and announced lunch was ready in the kitchen.

While Joe and Maddy ate their tuna fish sandwiches in dead silence, Mrs. Kowalchuck went into a litany of the trials and tribulations of widowhood, and worse, no other family member nearby or otherwise. She explained to Joe where her late husband kept all the paints, and went into great detail to explain how meticulous he was in cleaning and storing the brushes.

It didn't take Joe long to figure out what she was leading up to so he was prepared when she said the red stains from his drippings could still be seen and so what? if they were quite faint. He would have to repaint the porch —which needed it to begin with.

For two days in a row, after they left Mrs. Kowalchuck's, Joe and Maddy walked in stony silence almost to her home. He would remain on the sidewalk and watch her until she turned into the walk to her home.

It was on the third day's walk home that the inspiration for the cabin was born.

"Did you notice all the fishing poles on the wall in Mrs. Kowalchuck's study?" Maddy asked Joe.

He wrinkled his brow questioningly, then frowned indicating his interest.

This day, the two of them remained standing on the sidewalk a half block from her home nurturing the germ of an idea about a fisherman's dream cabin on a lake.

In between scrubbing, waxing, and polishing the living room, kitchen, and study floors, Maddy learned a lot about Mrs. Kowalchuk's late husband, most of it more than she wanted to know. But, it was while the two of them cleaning out the china and kitchen closets and washed every glass and plate and knickknack and bric-a-brac that Maddy garnered the most wonderful piece of news.

"Joe! Mrs. Kowalchuk owns an awful lot—no pun intended—of land on Lake Eagle Talon. Her husband was going to develop the land out there," Maddy said. "I got a real strong idea that she may be ready to sell after paying taxes on it all these years."

Then, Maddy drove the barb home when she asked, "Wouldn't you like to have a fishing cabin right on a lake?" Thus, subtly, deeply, permanently, the hook was set.

That was all the forward motion on the matter for almost nine months because right after they had satisfied the work that needed to be done at Mrs. Kowalchuk's, Peter and Paul stopped Joe walking home from school.

"Do you plan on seeing Maddy anymore?" Peter said nonchalantly edging in on Joe's left side.

"Course, we're not talking about the judge's orders," Paul said closing off the right side. "Don't think for a second all the Malloys are not grateful for what you did, but it doesn't automatically make you boyfriend material, if you understand what we're saying."

"You're not telling me ..." Joe started.

Peter put the palm of his hand before Joe's face to interrupt him. "We're not discussing anything, Joe; we just want to pass on an understanding. Our father and mother will see that you get a nice cash scholarship whenever you graduate high school to show the family's appreciation depending on your interpretation of our message: Stay away from Maddy. Find someone else. We will re-interpret that for you, if you wish."

"I hope you capeesh," Paul said. "Maddy hated private school so much she promised to eat spinach three times a day to be allowed home. She can be gone out of sight for six years, and she'll hate you if you make that happen to her."

"Or, maybe you want references?" Peter said. "In fact, you may know the fellow in town that has the St. Louis Slugger label imprinted on his ass from our last conversation with him?"

As Paul turned to leave, Peter lashed out, his knuckles digging into Joe's midsection making him blow. "Next time

I'll have to go with you to the hospital to have my first taken out of your ribs! Period! End of conversation," Peter said as he turned to catch up to his brother.

The following day, Joe slipped onto Maddy's bus standing at the rear until she came aboard and caught his eyes. They sat together, tucked away in the corner.

Maddy grabbed Joe's hand. "I know what you're going to say. Joe? Don't let them send me away! My mother went to parochial private school, so she knew. Those sisters are demons from hell. They make life so awfully miserable."

"They can't do that, Maddy!" Joe said.

"Yes, they can. My mother said if she hears we've so much as spoken to each other, unless we go through her— you know, the judge—she will ship me off."

"We'll just play it extra cool, like we are today," Joe said. "We'll find a way."

"We'll just stay away from each other. That's it." Maddy squeezed his hand with both of hers. "Too many people in the town owe their jobs to my father, including yours. He'll send him packing, Joe, I know that. You can't do that to your family. "

"Maddy, that's wrong! We're not out to do something wrong to each other!" Joe strained to keep his voice low.

"My stop is coming up," Maddy said. "We're just going to freeze it between us, Joe! Do you hear me? Don't even think of any notes. Let's wait for my graduation. Okay?"

As she got up to leave the bus, Joe buried his face in his hands.

Joe and Maddy did not seek out each other. Whenever they met or saw one other they exchanged friendly greetings—Joe shy, Maddy reserved. If they stopped to speak to each other, it was in an awkward moment and manner, both unsure of what direction to take, and always very, very brief.

It was just before Christmas, as if through some pre-arrangement, Joe saw Maddy enter a clothing store in the center of town. He waited a few minutes, then used the second entrance. He walked directly by Maddy without saying a word, but touched her lightly, and walked into one of the dressing rooms. Casually, Maddy took a skirt from a rack and went to the back of the store to enter the same dressing room.

Maddy scrunched her head down between her shoulders, a sign of her daring-do. She kissed him quickly. "You've got ten seconds ..."

"Maddy, Boyhowdie! do I like the way you kiss. I bought you a Christmas present. Just so you'll know, it's a brand-new, state-of-the-art spinning reel and rod. It's the newest thing," Joe told her. "It's called spin casting. You're not supposed to be plagued with birds' nests in your reel. I got you a Mitchell reel; they said it's the best. I really was going to get you a real-pardon the pun—fishing outfit, like a fly-casting outfit, but ..."

"You were curious about how this one worked?" she said.

He nodded. How did she know him so well? he wondered. "One day I'll have a cabin by the lake, you know I will. I'll bring the rod and reel there for you, whenever ..."

"Joe, you're so thoughtful. Thank you. I'll think of my beautiful present Christmas morning. And I have a present for you, another pen-and-ink. This one of a trout fly."

"They are so beautiful," he said. "You are an excellent artist."

"Just don't think exchanging Christmas presents changes anything," she declared. "We still have to be very careful. I love to draw. For a while I thought I would become a musician, a flautist—that's a fancy word for a flute player. My parents take me to Tanglewood in the summer. But, I've decided I'm going to be an artist. I've never done flies before. I usually do flowers. I love flowers," she said. "I can't wait for spring when my mom gets her flower garden going. Irises are my favorite, for painting, too. And you? What are you interested in doing?"

"First, I'm going to try to find a way to earn a living fly-fishing. Then, I like to work with my hands, I like to work with wood. But, I have to earn a living so I'm thinking I should become a professional designer of furniture. I don't know ..."

There was a loud rap on the door. "Miss? Do you need any help?" the store clerk asked.

Maddy's mouth dropped open. "This skirt is too big," she said opening the door and handing it out. "Could you bring me the next smaller size?" Maddy watched through the crack in the door as the clerk turned to go down the aisle. She looked hard into Joe's eyes for an instant, kissed him full and hard on the lips, then pushed him out the door.

When Maddy left the store, the clerk picked up the phone and made a call. "Mrs. Malloy? This is Frannie at the Clothes Place ... Maddy was in here for twenty minutes or so, alone. She bought a skirt. She just left.... . No, I didn't see her speak with anyone at all. You're welcome." When she hung up, she said out loud to herself, "See you in church."

Early that spring, Joe took Maddy's advice. He had approached Mrs. Kowalchuk about buying some of the land by the lake.

At first Mrs. Kowalchuk was adamant about not selling a single bit of it. Then, she softened somewhat when he explained he didn't want to exploit the property; he just wanted a place to build a fishing cabin he had always dreamed about.

"Just like my late husband," she said.

An impasse almost presented itself when it came to the price.

Because her husband had already laid out the parcels, she was able to show Joe the plat, and asked him—just offhand—which he would choose.

Although his eye was untrained, Joe was able to judge by Mr. Kowalchuk's notes and design the choice lot, which also happened to be the smallest and was the one he had reserved for himself. It was on the southeast end of the lake which meant it would have sun for a good part of the day. It included a small rise and was secluded. Her husband had put no price on that piece. Mrs. Kowalchuk had an idea of its worth, but said she would have it professionally appraised and then decide whether or not to sell it to Joe.

When Joe returned to learn the price he was dismayed. He had some money saved up, but he couldn't earn what he additionally needed if he worked all summer. To him

$1500 represented all the money in Fort Knox and for him it was just as accessible. This was something he wanted to do all by himself. He was not going to ask his parents for a loan.

When he told Maddy, she provided a new inspiration. "Mrs. Kowalchuk was talking about getting her house painted. It will cost more to do that than what she is asking for the land, so why don't you try to work out a deal with her?"

Maddy was surprised—delightfully so—and shocked that he kissed her on the cheek when the idea finally penetrated Joe's mind. Her thoughts went wild with that one when she tried to go to sleep that night.

Mrs. Kowalchuk was of the old school that believed land was more valuable than gold, but she was nobody's fool and knew a fantastic deal when it presented itself.

In exchange for the parcel of land on the lake which she had pretty much decided to sell to Joe anyway, Joe would paint the entire outside of her house and garage.

Joe was ecstatic. He knew Mrs. Kowalchuk was getting the best part of the bargain, but, really, it was the only possible way in the world he could get the land independently so it was worth it.

What Joe did not know was that when Mrs. Kowalchuk expressed some resistance about making the deal, Maddy offered to sweeten the deal by spending a half-day a week that summer cleaning Mrs. Kowalchuk's house. The two agreed to keep it their secret.

So, for the summer, every stroke of the paint brush for Joe, and every room dusted for Maddy, was done with the vision of the cabin on the lake becoming a reality.

"How's it going?" Maddy asked Joe mid-way through the summer. "Seems you're pushing onto nine days a week."

"Yeah ..." he said. "I'm not a pro so I don't know a lot of the tricks, but I'm learning. I just had no idea the scraping, scraping, scraping would take so damn long."

"What do you do when you're not doing this?" she asked. "I don't see you around."

"I'm fishing," he said.

"Why don't you take me?" she asked.

He looked at her sideways for a long time. "Because fishing is sacred, that's why."

Because Joe was a minor, the ownership of the property was transferred to Joe's father in mid-August.

Joe told Maddy he was going to inspect the parcel the following weekend.

Joe rode his bike to the lake. Maddy, earlier, had taken the bus and waited for him to arrive He was surprised but not unhappy to see her. Joe felt quite indebted to Maddy for her part in getting the land.

"Does your mother know you came out?" Joe asked.

"She warned me that you are a smitten fellow," Maddy answered. "She made me promise if you so much as cast a covetous grin at me. She really doesn't trust you."

"Do you trust me?" Joe said smiling.

"I could say I do, but ..." smiling wickedly, "... I guess I'll just have to prove it."

Joe took Maddy's hand as they started through the woodland. Neither one noticed because it seemed the casual, natural thing to do. She didn't pay any attention to it until Joe squeezed her hand tightly to help her over a fallen tree, then across a spring, and again up a gully. She liked the attachment so when he turned and caught her smiling at him, he glanced at their hands, raised his eyebrows and admitted to himself that he, too, didn't mind this indication of being an attentive escort if not of affection.

Almost forty minutes later they emerged into full sun at the edge of Lake Eagle Talon.

The lake was larger than either one of them imagined it would be. Joe estimated it to be a mile to the other side. They spotted only a few cottages which were mainly hidden. To the left he noticed how close they were to The Promontory, a cliff-like massive that rose a hundred feet and had the last horse chestnut tree at its erete that hung over the water. Actually, the lake seemed deserted.

Maddy turned and walked up the top of the rise.

"Where you going?" Joe called out. He ran to catch up to her.

Her face screwed up, and she put a hand on his shoulder. "I know there's a word for it, but I can't remember it. It's when you get this prickly sensation all over your body that gives you this silent message? Do you know what I'm talking about? Have you ever had it?" Joe shrugged. She started walking around as if she were looking for something in particular. "There's something spooky getting to me, Joe. It's just a feeling. Very strange. As if there are ghosts and figures sitting and standing around watching us. I think they want to make sure we don't upset this area. I feel it here, right here where I'm standing, the strongest. Mark the spot, Joe, mark the spot."

"You've got to be joking," Joe said despite the fact he picked up a fairly large stone and put it where she had been standing.

"Don't you believe me?" she asked.

"You bet I do," he answered surprise registering on his face. He nodded several times. "Put your hand on this rock. It was cool when I picked it up. Feel it."

Maddy kneeled to put her hand on the stone. Her head jerked forward as she looked intently into Joe's eyes. "It feels as if it's getting warmer!"

Joe nodded. He put his hand on top of hers. "Is there any doubt now this is our spot?" They stood, holding each other's hands, which formed a circle above the stone. "I don't know what this means, Maddy. It's beyond me. I've got to tell you, I care for you. Does everyone go through this ... ?"

"I don't know," she answered. "I care for you, Joe. This is something either very good or very bad. For the moment, we won't make anything of it at all, okay?"

"Okay," he said as he turned her to walk down to the water.

From where they were standing, the grading sloped down gently to the water forming a small, natural beach. To one side were huge, flat boulders that slipped out into the water that looked like beached whales. There was a slight breeze, which caused a rhythmic lapping sound as the wavelets rose and fell against the rocks.

Standing on the wide flat of the biggest rock looking out over the water, Joe was mesmerized. He remained motionless, hand on hips, feeling the heat of the sun, taking in the wonderland before him and thinking of what just happened with the rock.

His reverie was snapped when he heard the heavy splash beside him. Maddy had dived into the water.

She swam out a short distance, turned on her back, and waved at him. "Come on!"

"Are you kidding?" he shouted back. From what he saw, she was nude.

"Oh! Don't be an old poop! I've seen my brothers, and studied photos of The Da-veed! You know!" She turned swimming out, her little bottom breaking the surface.

Joe caught up to her. "You're some kind of crazy kid, you know that?" he asked.

"Yes, I know!" she said.

"You trust me," he said nodding for emphasis.

"I told you I had to prove it. Here we are. We trust each other," she said. "Come closer ..." she bubbled with her chin into the water as she took a mouthful. When he drew close, she squirted him. He ducked for a mouthful. Instantly, she moved to shallower water, her back to him. She swung her arm backward to splash him. He returned the favor, and soon they turned the water into a froth amid their yelping and laughing. In the action, he drew up alongside her. She turned, looked into his eyes, put her arms around his neck and kissed him full on the lips just as she did in her daydreams.

He started to protest, then felt her body make full contact with his. Smoke ran through his veins when he felt her nipples hard and erect scorching his body, her boobs squishy and soft. Automatically he put his arms around her and drew her close to feel every curve, bump, and hollow. Internal tidal waves rocked him. Then, electric currents zapped him from head to toe. His groin felt clamped in a vice.

Then, in an instant, it was over.

Joe turned; dug in and kicked hard to swim out full bore several dozen yards until he ran out of breath. He dove under water to explode out from near where they had been standing.

Maddy had climbed up on the flat of the rock and stretched out on her back in the sun.

"Do you know I can still smell your perfume?" he said, "but not lilac."

"Tres Jolie!" she said. "It's my favorite."

As if they had been following the routine for years Joe, dripping, moved up beside her and sat, scanning her closely.

"You're not shy?" he asked.

"Not with you," she said, "but Joe! Stop staring at me! You'll change the moment."

"I can't help it," he said, "You've got some beautiful pair of boobs."

"You're not shy?" she asked.

"I am really, but I have to meet your challenge," he said. "You know, it's a guy thing." This was something totally new for him. He couldn't help taking her in again. "You have a beautiful body."

"Thanks," she said, then impishly, "As compared to what?"

"To what I've seen in magazines," he answered cooly. "Yours, though, is like ... it's like it's just budding."

"What do you mean? Is that an insult?" she asked.

"No, not at all. Innocence is wonderful, you know? You're, well, you're only a kid, you know? You just have fuzz and your boobs are full, tight, nicely curved, not big, chesty, saggy ones like in the photos. And, you're innocent, as innocent as tomorrow morning's sunrise."

"Yeah! You talk like you're Casanova, don't you wish? You know what I wish?" she asked.

"Tell me," he said.

"I wish we get to see a lot of sunrises here on this lake, that's what," she said.

"You know what my brother, Sal says?" Joe looked at her hard sideways, "He's says he's going to steal you from me."

"What did you say?" she asked.

"That we got along but we weren't going steady, or anything like that," Joe said turning his head so she wouldn't see his face. "Sal and I are brothers but we're not close, you know? He goes his way, I go mine. He hangs out with an older crowd. You know what, Maddy? I have to tell you ..." he started.

"You mean, we're engaged?" she gushed teasingly, semi-seriously.

"Stop with the wedding march music, will you? You're embarrassing me! I've got the same excited, new feeling in me, too. Let's enjoy it!" he said. "I want you to know that I told my father this parcel will be in his name until I reach my majority, and after that, it will be in your name and mine. I feel you own half of this. You can bring anyone you want here to see as many sunrises as you'd like."

"I can't do that, Joe!" Maddy said.

"Of course you can!" Joe said.

"No, not that. I can't accept this from you. I've seen how hard you've worked, how badly you want to own this," she said. "I just can't."

"You've got nothing to say about it," Joe said. "Half of this is yours."

"Well, I give it back to you!" she said as she sat up quickly and reached to put on her clothes. "Don't you understand it makes no difference whose name is on the deed? We, you and I, are meant to be together. No! I'll say it differently, we are destined to be together! How do you like that?"

"Destined! You mean like we're meant to be together forever? And we have nothing to say about it?" he asked.

She looked at him through slits and grinned, then said, "Well, at least until prom nite."

"You don't know what you're talking about," he answered.

"I can prove it!" she declared. "How come we're not fooling around? You know! Anyone else would be making out like crazy. We're secluded. We're nude. I know you're hiding your erection. We like each other. What's stopping ... us?"

"Because you're the sister I could never have! That's why!" he said.

Her leg raised, her shorts mid-way up, she stopped, now her turn to stare at him sideways.

"Oh! For God's sakes!" he said as he, too, yanked on his clothes. "I am supposed to be your 'protector!' I told you that! At least that's the trip your mother laid on me at the hospital! You know? Like I'm the one to make sure no harm comes to you! I can't be grabbing any cheap feels on you after that! And, for what? For the rest of your life? Does that put our relationship on a super-high plane, out of reach of mere mortals, or what?"

"If that really-oh, truly-oh is true, what a relief!" she exclaimed.

"What do you mean?" He looked at her sideways until he guessed the thought. "Jesus! Maddy! What a friend you are! I am not queer!" He was relieved at the thought that when they had kissed in the water she had no inkling of his erection which felt so big it was ready to burst.

"I know that! For a second there, I thought your whatsis was broken not your brain," she said. "And you are right. Our relationship is on a different level, it is special. Sal and anyone else would find out pretty fast just how special. We respect each other, who and what we are, that's the reason we can do what we do, the reason we trust each other."

"Blah! Blah! Blah!" he repeated. "Maybe you just don't turn me on? Did you ever think of that?"

"Yeah?" she challenged. "The words 'statutory rape' aren't exactly an aphrodisiac!"

That made both of them laugh. It gave Joe pause to think about a lot of things concerning Maddy.

As they started out, they simultaneously put their hands on the rock. It was cool to the touch. They both raised their eyebrows questioningly.

"Joe?" Maddy asked. "I do, too, turn you on. I feel you deep in my heart. I love you."

Joe blinked his eyes rapidly. "I would be lying if I didn't say I feel exactly the same for you. I care about you so much. I stay awake at night remembering how I found you, how you scrunch up your cheeks when you laugh, the way you walk, how you smell, the touch of you as I carried you in my arms. I'm warned all the time it can never be for the two of us. Brad McEvily tells me all the time. Your parents have let me know for sure. So have your brothers."

"And you worry about what they say? They threaten you?" she asked.

"They don't faze me in the least. My concern is you. I don't want you to pay for something over which I have no control." He turned her face so he could look straight into her eyes. "I wish I were wise enough to know exactly what to do."

"At this moment," she said, "you'd have to be a real cidrule not to know to do this ..." Maddy put her arms around his neck to kiss him softly, warmly, for a long, long time. "Joe, I will love you until the day I die, I swear by this stone."

"My turn now," Joe said. His arms wrapped around her waist. He pulled her close. He kissed her exactly as she had kissed him, but for a bit longer. "Maddy, I will love you until the day I die, I swear by this stone."

They did not hold hands on the way out to the road.

The following weekend, Joe's father dropped him alone off at the lake with his fishing gear, sleeping bag, sandwiches, cans of pork and beans, canteen, and a trimming saw. Joe slowly hiked his land through the virgin forest taking in the lay of the land, the trees, and saplings until he got to the water.

Joe spent the morning searching out the metes and bounds of his land. When he returned to the hill overlooking the water. With the stone Maddy and he had placed as the center, he pushed four sticks into the earth and only moved them five different times to mark the four corners of just about the size and where he would construct the cabin. He walked far enough away so he could hold up his arms in front of him and gauge how the cabin would sit. Then, holding his arms in the same manner, turned to see how it would take in the vista to the water. To him it seemed a perfect fit. He did not know it at that moment, but he had put the cabin squarely in front of an ancient Indian circular fire pit which was directly before the stone.

It took until a bit after lunch to erect a fairly creditable and large lean-to, which he read about in the library books away from the location marked for the cabin but facing the lake. He lugged rocks and stones to build a firewall in front of the open side of the lean-to, which would reflect the heat of the fire into the structure.

That left him just enough time to string-up his rod and go after the bespeckled trout. This was serious fishing for supper, so Joe thought long and hard about what fly to use. He nodded in agreement with his choice and tied on his favorite—a ratty, worn, No. 20 gold hook black gnat wet fly. Standing offshore in his sneakers and jeans with the water just above his knees, he brought in two trout for dinner in two casts. He shook his head and stared across the lake for a long time at his unbelievable luck—not just the fish, but that he was the owner of the most gorgeous piece of property in the world. His entries into his fishing diary which he started some four years earlier were the proudest he had ever made.

He speared the trout with willow branches and worked them on a spit over the fire. The glow he felt inside was not from the heat of the fire. It was the calm. A pervading inner peace. He likened it to the purring of his soul. Not religious to any extent, he merely accepted the fact that he was in harmony with the universe.

It felt as if he had an audience. Then, he looked around, toward the water.

And there it was. Perhaps some twenty feet away, sitting upright on its haunches, its eyes boring in on his. It was not very big and blended in with the fading light. A fox. It was a silver fox with almost white-bright tips on its ears and the end of its tail, which was wrapped around its paws.

Joe had no idea how long the animal was watching him. It was plain unusual. A wild animal staring at a human? Something was going on. Joe realized the smell of the cooking trout may have attracted the gorgeous fox. Joe was mesmerized. A first experience. His thought: Was something expected of him? Yes. Of course there was.

Joe took one of the trout off the fire. Slowly he stood up. With his eyes averted, Joe slip-walked toward the fox. He kept his eyes downward. He caught the animal in his peripheral vision. The animal didn't move. When he had reached half the distance, Joe stopped, pushed the fish off the stick with his knife onto the ground. He nodded to the fox, as if it could understand his semaphore. Joe turned his back to the fox and returned to the fire, knelt and continued to cook his trout.

When he dared, he looked up. He found the fox standing up, staring at him, the fish in its mouth. It turned and pranced away, its tail straight up as a beacon.

Joe wished he knew more about such lore. He was aware that at one time the Mahegan and Stockbridge Indian Tribes lived nearby. The Mahegan Big Tent was on the Housatonic River in the center of Catamount. He would ask Maddy about all this Native American doings.

Would the fox visit again? Would there be other visitors?

After supper, sitting cross-legged before the fire, he instinctively froze holding a stick in the fire. The rattlesnake moved slowly under the stick. Mesmerized, Joe watched the snake draw up as if taking in the heat of the fire. Joe thought his heart had stopped but felt the bass drum in his chest marking time. The snake remained stock still for a total of 275 beats. Then, it moved off and disappeared. Joe wondered from where the serenity he felt descended upon him. Then, he knew, he really didn't care to know. It didn't matter.

He thought about the cabin location as he snuggled into his sleeping bag. It took a while to fall asleep. In his mind, in the far distance, he could hear the rhythmic beat of a drum accompanied by chants. Almost immediately he awoke to look at his wrist watch to find it was three hours later. Something woke him up. He got up on an elbow to stare into the darkness beyond the dying embers of the fire. He knew an animal was checking out his camp. He squinted and picked out the yellow slanted eyes moving just beyond the fire stones. It was a cat—but not quite. Joe watched it slink and sniff. What type of wild cat was it? It had a very distinct look. Its ears were pointed. The animal was black in color. At the end of each ear was a tuft of black hair. It had a short, stubby tail and long fur. Joe opened his eyes as wide as they would go. It was a lynx! He has seen photos, but it was unbelievable that one was no more than three feet away from him. Its wide-padded paw came toward Joe, but stopped in mid-air. The animal looked directly into Joe's eyes. The staring contest lasted for many moments. Unperturbed, the lynx sniffed around for just a bit more then disappeared into the blackness.

"Wow!" Joe thought, "I built my cabin in the midst of a zoo!"

Trying to get back to sleep, he thought of the location. How lucky they had come upon the fire pit. It was squarely in front of where the cabin would be built, directly under the rock Maddy and he had found, touched, and felt it warm. It was a canoe length in front of where the front porch would be. Perfect.

He decided to explore the area in front of the lean-to strictly from instinct. He ranged out from the Maddy stone. He became suspicious when the sharpened stick hit a rock. He moved over a bit, and hit another. When he struck a fourth rock he knew he had come upon something special: they were all the same distance from the rock in the center. Using the stick, he marked a circle. Digging at the periphery, he discovered the buried rocks formed a perfect circle. A chill slipped down his back. He wasn't sure what he had come upon, but he knew he had to be careful not to disturb some primal sacred soil.

He sat on the rock, his elbow on his knee, his head in his hand, as if to increase the power of his thoughts. Immediately, he knew three things. One, he would not disturb the circle by putting anything close to the fire circle. Two, whether or not this was a true mystical spot, he would accept it as such and believe it so; and only he and Maddy would know of it. Three, the rocks were not down very deep which meant he would not have to search very far to find conclusive evidence it was a fire pit. Within a foot of the surface, Joe brought up a chunk of charcoal.

Joe smoothed out the area. He moved the center stone so he could bury the charcoal under it.

He knew he had done the right and proper thing with the fire pit as he had with the bass he released. He needed no further confirmation about the solid foundation he felt in his soul concerning the meaning of the cabin in his life.

That night, there was mysterious affirmation as he slept in the lean-to. He awoke before sunrise to the smell of smoke. He rose on one elbow and looked about. Nothing. He sat up to look around the fire stones. A curl of smoke rose from the center fire pit. A circle of ghostly figures walked around the smoke in a slow, measured cadence.

Joe rubbed his eyes. Thick fog filled the distance. The figures held out their hands, palm downwards, cutting the line of smoke. One by one the figures turned away and floated toward the lake. The vision disappeared.

Joe got up. He walked directly to the fire pit. It was covered with dew laden grass. He leaned down to touch the stone. It was warmer than he ever remembered it to be. Only the shifting fog remained.

When he awoke in the morning, curious about the trout in the lake, he tied on a Parmachene Belle; a fly he considered couldn't catch a fish if it had an explosive tip. He was surprised when it brought in a trout much too big for breakfast. Then, experimenting with different types and sizes of flies, he caught and released five good-sized trout and one largemouth bass before he kept a small trout to satisfy his hunger. He spent the rest of the morning clearing out the space he had staked out. After lunch, he brought in a few more boulders for the wall; repaired a weak spot on the lean-to; and fell into a deep, happy snooze on dappled sunlit boughs. The activity, the location, the lean-to brought tranquility to his soul as he had never known before. He did not understand what was happening, mainly embracing the sensation of extreme, utter delight. To him, at that moment, it seemed the entire peoples of the world searched for such peace in any form. How lucky for him, he thought, that the entire universe's secrets—all the solar systems imaginable—were concentrated in his single being doing this singular, simple act of cognition.

When he awoke, he knew he had instinctively had done the right thing for his soul in acquiring the land. He was one of the luckiest kids in the world. He had found a refuge he would use for the rest of his life, he just knew it. He realized how vital it was to have such a spot, needed, as he once read, "to retreat from the trials and tribulations of the vagaries and vicissitudes of life." With exactly the same understanding, he realized it would be valueless to have this precious spot just for his own unless he could share it.

Joe gathered firewood, stacked it inside the lean-to for next time, packed his gear. He stood in front of the firewall and scoured the woods. Not a sign of the silver-tipped fox.

He touched their stone, and hiked out to meet his father
for his ride to his other home.

CHAPTER 6

JOE ACCEPTED Maddy's challenge a week later to teach her to fly-fish in fifteen minutes. When Maddy called, Joe asked her to come over to Brad's home where they could use the lawn for her first lesson.

"If you do this," Joe said, "I will let you in on the most fascinating secret in the world about my last stay at the cabin."

"Okay, I'm going to do this. Tell me now."

"Sacred secret. Can't."

"Boyhowdie! You're a bum!"

"Boyhowdie! You still don't know. Do this first."

"Are you serious?" Maddy challenged. "Fly-casting looks so difficult. I've seen the beautiful, long, looping casts you've made, and just as well the mess of coils others have made!" They were standing on the back lawn of Brad's home.

"That's fifteen minutes of hands-on instruction, which comes right after I explain a few simple principles involved," Joe said.

He spoke as he put his fly rod sections together.

In bait casting, he explained, the weight of the lure is used to take out a very light line which is used to bring back the lure or take in a fish. In fly-fishing, the weight of the line is used to take out an almost weightless lure, called a fly. The practical difference is that the energy used to cast a bait is similar to receiving a message in a letter—it is there all at once. The energy is all put in the lure. In fly-fishing, the energy is delivered a bit at a time much the same as receiving a message that must travel a phone line. Here, the energy travels the fly rod, and then along the length of the line. Technically, it was called kinetic impulse. Controlling the energy imparted in both types of fishing—which travels from the fisherman's hand to the rod to the line—is vital to the distance covered and the accuracy of the cast. When the energy runs out in the bait casting lure it falls, and in fly-casting the line collapses.

Using just the rod, Joe tied to the end a piece of white ribbon that was a half-inch wide and was just as long at his nine-foot bass rod. "Now, to learn to fly-cast," Joe said professorially, "one must watch the procedure, then do the procedure, finally, teach the procedure. Got it?" Maddy nodded. "So! We're going to make the ribbon fly—maybe that's where they got the term 'fly-fishing'—first in circles ..." Joe took the rod by its handle and spun the ribbon in circles, first slowly, the faster. "... and now in back and forth straight lines. Notice I've got my elbow close to my body. I saw a contraption they used to teach fly-fishing that tied the elbow to the body and made the arm move in an awkward, jerky manner. Then, just like using stairs with expensive oriental carpeting, the rule is go up the right side, and go down the left to keep the wear even. In this case, we go forward with the rod close to our ear, and bring it back a little further to the right so the rod and the ribbon do not crash. Now, I'll write your name ..." Joe spelled out Maddy in the air with the ribbon. Then, he spelled out "Joe," and finally wrote "fly-fishing."

"Hey! That looks like fun! When is it my turn?" Maddy asked.

"Now," Joe said as he handed her the pole. "Remember that as the tip of the rod goes, so goes the line."

Maddy made circles, then straight lines. With Joe's hand on top of hers, he guided her to make circles in front, and suggested she try making some on the sides, and finally to spell out her name. She ended by "air-writing" the word, "Neat!"

"The next step," Joe said, "is for you to teach me how to do that as if I've never done that before in my life."

Maddy knit her eyebrows and stared at him. "But there's nothing to teach!"

"That's what I've been trying to tell you about fly-fishing," Joe said, "it's easy. Now, here's the next exercise." Joe took the pole and made the ribbon sail back and forth in a straight line. "This is to show the importance of timing." Joe explained that until there was a "feel" for the line where it would be controlled by experience, the line had to be watched to understand when its direction was to be changed. Pointing to the ribbon, he slowed down his swing and showed where the end of the ribbon collapsed and fell before the rod went forward and again imparted energy to it. He brought the ribbon to a regular back and forth rhythm and indicated the loop that formed at the end of the line and how the correct timing brought it nicely into the reverse direction. Suddenly, before the loop had straightened out, Joe snapped the rod forward. The ribbon cracked like a whip.

"I have just broken the sound barrier!" Joe declared. "The speed with which the end of the ribbon was made to travel was faster than the speed of sound and we created a mini-sonic boom!" He handed her the rod and asked her to make the ribbon crack. As she got warmed up he reminded her to watch the ribbon go back and forth. The purpose of learning how to make the ribbon snap was because it was one of the things that should not be done with a fly on the end of the line because the snap would break it off.

"I can't do it!" Maddy complained.

"The ribbon won't snap if it's on a plane, a straight line. It must have the loop to speed around to break the sound barrier," Joe explained. This time he pointed to the ribbon and showed her where the ribbon formed a loop and was still loaded with energy and about to straighten out. "Now!" he shouted. "It's a matter of knowing your reaction time when to change direction." He did that several times until Maddy could see the point just before the loop straightened out at which point she should bring the rod forward sharply.

With the first snap, she screamed, "I did it! I did it!" It took several more attempts before she repeated it. Gradually she caught the technique, making the ribbon crack several times in a row.

"Now, teach me," Joe said.

Maddy was pleasantly surprised to find she could identify the spot on the uncurling ribbon when Joe should snap the rod forward.

Joe took off the ribbon from the rod, and strung it with a fly line with a hookless fly on the end. He stripped off fifteen feet of line and cast it on the lawn straight in front of him. "This is going to be a one-handed cast because I'm going to capture the line coming off of the reel under my hand on the handle so no line will go out. Got it?" Maddy nodded. He made her stand to one side so she could watch him sideways. With a quick upward stroke he pulled the line off the grass, had it fly up, "Remember to watch it!" he cautioned, then he pulled the rod forward and let the line land in front of him again. He did that several times. "Your turn," he said and reminded her to keep her elbow in.

Maddy took the rod and made a half-dozen casts. "When do we get to the hard stuff?" she asked. Handing the rod to Joe, she mimicked him, "Try to keep your elbow in and your eye on the line ..." Joe deliberately pulled the rod forward too late. "No! No!" Maddy said. "Watch the loop, and just before it all straightens out, cast forward!"

Joe looked at her feigning a slack jaw.

"Let's get with it, Joker," she said, "your fifteen minutes are fast running out!"

"OK," Joe said. "What we were just doing is called the 'back cast.' When you were making the back cast, where were you trying to put the line? Point the direction for me."

Maddy stared at him sideways suspecting a trick. She turned around and pointed behind her.

"That's where the line may go, but in your mind, you should try to throw the line directly over your head!" Joe made the tip of the rod follow a straight line up arcing near the top of the throw sending the line sailing upwards and floating behind him. "If you think you have to throw the line behind you, you will automatically make the tip of the rod form an arc from the ground to the end of the cast. Instead, try to throw the tip of the rod directly above your head. What that does is make the back cast float high above the ground behind you which is critical. If the line is not up high on the back cast, it may start to collapse and several things may happen. It can hit the ground behind you. It will loose the energy quickly and not even open the loop. You can have the line drop, and tie what is called a 'wind knot' in your line." Joe showed her how to combine throwing the line high to the rear, then instead of letting the line land in front, he cautioned Maddy to watch the front cast and to make the back cast just before the frontwards loop opened up. He explained keeping the line in the air is called "false casting." The three main purposes of false casting, Joe explained, was to dry off the dry fly so it will float on the surface of the water; to take in or to let out line, or to both dry the fly and alter the length of the line and to change the direction of the fly to land at another area.

Joe was delighted to hear Maddy sound like a drill sergeant as he deliberately fouled up his casting so she would correct him. Her hand-eye coordination was impeccable so she picked up the technique of fly-casting very quickly.

"Okay! No more fooling around," Joe said, "we've got three minutes left and I've got to show you the two-handed fling!" Stand on the fly line just where it's touching the ground, he instructed. He asked Maddy to tell him what happened when he suddenly raised the rod as if he were trying to lift the line from the water.

"The line stayed where it was, but the rod bent way over into an arc!" Maddy said.

"Beautiful! You get a gold star!" Joe said. There are two principles at work. The first is the weight of the line on the water. That must be overcome. In addition, there is the cohesive force of the water on any object laying on the surface of the water. If you could lay a needle down gently enough, it would float on the surface because of cohesion. To quickly overcome weight, cohesion and gravity of the line laying on the water, we use the two-handed cast. It takes some coordination, but you know you've got it when you do it! "Here's how," Joe explained.

As the right hand pulls back the rod to life the line, the left hand reaches up as far as it can to grab the fly line and yank it down to help snap the line free of the cohesion and give it an added impetus to get into the air.

It took more than three minutes for Maddy to coordinate the pull-yank of the two-handed cast, but with her first successful cast she let out a scream of joy!

"I did it! I did it!" she shouted.

Joe beamed from ear to ear.

"What are you smiling about?" Maddy asked.

Joe looked at her benignly and said, "What do you know? I've got a fishing buddy!"

The smile on Maddy's face slowly disappeared as Joe spoke about various other casts, such as the roll cast; the various knots one needed to know to attach flies and lines; how to mend a line; and how to avoid wind knots.

"Class is over." Maddy said. "Now tell me the secret."

"What secret? Oh! It's not much." Maddy stared him down. "I had two visitors at the cabin."

"What?"

"I was alone. It was a vision. Beautiful. Just gorgeous."

"A girl?"

"Yes, I think. Douse the fire in your eyes. It could have been a vixen, but a little bulkier. More like a reynard. It was grey, silver tipped ears and tail. So special."

"I've never seen a fox in all the years I've lived here."

"Wait'll you meet this one. It ... it didn't seem real. You know?"

"Ethereal?"

"Yeah. Ethereal. Ghost like. But this ghost can eat a fish."

"What about the second visitor?"

"Actually, I don't think you want to know about it."

"Not fair! You come right out with it!"

"A rattlesnake."

CHAPTER 7

GRADUATION. The word conjured many things in Joe's mind, but one event more than any other. It happened to be his own graduation from eighth grade and his best friend's celebration party.

It was in Brad McEvily's back yard thrown by his parents. Almost the whole graduating class was there, including Mr. Thompson, their home room teacher.

Mr. McEvily pretty much cleared out the floor of their barn, strung lights, installed a speaker and turntable, fixed up a dance floor, and strung crepe paper from pole to pole to make it look like an arbor. Because he liked to be thought of as a progressive, Mr. McEvily had set up a keg of beer in the darker corners of the barn, as if it would make it more acceptable to anyone who disapproved in the slightest, like his wife. What the hell! He wanted to be in on this innocent "rite of passage" compared to his own when Uncle Lenny took him to Hudson, New York, for his first visit to a whorehouse. He also learned the town originated the term "red-light district" because establishments lit a red light on the porch when they were open for business.

Mrs. McEvily had come up with tons of sandwiches, cakes, pies, sodas, and had a wild array of games to be played. She prudishly asked her husband to remove the ladder to the hay mow. Instead, trusting soul that he was, he put up a small sign that read, "Hay Mow off-limits," with an arrow pointing upwards. The blizzard of hay falling on the dancers was the clue that the sign wasn't working.

Early in the evening, Joe was attracted to the joyful voices of the male chorus of the Chug-a-lug society. He followed the throbbing beat to the far, dim corner of the barn where stood the beer keg. Curious as ever and always, Joe moved through the ring of merry-makers to the inner circle. He watched as a pitcher was filled with beer. "What's happening?" he asked. All eyes focused on him.

The lad holding the pitcher said, "Congratulations! On your graduation!" and handed him the full pitcher of beer. The initiators told Joe they would first sing to honor him, and then, on command, he was to chug-a-lug the beer.

Joey smiled broadly, and was much pleased to be selected so quickly. He felt honored.

So, they sang:

> Here's to Joey,
> He's true blue,
> He's a drunkard through and through,
> So, set them up high,
> Celebrate the day,
> If you don't go to heaven
> You go the other way!
> So ... .
> Drink! Chug-a-lug! Chug-a-lug! Chug-a-lug! ...

When the chorus commanded, "Chug-a-lug!" and so long as there was beer in the pitcher, the honoree continued to drink. In this case, it was Joey who guzzled and guzzled with abandon and joy.

Joey was such a good sport about downing his first pitcher of beer, that the meanest cabal of fourteen-year-olders macho peer-grouped him into two more in the space of a half-hour.

It did not take much to be notorious in a small town. Joe had held his own at long-distance peeing. Less than twenty-minutes after his last swallow from the third pitcher, he set a remarkable record of seven feet, three inches with regurgitated hops and malts. The record stands in Berkshire County to this day. The amazing projection, however, to this day is beyond Joe's recollection.

What Joey remembered of graduation then was throwing up his guts for the next thirty-three days whenever he took anything by mouth stronger than ginger ale.

He was reminded of graduation every time he passed a bar and got a whiff of its stale aromas which gave him the onset of what he called false, wrenching labor puke spasms.

Maddy's graduation, though, was something completely different. It sent the chills right through him when he thought of the three big events going for her. The major excitement was brought on by the gift he bought for her. Second, the judge who had made it possible for him to be her date for the graduation party which was to be held at her best friend's house. And, third, they would both be going to the same high school in the fall.

He had no reservation about going into his cabin savings to buy her a present. Besides, from the past September to this early spring, progress on the cabin did not depend on available funds. Most all of it was grunt work, clearing the line of the road to the cabin from the blacktop. For that, he marked the easiest path around large pine trees and skirted outcrops. It was going to be just plain, difficult physical labor. The pleasantest chore, he decided, was to clear the area he designated for the lay of the cabin. He had put a lot of time and thought into the plans. He made drawings upon drawings, and sketches of every sort and description. He borrowed and studied books from the library and spoke about the cabin with anyone who not only would listen but who offered a viewpoint or was interested enough to make any kind of a suggestion. The shop teacher had taken a sabbatical to build and live in a cabin in the wilds of New Brunswick, Canada. He spoke as if he were the original Dan'l Boone. Besides, he had a lot of advice but none of it structural. His strongest recommendation was for Joe to lay in a huge store of canned foods. For his stay in the wild, the teacher had planned to live off the land. The one moose and the deer he shot did not feed him for long. The wild animals in the area of his camp fell in love with the teacher as a bountiful provider. When it came to preserving his catch, the teacher proved to be as smart as a fallen log. It was just ten days after the shop teacher got there, in his haste to return to civilization, he left behind a ton of equipment he had portaged in by one day trips. According to the inventory the teacher let Joe scan, there were two expensive rifles, two axes, complete fly-fishing equipment, cookware, a one-man two-handed saw, and among many other items, provocatively two dozen Shiek condoms. The teacher left it all, traveling only with the first snowflakes and an empty, growling stomach. He considered himself fortunate to be alive. The teacher asked to see Joe's intended cabin, but Joe put him off. The cabin was his thing, and it was staying that way. The graduation present he bought Maddy would delay only slightly his timetable. He used the money to buy her a brand-new flute. It came as an easy decision. That was when he made another important decision about the cabin: It would go easier if he had help.

His brother first mentioned the idea. Salvatore liked the thought and offered to lend a hand. Joe said he would think about it until he mentioned it to Brad. Joe was astounded by his enthusiasm, and even more so when he mentioned all the volunteers.

He was invited to and attended Maddy's graduation concert performed by students. She had a solo part, and she was rewarded with an overly-long applause. He was struck by how professional her demeanor and how beautifully she produced the notes with nary a clinker as several of the other students produced with accompanying unintentional snickers in the audience. Joe several days later could still hum a few bars of Maddy's music although he couldn't remember the name of the piece. The fact was that Maddy, as almost all the students, rented their instruments. Parents didn't want to make a huge investment only to learn a short time later they would pay their child not to practice the instrument at home. For them, rental was the wise way to go.

Joe knew Maddy could be as fine an artist as anyone in the world; but he was absolutely positive she was just as much born to play the flute. So, he bought her one. He was determined she should have one available to her for the rest of her life even if she never played it again. He brought it to her when he arrived at her home to escort her to her graduation party. He was there at the judge's order, and took advantage of the situation. What could her parents say? He would rely on the authority of the judge! Joe was

nonchalant, pretending to study the binding of some books
as she unwrapped it. He wanted to catch her reaction, so
he cast glances at her quite often. By her shaking, he knew
she had guessed by the case what it was, but it wasn't
until she opened it that her eyes and mouth opened wide.
She stared at the instrument for the longest moment,
looked at Joe, then ran out of the room with it.

"Mom! Look at what Joe ..." she started.

It took at least a half-hour for Maddy to stop crying,
and get her face back to some semblance of normalcy.

Her mother was stone-faced. Her father dug his hands
deep into his pockets and walked in and out of the room.

When Joe thought it was the right moment, he
explained to her parents, "I knew you would buy her one
because she is a gifted musician, but it was something I
felt I needed to do to show my gratitude not just to Maddy,
but to the Malloy family. I hope you will kindly allow her to
accept the gift. I know it will please the judge." Invoking
that theme would stand him in good stead he knew.

Mrs. Malloy stared at her husband. He stared back. He
shrugged, threw his hands in the air, and walked out of
the room. Mrs. Malloy moved her lips back and forth
rapidly as if she were trying to kiss a hot iron. Finally,
resigned, she said, "The judge would approve."

Maddy with Joe as her escort were invited to a
graduation party at Mary McBride's, her friend's home. It
promised to be exciting and fun-filled. Joe and Maddy were
greeted as if they were a royal couple. The party seemed to
move up a notch with their arrival. The laughter and
chatter went up a few decibels and what residue there was
of party-shyness evaporated. With the boys wearing suit
coats and ties, and the girls in flouncy party dresses, it was
the unofficial indoctrination into adulthood, so the attempt
at a degree of sophistication pervaded the air. There was
talk of running over the New York border where the
drinking age was lower with the accompanying initiation of
sitting in a bar and ordering something as daring as a rum
and coke. It was all talk. They knew of no one who had a
car or a driver's license, and this type of excursion didn't
start until high school.

To assure the success of the party, Mrs. Malloy at random would grab a boy and a girl, escort them to the dance area, make them face each other, and get them started on a zombie two-step. Joe was pretty good at evading Mrs. Malloy but eventually was nabbed and matched with a girl named Serena. He felt awkward at first even though they were moving together pretty smoothly. Then he almost lost it when she kept jamming her boobs into his chest. His eyes popped open when it first happened. The next time, he glanced at her. She looked into his eyes and broke into a smile that indicated mischief. It would have bordered on wickedness if she knew what she was doing besides sending the message: "I've got tits." It seemed from thereon she was determined to give him a full body-to-body massage but only because that was how her girlfriend had to guide her around the floor as she was hurriedly taught to dance. Joe thought it was quite enjoyable, until he suddenly was aware she had stirred in him something deeper. His mind was set to go into shock. Praying he was fast enough, he pushed himself away from her. That's when he heard: "Here's to Maddy, She's true blue ..."

He left Serena with her smile sluicing off her face, and headed for the chorus circle.

Maddy, beaming proudly, stood in the center holding a pitcher of beer.

... She's a drunkard through and through ...

Joe pushed his way through the choristers to Maddy's side. He covered her hand holding the pitcher, and his other at its bottom. He said, "This should wait for some other time..."

... So set them up high
Celebrate the day ...

Maddy turned to look at him, the smile turning into a frown. "What are you doing?" she asked.

"I don't think this is such a good idea, Maddy," he said.

"No!" she replied tugging at the pitcher, her anger flaring. "You don't own me!"

"You let it go, Maddy," he said calmly. "It doesn't prove a thing. Take my word for it."

"I don't need or want a baby-sitter!" she exclaimed fire dancing in her eyes.

If you don't ... go ... to heaven ... .

The songsters eating up the drama unfolding.

"You came with me, Maddy," he said. "I should take you home."

"Well don't you worry about that!" she said. "I'll find my own way home."

"You are right; you are your own boss," Joe said turning away, cutting through the crowd.

For five seconds there was dead air. Then:

Here's to Maddy
She's true blue!
She's a drunkard through and through ...

Joe, shaking his head, walked outside and stood by the garage looking up at the sky shaking his head. He shrugged several times. Then, he spotted the basketball, and the hoop hanging over the garage doors. He started shooting baskets, moving further and further away from the hoop, and moving around in a semi-circle. Ordinarily, he was the world's worst free-shot but this night he was rarely missing.

Less than an hour later, Serena ran up to him. "Joe? Your date has really been partying."

"Are you talking about Maddy?" Joe asked. "She kind of 'undated' me."

"I'm not here to make myself available, Joe," she said, "whatever you think."

"No, of course not, Serena," Joe said. "Everyone has a good time at a party."

"Shooting baskets?" she stared at him. "I'm here to tell you I don't think Maddy is used to drinking beer. She was in the house, on the way to the upstairs john when she upchucked from one end of the living room carpet to the other. Mrs. McBride's with her in an upstairs bedroom."

"Thanks, for coming to tell me, Serena," Joe said. "I owe you."

Joe walked into the house and the smell of vomit. Without thinking twice, he took off his jacket, found the bucket, mop, dustpan, and cleaning rags. He steeled himself to the smell, and went into the living room. Maddy had left a pretty good trail. He opened all the windows and doors. Joe used the dustpan to pick up as much of the slop as he could and put it in the bucket, then emptied that in the downstairs john. All the while he fought to keep his heaving stomach under control. Finally, on his hands and knees, he used a damp hand towel to really clean up the carpet. He used the vacuum cleaner to get it as dry as he could. Finally, he found a deodorant spray in the laundry room and applied it in strategic spots.

Joe had just put away the last of the cleaning materials when Mrs. McBride came downstairs. She stared at the carpet, her brow furrowed.

Joe walked up to her. "It was just a spot or two, here and there, cleaned up in a jiffy," he told her. "How is Maddy?"

"I think I should drive her home," Mrs. McBride said.

"I'll go up and get her, and meet you by the car in front," Joe said.

Maddy could barely make the stairs at her home, and with Mrs. McBride leading the way, Joe picked her up in a now familiar way, carried her through the doors held open by Mrs. McBride and Mrs. Malloy. Before Mrs. Malloy could say a word, Mrs. McBride announced, "Maddy got a little sick on some beer!"

The words stopped the panic registering on Mrs. Malloy's face. She nodded rapidly. "This way!" she ordered, and headed up the stairs to Maddy's bedroom, Mrs. McBride following.

Joe returned to the front door alone, where he confronted Mr. Malloy.

"What the hell did you do to my daughter?" he asked.

"I didn't see her drink anything, Mr. Malloy. I wasn't with her all the time at the party, but it seems she got sick on beer," Joe said.

"Thank you for bringing her home, Joe," Mr. Malloy said. "I want to make this very clear. I don't expect to see you with Maddy ever again. Is that understood?"

"Goodnight, Mr. Malloy," Joe said as he walked through the door.

Mrs. McBride called out as she came down the stairs, "I'll drive you home, Joe!"

"Thanks, Mrs. McBride," he said. He explained he'd rather walk and keep the good company of the stars.

The next day, Joe went to Maddy's house to drop off a six pack of Budweiser. He rang the bell, put the beer by the door, and left. The note on it read: "I'm sure you'll appreciate some hair of the dog that bit you."

Joe and Maddy didn't talk to each other face to face for two weeks thereafter. Then, they passed one another in the lobby of the Capitol Theatre, he with Brad en route the balcony, she with Mary to the orchestra. Maddy's eyes flared, Joe nodded as they said "Hi!" to each other.

Ten minutes into the feature film, as if by some spacial sensory pre-arrangement, Joe and Maddy met by the candy counter. It was a matter-of-fact that they expected each other.

"Is this strange?" Joe asked.

Instantly she said, "No."

"Let's go take a walk," Joe said. He held the door open and led the way out.

They went a short distance without speaking, the air between them thick. They took turns sneaking glances at each other. In an unguarded moment, the back of their hands brushed together. Each reacted as if it were an electric shock and they widened their gap. It was not a challenge to see who would be the first to speak, but rather they each were searching for the exact words for an opening phrase.

Finally, Maddy: "You've been avoiding me. Long time."

"Not really," Joe said. "I've been chasing tail and, you know, going crazy..."

"The cabin? Fishing?" she asked. "Or does 'chasing tail' mean someone else but not over me?"

"Yeah! Work and ... I'm seeing someone else."

"You what? Do you want me to have you talk to my brothers? Do I know her?" she asked.

"Look! I'm just playing the field," he said. "You should, too."

"Why?" she asked him firmly.

"Because I can't, you know, fool around with you!" he answered. "On a date I like to swap spits and get a feel, and give and get hickeys, and sometimes she gives my hard-on a grab. It's something new. It's growing up. I like it. It's a lot of fun."

"You can do that with me," Maddy replied.

"Are you crazy? No, I can't," he said. "Your brothers would kill me, and I'd hate to think of what your mother would do."

"But if I say it's okay, it should be okay," she said.

"I just can't do that kind of stuff with you," he answered.

"Just forget it's me!" she said. "Did you ever think I'm curious about that kind of stuff, too. Hey! I never grabbed anyone's hard-on, and I'd do that with you if I had to do it with anyone. I'd want it to be you?"

He looked at her for a long moment. "It never occurred to me that you'd ..." They walked a half-dozen steps. He stopped. She turned to face him. "I can't use you like that. Look! I'm more interested in the stuff I'm doing than the person I'm doing it with. Can you understand that? I care too much for you. Maddy? When I told you I loved you, I wasn't playing. I meant it. I mean what I'm saying now. There will be plenty of time for each other."

"You're being a goody-goody. Too bad!" she said.

"Wrong! and you know it. Kissing you, you know, like when we were at the lake, is okay. I-I mean, it's great and that's fine. But, feeling you up and touching you in crazy places just makes it all seem so ... cheap," Joe said. "I think the word I'm looking for is 'demeaning.' It makes me think I'm treating you like a half-a-pound of ground round at the meat market, making you something less than you are. Like, what kind of a girl allows herself to be mauled and poked in her crotch just because some guy is curious? The girls want me to do that and what the hell, I like fun as much as the next guy ..."

"You're not the only one in the world who likes that," she said. She started walking and he caught up. "I like all that romancy stuff, not the stupid kissing games they play at graduation parties ..." She paused realizing she had just stepped on a very sore area. "Some of my girl friends say they get into some real heavy stuff. I mean, like heavy! They grope and stuff and they make the guy go crazy. They say oral sex is not sex. They like it and want to know what it's all about, too."

"And you're not?" Joe asked.

"Of course I am! I told you! Maybe even more than anyone else. Mom talks about this hot Italian blood," she said looking directly into his eyes. "But I can wait for you."

"Oh! No you don't!" He stopped, spread his hands and pushed down as if he were holding down a board. "I don't want that responsibility."

"Say you don't like me?" Her walk turned to a swagger.

"I already told you I did."

"Tell me again."

"I not only like you, there's something special between us."

"I know. I love you, too. So? What's the problem?"

"I'm not the smartest guy in the world, Maddy," he said. They were standing semi-obscured facing each other, she with her hands on her hips, he with his arms folded tightly over his chest. "I know this. We have only one chance at this life, at this time, at this moment. When it's gone it's gone. It's not first grade where we're allowed to erase and start over. If we miss a chance to learn what other people our age are like, we may regret it forever. I don't want you and me to end up a statistic: 'Well! Did you hear? Maddy and Joe had one of those starter marriages!' When and if I ask you to marry me it will be because I'll know where I'm at. I'll mean it, and mean it with all my heart and soul. I'll be yours forever. When I say it, consider it done. My word is my bond. I'm not going to waste my time trying this type of girl and that type of lady or who knows what kind of woman! I want life to be fair with us, Maddy, I don't want to stack the odds against either one of us, or both of us. If I sound definite it's because I am. I've thought about it a long time. One of the major considerations? Your mother and father. I don't want them to think any less of their daughter because she likes someone on the unapproved list …"

"Don't pay any attention to that!" she said. "They love me! They'll come around!"

"How about them expecting you to come around? People have been going to war over religion for centuries. You and I are not going to stop it. Let's just cool it until the future is a little less foggy."

His posture relaxed. His arms fell to his sides. Maddy looked up and down the street, folded her arms tightly over her chest, and let her foot swing on her heel.

She said: "What the hell do I know, Joe? I'm only a kid. Yeah, what the hell do I know? Do you know the twins, both of them, Peter and Paul, are talking about enlisting in the navy or something so they won't get drafted into the Army? What the hell's going on? They're just kids and they're volunteering to get their heads blown off!"

"My brother, Sal, same thing. He says he's bored hanging around. He doesn't want to go to college no matter what Pop says. He wants to put on a uniform, play grown up, and drink beer Saturday night, and fool around with the girls. He and his friends talk about it as if they're going to do kindergarten all over again. They think the soldiers they see using crutches with their pant legs pinned up lost their legs in the sandbox stepping on pee-pee!"

"You may have been right at the party, but you let me have my head. I guess we all have to learn about this world," Maddy said. "I guess you and I have to trust each other's judgement. If by putting me off you expect me to become an emotional teen-ager right before your eyes, it's not going to happen. I'm not going to go all weepy on you. Jeez! You should see some of my girl friends go through a box of tissues! Look! The way I see it, one way or another we're going to be in each other's lives no matter what pronouncement you make."

"If you say so, that's it."

"Until something better comes along then, we're going to look out for each other," Maddy said. "You should know a couple things. Everyone at home blames you for what I did at the McBrides' party. Look out for Peter and Paul. They may come looking for you."

Holding up a hand and wagging it, he added, "No problem. Thanks." He reached over, grabbed her by the shoulders, and pulled her towards him. He stared into her eyes for a long moment, then kissed her full and long on the lips. Their lips parted. Joe said, "I love you, Maddy, I love you with my whole heart and soul and being. I love you."

"I love you, too, Joe, you are my whole and entire world. Don't let anything happen to you," she said. She kissed him hard.

She tilted her chin high, a smirk on her face. She patted him on the chest. "Now tell me it isn't as good as you get?"

The tears started rolling down her cheeks. "I need something to make your essence mine. So I can dream and remember. It won't take anything away from us. We love each other. What's so wrong?"

"Let me go, Maddy. You're going to drive me crazy." He grabbed her and kissed her gently with all the sweetness he could muster. "I love you, Maddy. I always will."

"Don't run away, Joe. I'm sorry I cried. I want what I want. I didn't see it your way at all." She walked up behind him, put her arms around him, her cheek against his back. "You are an honorable man. I am proud of you for that. We're in a room with no exit and a stupid clock. We'll just have to wait."

Joe turned to face her. He held her. "It's okay. Now, we have an understanding, right?" he asked. He anticipated her lifting her chin, wetting her lips, opening them a bit, as he drew close, "There was something else?"

"Yes. We had a serious dinner meeting about a week ago," Maddy said.

"Oh! Oh!" Joe answered understanding completely what she meant.

Dennis Malloy accepted no excuses for everyone not being present at the dinner table. He grew up in a family where communication was treated as a disease. As a result, the family was fractured because of misunderstandings, wrong assumptions, and bad guesswork. Dinnertime for Mr. Malloy meant learning the art of conversation, worldly enlightenment, and problem solving on any level.

On this particular night, on the agenda was Mrs. Malloy's concern about her daughter and a guy named Joe. She couldn't come right out and say Maddy and Joe were seeing each other, but her mother's heart was telling her trouble was a-brewing. She insisted it be stopped before it began. She had no reports from anyone in town that Maddy and Joe were seen together, but that didn't mean a thing. She asked Peter and Paul directly if they had ever seen or heard of their sister being seen with Joe.

Peter said: "Come on, Mom, I'm not going to rat on my sister! That doesn't mean I know anything, just that I'm not going to rat on my sister!"

Paul said: "Neither will I, but just to close it down, no! I haven't seen or heard anything about the two of them being together."

Peter said: "It's no big deal!"

Paul said: "It's not like the wedding march is in the air! Ask Maddy! It may be just an infatuation! Maybe not."

Mrs. Malloy said: "Is that so? I read where it costs parents a quarter of a million dollars—a quarter of a million!—to raise a child and put that child through college. If anyone at this table thinks we're going to put that kind of money into any one of you, and then have an infatuation trash it all and throw all the work, and time, and love, and expense on the garbage dump, then we have raised a bunch of idiots! For that kind of time and attention we expect, we demand a return on our investment! We do not expect to be embarrassed by whatever mangy creature any one of you may drag into our family! I won't have it!"

Mr. Malloy said: "What your mother so eloquently expresses is that a purebred bitch that is bred by a cur no longer has any purebred standing ever! Ever! Let me assure you, we are not snobs, but we do have standards. If there's one thing the Malloy's have, it's pride! Yes, pride! I will disown any one of the three of you that brings home an anchor for a spouse. The world is tough and difficult enough without our emotions enduring such a trying situation."

Peter said: "Dad, people have no control over their emotions! If they fall in love, they fall in love! Who's to judge right or wrong? Is it better then to live without that love, or without your parents?

Mrs. Malloy said: "Don't even insinuate ..."

Mr. Malloy said, interrupting: "No! Let me answer! These family council dinner meetings are the bond that keeps this family together. We can say anything and everything we feel is important. We air our concerns. We educate, we teach, we learn, not just parents to children, but children to parents. That's been our strength and value. In all this time, we have never had need for an expletive ... until tonight. You are never to introduce into this family anyone who is not equal to the level of this family, in education, intelligence, finances, social standing. If any of the three of you just think of bringing anyone here of another race, religion, or color, my word to you is very plain: Don't the hell do it. Almost every woman marries below her class, except your mother, of course. Don't you do it either! Bring home a hippie, a motorcyclist, a pansie, a layabout, I'll disown you before you hit the sidewalk."

The five of them could hear only their own breathing for several minutes, a jumble of thoughts ricocheting through their minds.

Finally, Mrs. Malloy said: "What your father wants you to understand is that you should stop anything of that sort before it begins. In Peter and Paul's case it will be Harvard or Yale or Princeton where meeting the right people is a priority. For Maddy, it means camp through the summer, and private school thereafter."

Maddy said: "I won't go!"

Mrs. Malloy said: "You'll do as you are told."

"Maddy said: "No, I won't. I'll run away first."

Mr. Malloy said: "Listen to your mother, Maddy, she knows best!"

Maddy said: "No! She doesn't know best! Why should I be punished because I'm born into this snob, racist family with all these rules and regulations? No matter what you both think, I'm just a usual and ordinary person! There's nothing special about me! I don't belong to a "class." I don't wear a halo around my head! I just want to be with my friends, and have a good time. You two picked Catamount to live in, I didn't! And a person by the name of Joe and his family, whose father works for you, also happens to live in this town, and I've got to pay a penalty for that? That's both insane and irrational!"

Paul said: "Does Joe have a sister? ... Sorry. I was trying to be funny."

Maddy said: "Another point! When I'm of age, won't I have the right to marry whomsoever I please? Rich, poor; black, white; smart, dumb! It won't be my choice about whomsoever I fall in love with!"

Mrs. Malloy said: "Men don't have a choice! Women do! Men have needs: a mate, a house manager, a cook, a hostess whether he lives in a trailer or the Taj Mahal. In return, a woman makes a determined choice of only two things: Does she want his children and his status?"

Maddy said: "I don't believe love can be so calculated."

Mrs. Malloy said: "It may not be the first time, but it always is the second time."

Maddy said: "I would think you'd rather share my true happiness with someone I love rather than anyone with financial and social standing!"

Mr. Malloy said: "You are right, Maddy, of course, about finding true happiness. I say it's a rather expensive way to feed your ego. If you are lucky with the right Mr. Right, but don't ask anyone outside your family about this. Everyone pays lip service to the brotherhood of man, social equality, no prejudice; but in their hearts where their minds bed down self-interest and hate have a home. If Christmas has any meaning at all, it is easier to celebrate Christmas with a Christian rather than with someone who throws chicken bones to predict the future. If you are going to take up with a three-legged, one-eyed mangy cur you should not ask nor seek understanding, sympathy, or sharing of your martyrdom. You want your bucket of love filled to the brim with love no matter what it cost you, whether you marry an asshole or the Prince of Denmark. You realize, it is a form of insanity for which only death is the cure. You don't have to agree, merely understand."

Mrs. Malloy said: "You may think your parents are off the wall. We know whereof we speak. Let's say this thing with Joe was instigated by the judge. Okay, it could just wash over. Let's go on the basis of the best way. Maddy, if you promise me you will not contact Joe in any way, shape, form, or manner while you're away at camp, it will be proof enough, and a good reason for you to attend Catamount high school in the fall."

Maddy said, with no hesitation: "That's no problem! I just have to be with my friends in the fall. I've always liked the regimen and fun of summer camp. I won't mind going just to prove myself to you, if I must. I have to say I understand what you said Dad, but I do not at all agree with your bigoted ways. It is corrosive. It is destructive. It's a very narrow view toward developing our world as a friendly environment."

"I must interrupt you, and I apologize," Mr. Malloy said. "You will not understand what I say until you reach the educable moment. What is the educable moment? When the rent can't be paid; when the bank forecloses; when you find yourself digging in the dumpster for food. At that educable moment, you will not have enough pride left not to ask your family for help."

"Isn't that a rotten wish you'd like to have come true to pat yourself on the back!" Maddy half stood. "You put down Joe, yet you value his father for the financial rewards he brings you and your company. I believe there is a term for that."

Mr. Malloy snapped: "It's not hypocrisy! It's business! I don't have to go to bed with him!"

Mrs. Malloy said: "You keep your promise, Maddy, I'll keep mine. You may be excused."

When Maddy had left the room, Mrs. Malloy turned to Peter and Paul. "Just to be sure there is no misunderstanding on anyone's part, I expect the two of you to convince Joe it is the best plan of action to leave your sister alone. Need I say anything more?"

Paul shook his head. Peter said: "We got it."

Mrs. Malloy said: "This stays between us. Just make sure you both dot every 'I' and cross every 'T' so he really understands."

A week later when Peter and Paul confronted Joe by the park a short distance from his home they were carrying short lengths of rubber hose.

Peter spoke first. "This will only take a second, Joe, just hear us out first. Okay?"

"Okay, what's up?" Joe asked.

"We're supposed to convince you to stay away from Maddy," Peter said.

"We're supposed to beat the crap out of you with these rubber hoses," Paul said, "but it's not in our plan."

"No, it's not," Peter said. "You can tell anyone anything you want, but this stays between us. We can't forget what you did for Maddy. That's more than good enough for us."

"Yeah!" Paul emphasized. "You get in trouble on your own."

Joe looked from one to the other. "You know? I'd love to have you as in-laws. I always envied you two. Who lefty and who's righty?"

"Pete's righty."

"And you talk your own language?"

"Haey, ew evidr eht srehcaet dna rou stnerap yzarc."

"Ruo stnerap og tihs-epa esuceb yeht wonk er'ew gnidih ffuts."

"Boyhowdy! I'm impressed," Joe said.

"That's not the end of it. Pete sits on the john and I fart!"

"Yeah! He gets a hard-on and I wear it!" Paul said. "One thing's for sure. We absolutely, positively are not going to go into the service together. Under no circumstances."

Joe looked from one to the other. "Well, about tonight, Hey! Shouldn't I at least bloody a nose and blacken an eye to make it look good?"

Paul said, "Let's not and say we did. We like the idea of the cabin. We don't want to lose out. We're crazy about the idea. It's like a major clubhouse."

Peter and Paul exchanged glances then looked at Joe. All three burst out into laughter.

So, when Maddy told Joe she was going away to camp for the whole and entire summer he was not entirely surprised. Joe sat on the curb and held his head. He wondered how he would survive the summer. He decided the best way was to keep each other in their hearts and minds. "Maddy? What time is it now? Exactly."

Maddy was taken aback with the quick shift in subject. She peered hard at her wrist watch in the dim light. "It is precisely seven-fifty-five."

He stood up. He held both of her hands in both of his. "Maddy. No matter where we are, or what we're doing, if only for a split second, we will concentrate as hard as we can on each other. I've read about E.S.P. About a mother waking up out of a deep sleep, and sitting straight up in bed at the exact moment her son was killed in action. I don't know if it's a matter of actual fact or not, but I have to believe in something concerning you and me. I want to believe you and I can communicate even though we hundreds! Thousands! of miles apart! So, at seven-fifty-five p.m., every day, it will be our moment. Okay?"

Maddy apologized. She was thinking so hard about Joe, she didn't hear what he said.

CHAPTER 8

FROM THE moment Joe knew he was going to get the land, he started drawing structural plans for the cabin. First, he drew a plat of the property to scale. He roughed in the road. He situated the cabin on the drawing more or less where he thought it should go.

Then, throughout the past school year, he spent hours upon hours making meticulous plans of the cabin itself. He went through every book on building a cabin that was in the school, town, and neighboring libraries. He studied architectural drawings, and looked at hundreds of photographs and paintings of cabins.

Finally, after scratching out drawings on reams of paper he settled on a design and the specifications he wanted. He made builder's drawings on large sheets of paper with front, top, and side views. He signed them, "JOSEPH CARUSO, GENERAL CONTRACTOR." It was a private joke. Two summers before, he worked mornings as a gopher for builder Sven Johnson. Mainly he did odd chores like stacking wood, going for coffee and sandwiches, keeping the office swept out, sharpening saws, and washing the boss's pick-up. He was told he would be the Assistant General Contractor. "What does the Assistant G.C. do?" he asked Sven.

The boss told him it wasn't what he did, but as Assistant G.C. he was to take the blame for everything that went wrong with any project anywhere. "But! ... " he started, then realized he was being teased.

Sven very much figured into Joe's plans to get the cabin built. Sven welcomed Joe's availability. The arrangement was that Joe's salary would go for buying the building materials, which Joe would get at wholesale prices, plus,

Sven agreed to deliver whatever was needed right to the site. Joe would start full-time as a carpenter's apprentice as soon as school was out.

Joe planned on a very full summer.

Joe knew exactly who was going to be the project Assistant G.C. for the cabin although Maddy didn't know anything about it until she started high school that fall term.

Joe's father had given him a philosophical outlook because he knew Joe would want the cabin to be constructed and useable by yesterday. His father knew he was ready to throw all his forces and energy into the project. He also knew that unless he could rein in the youngster's enthusiasm Joe might not overcome early disappointments. Not because Mr. Caruso, as a very successful salesperson, knew his son but understood human nature also. He made him aware of the realistic aspects of unfulfilled visions. They could cause not necessarily the abandonment of the whole idea, but a satisfaction with settling rather than achieving. He knew Joe would be more disappointed in himself than a cabin that remained no more than a lean-to.

When Joe first heard him urge patience, Joe was ready to dismiss his admonition. He was young and strong, and he would race with the wind to have his cabin. Then, his father's logic reached him. Yes, as there was in life, there were uncertainties, vagaries and vicissitudes. He had heard about those before. The words sounded familiar, and then he remembered them. "You may plan to work seven days straight," his father said, "but only the forces that be will tell you when you can do that."

When school let out on Friday Joe noticed the weather had turned unseasonably warm for May. He had already decided he would share the majesty of the spot on Lake Eagle Talon with those of his friends who were interested. He would seek them out one by one.

He told his brother, Salvatore, there would be a work crew at the lake Saturday starting at about two, going through a picnic supper and he would bring the fixings ... and the beer. He suggested he bring a saw and/or a shovel and be prepared to work.

As he encountered Richard Thompson, Paul, Peter, and Gerard Malloy; Brad McEvily, Sven Johnson, and Fred and other classmates, he told them the same thing he told his brother, Sal. Whether they came or not, he asked them to keep it to themselves because only those that were there the first day would be what he called, "plank owners." After that no one else would be asked to join.

By early afternoon the next day, they began to arrive. As they did, Joe read from the list he had prepared of the work that should be done.

Joe asked Richard, Brad, and Fred to follow him to a spot a short distance from the camp fire to dig out a slit trench for sanitary facilities.

All three Malloy brothers were asked to clean up the area around the fire pit to use as a gathering area. It was only a short while after they had taken off their shirts and started digging that they called Joe over with some startling news. They had uncovered eight flat rocks evenly spaced around the fire pit. Sven pointed out it had to be an omen of some kind: eight of them and eight flat rocks? He believed they may have uncovered an Indian campsite area. Joe said he would research it at the library.

Joe and Sven went out to cut deadfalls into firewood to be stacked near the campsite.

Sal was put in charge of Commissary. His job was to keep the beer cold by storing it in the water near a spring. Then he had to cut long sticks on which to pierce the hot dogs to cook them, and preparing "Y"-shaped branches on which to toast the rolls. His chore also was to get a fire started and have it burn down to coals so he could position the cans of baked beans around it to get them hot.

As they completed their chores, the next big project was to clear the area where they were to build the cabin.

The creative manifestations of dering-do went on all afternoon.

One took care to lie down and rest because one would awaken, try a step, and find his face plowing up dirt, his laces tied together.

One would not fall too much asleep for fear of waking to find a hand in warm water and a circle of friends looking down watching as he peed in his pants.

Hiking boots were best for inserting book matches head first into the crease at the ball of the foot and lit. A variation of the snake-bite war dance usually took place.

Signs surreptitiously taped onto a back won the greatest applause for the day. The winner: I give full-breath blow jobs.

The slit trench: You'll find it when you see the musette bag hanging on a tree, which holds the toilet paper. Either way, watch your aim?

Don't make the fire so big the fire department responds.

Next time to clean off the rocks around the fire would you kindly bring a vacuum?

We need a clothes line to hang things ...

In the center of the ring of stones, the fire from chestnut snapped loudly as it burned down. The surrounding rocks had been washed and polished. The earth from the sitting stones to the fire was tamped down with heavy flat stones. Small holes around the fire pit were made lined with stones to form pockets, which held "Y" sticks on which skewers of wood held meats for smoking for roasting. This was especially useful when Joe's father brought a half-dozen prepared rabbit for dinner.

The tamped earth angled away from the fire circle to keep rain from cutting ruts. The hard work showed by creating the aura of a sacred meeting place.

Some two hours later, Joe—ever the playboy—stood at the bottom of the fire circle and looked around hard at the other eight who had gravitated to the fire as they completed their work. All had their shirts off. Joe unbuckled his belt, shucked off his shoes, slid off his socks and underwear as they stared at him. He turned, ran toward the water, splashed past the rocks and dove in.

Every single one of the others whooped and shouted as they stripped and joined Joe. They dove, swam, belly-flopped, splashed and shouted. They relished the relief, but even more, they were ecstatic over the plain, pure camaraderie. There seemed to be an attachment, one to the other.

With an unannounced command they suddenly stopped what they were doing.

The eight in the water turned toward Joe who was standing high on the flat rock. "Are we not all brothers?"

There wasn't a moment's hesitation. The collective voices shouted, "Yes!"

"Is this not a worthy brotherhood?"

"Yes!"

"And so must we prove our worthiness! It is so decreed by the Sachem of the Mahagawany Elders, the keepers of Lake Talon Eagle."

"What's this proof you need?" Sven asked.

"I will go first. Sven, cut sticks in descending lengths and have each of you pick for the next in line to follow me. One at a time, we will go, prove our worthiness, and take our place by the fire."

"What are you going to do," Sal asked.

Joe said: "This all came to me one night when I was camped out here. It was as if I joined the spirits by the campfire. They told me. It would be satisfactory for them. It will be satisfactory for the group. I will leave here and walk to the Promontory, there, to our left. I will climb to the top. At the top, I will climb the horse chestnut tree to the very top where there are still clusters of the spiked horse chestnuts in their shells. I will break off a cluster of the chestnuts to prove I was at the top of the tree. From there, I am to dive into the lake, return to shore, and place my chestnuts on the first open seat starting from the top going to the right."

Peter shouted, "For God's sakes! That's almost a 150-feet high!"

Sal said, "At least!"

"You can count me out!" shouted Brad. "Come on, Joe, you know I can't do heights! I can't even go up one step on a stepladder and get a nosebleed no less get up to the top of that tree! And then to take a swan dive down? I can't do it. Sorry. Count me out."

"Brad, I'm very sorry," Joe said. "We have known each other almost all our lives. I know you don't like heights. I've always known that. I don't know how many of us right here right now, including me, is not shaking at the thought of proving worthiness."

"Then why do it? Make an exception, for God's sakes!" Brad said.

"I would make an exception for you, Brad. How much more of a buddy can you be to me? But the spirits of the fire will not allow an exception. They never had and they never will. For one to sit by the fire he must be trusted. He must be trusted that he will do his duty no matter what the challenge. He must prove that before the challenge. He proves it by showing he can overcome fear in all its manifestations. Once he has mastered fear, then he will always meet any and every challenge. Why? Because that is the way these men are made."

"Can't I make an appeal to the group?" Brad asked.

"Brad, draw your stick, and do the best you can. I must hurry because this all must be done while we have the daylight. You must be back here in eleven minutes with a cluster of horse chestnuts or to pick up your clothes. Then, the next in line takes his turn."

Joe turned and loped toward the Promontory.

He felt his heart pounding in his chest when he was about half-way up the Promontory. The mount rose sharply up the top. His heart sounded like a bass drum as he scrambled over the last ledge to reach the erete.

He ran to the base of the huge tree and threw his arms about it. He guessed it would take somewhat less than three stretches to reach around it. He looked up and was dismayed to see he could not possibly reach the first leader that would enable him to climb the tree. He needed a ladder. He couldn't jump that high. He thought about leaning short, heavy branches against the trunk and using those as footholds to go up higher. On the first try the branches slid down making him crash to the ground. He tried again. This time when he crashed down he skinned a knee and elbow. There was no way he could get up on the second branch. He would be the first to fail. What irony, he thought.

The pressure of time made his mouth go dry, the anxiety causing him to make hard fists. He looked around. When he saw the birch bark trees close by, he remembered the poem from his English class, "I am a swinger of birches!" He offered a silent prayer to Mr. Frost.

He chose the largest birch tree that was closest to the tree. It had almost a five-inch diameter. He estimated it was tall enough when bowed to reach the second leader on the chestnut tree. He grabbed the tree with both hands, and started shinnying up. Up! Up! He gripped with his ankles and then moved his hands higher. Using ankles and hands he made his way upwards. He clambered until he felt the tree beginning to bend. He checked the distance to the huge tree and estimated he was lacking another five feet or so. Could the birch take it?

He inched up, higher and higher. When he thought he had gained his own height, he swallowed hard, and took a deep breath. He held on and let his legs swing loose. Slowly, ever so slowly, the birch bent. At least it was headed for the tree. Joe moved his hands up higher with the trees' descent speeding up. He saw himself about to crash into the tree. He let go. The birch swished toward its original place. He aimed himself to land on the first leader two feet below him. Right on the mark! He embraced the tree as the force of the crash made him blow hard.

He looked up and saw the path, step by branch to the top. Breathing rapidly, he grabbed and stepped, grabbed and stepped upwards. Now, out of breath, he looked down. He had not yet reached the new clusters of the horse chestnuts, but to his dismay, he was still over land! He would have to make his way even higher over the diminishing sized branches until he was clear of the arête. Now his pace became more measured as he tested a foothold. The branches began to bend under his weight. His eyes bugged out waiting for the snap of the branch as he put his weight on one after another. His hands almost cramped he held on so tightly.

At last he saw water beneath him. He saw a spiked cluster nearby. He put his hand on it, then hesitated. Not everyone could reach as far as he could so, altruistically, he would leave the close in cluster for someone else. He saw one just beyond his reach. He dared not step out further on the branch. If he was to take the cluster further out, he would have to bend his knees, and lunge out, grab them—hopefully—and dive into the water. If he missed the cluster it would mean another climb up to the top, another swing on the birch, and another attempt at the diving grab!

He bent his knees, made himself feel like a bird, and threw himself outward, his hand stretching toward the cluster. Throwing his arms out wide, he found himself soaring through the air, his mouth open wide with exhilaration.

He hit the water like a bathtub making a landing. It knocked the wind out of him. He sank, sank, sank, and then started kicking hard to get to the surface.

When he did, he smiled broadly. He saw the cluster of spiked horse chestnuts in his hand!

He swam hard for shore and loped back to the campsite, where, wearing only a loin cloth, sat at the first stone at the fire.

Richard left the camp area. He returned wearing a huge grin, his left hand behind his back. He took a seat next to Joe.

Paul, Sal, and Sven did the same thing, filling the seating spots next to each other.

Fred, Peter, Gerald, and Brad remained.

Sven called out Fred's name. "Fred! Where the hell are you? You're up!"

Everyone looked around.

"He's not in the water," Peter said.

"He's not taking a leak or he would've passed me," Sal said.

They all grew quiet. They looked around. They looked at one another. They all turned away from each other, the unsaid was left unsaid.

"Brad!" Sven called. "You're up!"

All eyes were on Brad down on his haunches by the water's edge.

Brad swiveled his head to stare backwards at the fire pit. He rose, his face black. His eyes darted from one friend to another. He rubbed one fist hard into the palm of the other as if he were trying to rub off the skin on his knuckles.

"Time," Peter said.

"Pete! Do me a big favor. Go ahead of me, please. Just help me out," Brad said.

"Look! The more you think about it, the less you'll be able to do it," Peter said.

"You look!" Brad said. "You have no idea how terrified I am of heights. Now goddammit! Do me this favor!"

Gerald held up his hand. "Go ahead, Pete. You gotta give him his head on this one. I will, too, if he asks."

"Sorry to say," Joe said. "We're running out of time. Let's do it!"

"Yes. Please," Brad said. "I'll go last?"

Peter and Gerald took their turns and joined the group.

"Shit!" Gerald said, "I hope he makes it!"

The others nodded.

No one was really keeping time. Each one kept himself occupied by scratching the earth with a stick, digging a heel into the ground, or tossing stones out into the lake. More time passed.

Sal threw a stone as far as he could out onto the lake. "God-damn, fucking, son-of-a-bitch!"

Joe said, "Relax. He'll make it. He's one of us."

"I hate to mention it," Sven said, "but just how much time do we give him before we give up?"

Richard spoke up. "Look! He's got to work through it. Let's give him all we can."

It was less than five minutes later when a whooping war cry was sounded on the trail from the Promontory. Everyone stood up and stared at the trail. Brad leaped into view holding what looked like an Indian lance above his head in his right hand. He leaped and bounded his way toward the fire wearing a broad grin while yelling as loud as he could. When he got to the others, he was wet, his head hanging so low his chin almost touched his chest. He took two steps haltingly, then jumped into the air, "Holy Shit! Look at what I got!" He held up a cluster of horse chestnuts!

The other joined in the cheering, whoops, and cat-calls, whacking him on the back, rubbing his head, and grabbing his arm.

Joe said, "Come, Brad, welcome to the fire circle."

They all took seats around the fire.

TRANSLATION FROM THE MAHAGAWANY LANGUAGE:

JOE: *I am proud to sit with you at council fire, my brothers.*

MEMBERS: *As we are with you.*

JOE: *Why did you all laugh when you first saw me with the cluster?*

SAL: *You wore a white stripe from your chin, down your chest, across your belly, down your pisser, inside your knees, and down your ankles.*

JOE: *Ah! From the birch tree!*

SVEN: *We didn't make the connection until we were atop the mountain and saw that the birch tree was the only way to get to climb the chestnut tree!*

PAUL: *A white stripe in the front means no yellow stripe on the back!*

BRAD: *You can bet the farm on that!*

PETER: *That's how we watch each others' backs.*

MEMBERS: *Each of us sees the other in ourselves.*

JOE: *Brad. We are especially pleased to find you with us.*

BRAD: *Do you think for one second I was going to miss out on this? I surprised myself and also, I pooped and screamed a lot. I hope you didn't hear me. I really don't know how I did it. I believe I just wanted to be one of you more than anything else in life—even death, if it had to be. I realized worse things can happen to a person besides death. I hypnotized myself and screamed a lot. When I saw the trail leading to the promontory, I just positively knew I had to do everything without thinking. I ran just as hard as I could. I didn't see the vines that crossed the path close to the earth. My foot got caught and I went sprawling, my arms out before me... ."*

SVEN: *Hey! That's what happened to me!*

BRAD: *You won't believe! My right hand fell right on the top of a flint lance point that was stuck in the ground! When I got up I realized what it was. It was a sign! A sign for me! To screw up my courage, every single bit of it, and do what I had to do. It seemed I did everything in a dream world. I know I left the lance stuck in the middle of the path. I was determined to go back to get it. If I was a little late getting back, that was the reason. Before I knew it, I had the*

*exhilarating feeling of swinging off the birch onto the
chestnut tree! I was so proud of myself I cried with joy! I
saw you all left the closest cluster for me, and I thank you
for that. I thank you all for your guidance and help in
making me a better man than I thought I was. Now, where's
the fucking beer?*

RICHARD: *Joe, I just noticed! When did you get that?
It's a tattoo on your right shoulder of a Silver Fox!*

JOE: *How lucky am I! I see my Spirit Guide has come to
me.*

PAUL: *Richard, you've got a tattoo, too! I can't make it
out.*

PETER: *It's an otter! Paul, you've got a dog! What do I
have?*

GERALD: *You're lucky you got one. It's a crow ... no,
wait, too big! It's a raven!*

SAL: *Gerald, I can see you have an owl and Brad has
a ... what the hell is that?*

SVEN: *Brad, you really earned it. It looks to me like a
wolverine. Sal has a squirrel, and can you believe? Look at
what I've got? A mountain lion? No, let's call it a puma!*

JOE: *My fellow braves, we can be proud of ourselves
and each other. I must embrace all of you as plankowners of
the soon-to-be spirits cabin of Lake Eagle Talon. My father
holds the title but when we all reach our majority, the title
will be put in all of our names. Your share can be passed on
only to another who has passed the test. That is our solemn
pledge. As you all must realize, each and every one of us
has conquered fear. Nothing we encounter in our life will
ever cause us to tremble. Fearlessness is us, the warriors of
Lake Eagle Talon. We must wait each of us for our Spirit
Guide to make itself known to us. Now, as Brad says, I'm
hungry! Where the fuck are the hot dogs?*

CHAPTER 9

The mere mention of the cabin generated heightened enthusiasm among the members. It was the most exciting event in their young lives. Among themselves, they noticed that all of the members, Brad especially, walked taller, with a bit of a swagger, and a proud air. It was an unspoken rule among them that they were never to speak about the cabin while at school.

In the loosest of unions, they all agreed they would appear at the cabin-site whenever they had the time to do so. They would stay as long as they were able, do as much as they were able, and bring their own food and drinks. Joe would leave in a waterproof canvas bag a clipboard with a list of work to be done. Young, anxious, and interested it was no work at all. They were enthusiastic about everything and anything to do with getting "their" cabin situated.

Joe understood exactly what his father meant when he and the crew planned three weekends to cut in the road, and got rained out on two of them.

The road wasn't as difficult as Joe thought it was going to be. He took the time to scout several paths. He chose the one that seemed natural to the lay of the land even though there were a couple obstacles—a stump, a boulder—that would need special attention.

At those times when the members were going to the lake they settled into a routine. They declined any offer to drive them there and pick them up. There was a certain independence they enjoyed when they rode their bikes. They could go and return as they pleased. They would fix a tuna fish sandwich, pack five or six chocolate chip cookies or a couple brownies, grab an extra "T" shirt, and load everything into their saddlebags. They strapped whatever tool they needed across their backs, and were off.

Joe was surprised not any were interested in camping overnight. Sven, for example, had a girl friend who insisted on his companionship over the weekends. Otherwise, he had a business to run. His brother, Sal, enjoyed coming out during the days on weekends, but he positively would not give up his weekend dates. Oftentimes, Richard, a grade school teacher who lived on a farm, didn't really have that much free time, but when he was at the site, he did the work of three men. He was with them only a very short time before he was called back into the Army reserves for duty in the South Pacific.

Joe found the work with the brush hook went fast and was fun. He was able to whack down fairly big saplings and knock over underbrush with carefully aimed deft strokes. Whoever was there cleaned up as he went along either cutting brush into small pieces or stepping on it to have it lay close to the ground. He noticed he was developing quite a physique. Where it used to take a couple cuts to knock down a large sapling, now a deft, well-aimed stroke was enough.

Then, there came a choice of either cutting down some trees and getting rid of a boulder, or making the road longer. He decided the boulder was a challenge, but it would have to go. He wanted to save the trees. After poking around a bit, he decided on a plan. It was plain pick and shovel work. Those were the tools available to them. They dug a hole right in front of the boulder. They dug down to its bottom, and removed the dirt to at least half of its diameter. With that, Joe was able to estimate its size. The work party continued to dig the hole in front of it down to one-and-a-half the height it was above the ground. Then, from above, they removed the dirt on the boulder's sides. Finally, he thought they had moved enough earth. He used the pick as a lever, stuck it behind the boulder and got it to wiggle. He smiled to himself. His plan might just work. Savoring the moment, a half-dozen hands moved the boulder an inch, then rocked it again another six inches. Then, exhaling hard three times they all exerted every bit of effort they could against the pick handle and the boulder

gently rolled and dropped into the hole with a "THUNK!"
That was emphasized by a cheer that rang all over the lake.

They all agree to wait until after lunch to do the
gratifying chore of filling in the hole and leveling the road.

That afternoon, again Peter, Sal, Gerald, and Joe used
a shovel, an axe, and a come-along to muscle a stump out
of the road.

In his early thinking, Joe didn't want a road right up to
the cabin strictly for the privacy. He thought of putting a
chain across the road with a sign but knew it would attract
the attention he didn't want. He also knew he was
establishing a perfect lover's lane which would also attract
attention. He decided on a simple sign nailed to a tree by
the entrance which read: Private. He needed the road to
have building materials delivered. It would save time
besides making the whole job easier for him and the crew,
besides more fun.

Joe hoped to have the road completed and the post
holes dug by the time school was out.

Even if he wasn't a bit ahead of schedule, he decided to
quit work for the day when he was there alone and came
up with the thought that his mother would really
appreciate some fresh trout. Besides, it had been at least
three days since he made an entry into his fishing diary
that didn't end with the notation: "Released."

Joe used a hollow in a huge tree close-by the lean-to as
a cache for his fishing equipment. He retrieved the rod
then decided he would try a spot a short distance from his
land. Because of the time of day with the sun waning, and
the bug activity just above the surface of the water, he
decided to use a surface fly of his own making. He wanted
a fly that could be dried off with only one or two false casts.
He decided a pale green ball of feathers, more or less, with
a mayfly tail aided by surface tension would keep it afloat.
Up to today, his faith in the lure was greater than its
success, but he decided to go with it anyway.

He watched the line lay out on a medium cast, the
tippet arced to let the fly come down gently to float onto the
surface. It barely disturbed the water. Joe let it sit as he
looked around to see if a fish was snuffling the surface. A
fish would work the area just below the surface keeping

their dorsal fin submerged but roiling the water as it took slow rising food.

With his eyes off his fly, he wasn't prepared for the explosion when the bass blasted out of the water for the fly. It made a "WHOOMPP!" as its mouth snapped open just before it hit the surface to inhale the fly. Joe knew by the tug it had set the hook itself, and that the fish was a beauty. With his rod bent in a narrow arc, the fish stripped line, the reel whirring in a high pitch.

Joe knew he was in a tough situation. He was grateful he had left his vest and net on shore. The water was above his knees and he wasn't sure of the shoreline fall-off, so he knew he was anchored to the spot. Also, he had no idea of underwater hazards—trees, rocks, weeds—that the fish would use to evade being killed.

When the line backing started going out, Joe knew he had to try to stop the fish from sounding or at least turn it around. He held the rod high above his head and yanked the rod back and forth a half-dozen times. He felt the tension ease a bit. Perhaps the trick had worked! He started taking in line. The hope was to have the monster jump. "Come up and get a sun-burn!" Joe shouted, "You son-of-a-gun!"

Joe was quite aware he wasn't a-looking for a monster bass when he made his cast. He was using a number 18 hook which was not going to take much of a hammering. So, as gingerly as he was able he started to retrieve line. He tried to keep it slow and steady, trying to have the vibrations from the line to the pole to his hand signal him in enough time to slack off. If he brought in this fish, he knew he would have to be more than lucky.

He could see the nail knot where the backing joined the fly-line, and prayed harder. Another thirty-feet and the whale would be at his ankles. Then, the line went slack! Immediately, Joe dropped the tip of his rod. The Colossus was going to reach for the sky! He would come out of the water, his tail slapping at the hook. Tension on the line would help him get free.

As a canon-ball blowing out of the deep, as graceful as a hanging ballet leap, the dread-naught sailed dreamily for the sky, prisoner yet to the whisp of line.

It landed flat on its side creating a spectacle of an exploding froth.

Joe went slack-jawed; his piscatorial duties forgotten until the rod vibrated then tensed in his hand. By second sense, Joe took up the slack regaining a tight line. This time, instead of using the reel, he took it in quite delicately in a one-handed roll-up as his right hand kept the tip of the rod close to the horizon. The like jerked several times. Joe knew the fish was swagging the line, shaking his head violently from one side to the other.

Then, a sudden release. The fish came up again: Not as high, not as graceful, not as beautiful as the first time. The return splash half of his first waterfall.

Joe knew to bring the behemoth in he had to keep the hook from tearing free. That was the worst case scenario, which he usually considered first. Joe focused intensely on the vibrations coming in from the line. Keeping the line in his hand with a steady drag, the fish ran in wide arcs. Joe could feel the giant's energy ebbing as he slowly, slowly took in line. Finally, with a prayer every inch of the way, Joe switched the rod to his left hand locking all the line he had taken in. Gently, he brought the tip of the rod behind his head enabling him to get the line in his right hand. Slowly, he followed the line down, murmuring to himself in almost a hypnotic way, he could see the flash of his belly as he swirled. Joe put his face under the surface of the water so he could grab the fish's bottom lip.

Joe got a thumb in the bass's mouth and clamped down hard as the line parted above the fly.

Face and fish burst through the water.

Joe held up the largest bass he had ever seen. He couldn't believe its heft although it had a huge, distended belly. He stared at it for a long time as it waggled in his grasp. His mind could not comprehend the size of the monster. The fly and a bit of the tippet dangled from the side of its mouth.

He moved to the shore.

He placed the bass in his landing net so he could weigh the fish. Discounting the weight of the net, the bass was ten pounds, seven ounces, a record fish for Massachusetts for sure.

Joe thought about his decision for just a short while. He was ready to give up being a record holder and the notoriety that went with it. It had little significance in his thinking. Sharing the lake with this king was all he understood or needed. He waded in a short distance, checked that the fly would cause the fish no trouble because he was going to leave it there. He thought the fish had earned it so the fly would never be used to catch a lesser monster. He lowered the bass into the water, and watched it barely move as if stunned, then, before Joe knew it, the fish was off.

He would really feel good making this entry in his fish diary, but best of all, he just relished the strange but marvelous feeling he had not just for the camaraderie, and the cabin coming along, but for the feeling of spirituality the experience of the cabin has brought to him and his friends.

Fishing didn't work so well for a fast completion of the cabin, but he understood it was the best foundation for it.

Joe decided right from the beginning, his cabin would not have a dirt floor. They would dig post holes about six feet apart on which to put up the structure. Checking the lay of the land, and the position of the cabin which would have an end to the water, the posts would run from six inches above ground at the back to about 36 inches above ground at the end facing the lake. He planned on a porch and an area under it to store a canoe.

Joe was filled with enthusiasm and charged with vigor when he strapped the post-hole digger on his back and set out to dig all the post holes in that day. How great he thought if two or three of the others showed up. They could get this chore done before sunset.

The posts would be five five-feet apart on the short side, six-feet apart on the long, with a third row down the center for a total of 22 piers. The cabin would be twenty feet by twenty-four feet with a six-foot wide porch on the short side facing the lake.

Brad, Peter, and Paul showed up late that Saturday morning. With tape measure, stakes, and blue prints it took them all morning to lay out where the holes would go —but exactly!

The first time he raised the digger up high and brought it down into the earth he knew he would have to revise his work-time estimate. The previous day Sven told him if he was lucky he could dig a hole in a half hour. Despite the fact that they had a very efficient digger, the area seemed to be a garden of rocks and roots. The post hole digger Joe borrowed had the usual opposing semi-circular shovels each attached to a long handle, but this digger had a third little shovel inside the other two that operated to keep the dirt from falling out once it had been dug up.

Taking turns, the four of them made fairly good progress when they just encountered earth. It was when they brought the digger down and it "Clanged!" against rock that their bones rattled and they became unsettled. Soon, they came to understand their opponent, and settled in to emerge victorious. What that meant was that the entire weekend was spent digging holes for the piers. Instead of taking the post hole digger home, he envisioned rowing out to the middle of the lake, and dropping it overboard.

At the end of first full week of work when a varied number of members showed up, Sven made two trips out to the lake in his pick up loaded with cement, sand, a mixing trough, a hoe, and enough boards cut to make forms for eleven piers. With Joe, Sal, Gerald, and Sven pitching it, it allowed them to pour all the piers in two batches.

Joe alone camped overnight and the next morning started in nailing the forms together and reinforcing the tops with a wire strap. By that time, Sven, Paul, Peter, Brad showed up, they all worked to set the forms in the holes. Sven started the crew mixing concrete. They put cement, sand, and water in the mixing trough and chopped mud. When the batch was mixed, they shoveled it into the forms. Sven used a string tied to a bolt to plumb each pier with a helper using rocks to hold it in place. Then, Sven pushed a bolt into the wet concrete in the center of the pier, which stuck out with some several inches of thread showing. It would be used to bolt down the sill.

By late in the day, they had all eleven piers hardening and were ready to go home. Joe stayed behind to go fishing. He took home three trout to his mother for dinner.

Early the next morning, Joe, Sven, Brad, and Paul were back at the site. Gingerly they removed the forms from the piers and set them in the other holes. They started the routine of mixing the mortar and filling the forms. By mid-afternoon Sven had re-checked the plumb of each pier. He ran a string from corner to corner to make sure the top of the piers were on a plane. Then, he ran the string from an opposite corner, saw it was over the center stone which put the fire pit dead center of the cabin; then, ran the string from the other opposite corners to make sure the centers were pretty close to make sure he had made a square and not a trapezoid. Sven pulled a six pack out of his cooler, passed out the beer and hailed each and every one for a job well done.

Joe was not unhappy the next day was misty and rainy. It was a perfect excuse not to go to the cabin. Not that he was loosing his enthusiasm, but he worked a hard week, eight hours a day, for Sven. The work with Sven was demanding and tiring. Sven was not a taskmaster, but he expected his workers to give him a day's work for a day's pay. Sven took time with Joe to show him how to do a particular job, or make a special cut, or the proper way to toenail. He showed him how to use a carpenter's square to cut a birdmouth in a rafter. "Be sure you use two sixteen-penny nails to nail it down!" he would caution Joe, "because the building inspector will close us down if there's anything less!"

Joe's work with Sven meant a lot of lugging and a lot of hammering. He also watched very closely how a building went up. He would put the information to good use when they put up the cabin.

Joe missed the next night at the cabin, too, when Brad called him to go fishing. Joe enjoyed his company. The two of them got along, so Joe liked not to turn him down. They would go to nearby streams to catch the evening rise. Occasionally, they would agree on night bass fishing, but because both worked and were tired they made them early evenings.

Joe also lost time at the cabin when Mrs. Kowalchuk would call to have some small, odd job done. She always offered to pay him, but Joe refused. He had a soft spot for her, and, besides, she always had a huge batch of brownies ready for him to take home. She always mentioned the last time Maddy had been there, and always complimented her on what a thorough worker she was. "Course, I tell Maddy the same thing about you!" she told Joe.

When Joe returned to the cabin after work that week, with Sal, Brad, and Paul they were able to remove all the forms from the piers. Remembering Sven's admonitions, Joe checked again that they were plumb and filled in around the piers. When that was done, they started taking the forms apart because he had taken Sven's advice and would use the wood as part of the flooring.

After work that Friday, Sven delivered to the cabin site the ten- and twelve-foot sills and all the floor joists. When Joe realized there was no power at the cabin, and that they would have to use hand saws to cut any lumber, he got permission from Sven to use his shop to pre-cut whatever he needed. He did that with all the bridging used to stabilize the floor joists.

"Take your time putting in the sills," Sven cautioned Joe. "You want to have your building a square not something else."

During lunch breaks, Sven often sat with Joe explaining the intricacies of the building trade. At one such meeting, Sven lectured on the Pythagoreum Theorum. "'A'-square, plus 'B'-square equals 'C'-square," he expounded. "A square or a rectangular building must have four ninety-degree angles, one at each corner. To confirm you have a ninety-degree angle, check with Pythagorus," Sven said. "If you take three consecutive numbers, for example 3,4,5, and measure the distance of each of the first two numbers exactly out from a right angle, then the measurement from each of those points to the other should equal the third number. That will work with any number. For example, if I multiply the numbers by ten, I will have, say, thirty feet on one side, forty feet on the other side, and the distance between those two points will be fifty feet. If it's not, it's not a right angle. If it's not a right angle, you won't have four ninety-degree angles needed for a square or rectangle."

Joe's brow remained wrinkled as he listened. Then, said to Sven: "The cabin will be twenty feet by twenty-four feet. To be sure I make right angles at the corners, I should measure down on the left side, say, from one corner, say, ten feet. Then, measure up on the right from that corner twenty feet. When I measure between the ten-foot and the twenty-foot marks, the hypotenuse should be adjusted in or out until it measures thirty feet!"

Sven smiled. "You go to the head of the class! Do that at all four corners running a string and you will have a rectangular cabin! It may be easier to determine if you measure from opposite corners and get the same figure. Where the two lines cross is dead center."

Joe with Peter's help, drilled holes for the pier bolts and set the two twelve-foot sills on one side first. In the shop, Joe had cut forty-five degree angle cuts in the sills that would be at the corners. Using the point of the forty-five in the sill he ran a string to the short corner which he set as a guide for the two ten-foot sills using the 3-4-5 method. He set the sills on top of the pier bolts and whacked the top of the board to make the bolt indent the sill. He turned the sill over, drilled the bolt holes with a brace and bit, and set the short sills. He did the same thing to set the other long and short sides. He rechecked the measurements at all four corners with both of them beaming as the numbers came out right.

They nailed two-by-eights together to make the center support which he ran down the center piers.

The next chore would be to run the floor joists sixteen-inches on center and put in the bridging.

When Sven delivered the joists, he took time to help Joe, Sal, and Paul put them on top of the sills. "Two men handling these ten footers is fast work. One man doing the same thing comes out three times as long," Sven said, "but setting them up here will make it a little easier."

Joe tried to tell everyone there how much he appreciated all they did to help complete their dream cabin. All of them started talking at once and wouldn't let him get into it.

Joe didn't fully realize what Sven was telling him as they were going over the blueprints when he urged Joe to push the work to get the cabin closed in and finished as much as he could before winter set in. There was something about Sven registering for the draft.

"You're not concerned, are you, Sven?" Sal asked. "You're married!"

"Yes, I'm married. It would be better if I had five, six kids; and even better if my wife and I weren't separated," Sven said sadly. "I asked if I could put off getting drafted for just two months so I could finish the house we're working on. I would make it up by adding on at the other end of my enlistment. Do you know what they told me? 'Sure! But supposed you get killed how are you going to make up the two months?'" Sven roared with laughter and slapped his thigh resoundingly at the noir joke on himself.

Some evenings, Joe wondered where they all got to strength to go swimming and play touch football after swinging a framing hammer all day long.

They were all spurred on by Sven's praise of their work and progress. He was the professional builder and his praise was much valued. Sven estimated that it should take two workers five weeks to complete the cabin. At the rate they were working, Sven estimated they would have a good chunk of the cabin done by Labor Day. He was working six days a week as it was to get his contracts fulfilled, but even so, offered to help close it in if the progress were delayed for some reason.

Joe allowed Sven to talk him out of thick, diagonal flooring. Yes, it would add strength, but there would be a great deal of waste and a lot of hand sawing to trim off the excess. Tongue and groove flooring would work out just as well and be a lot faster. Joe was surprised at how fast the crew put down the flooring.

Joe was substantially spurred on when Sven started delivering the two-by-four framing studs.

He knew all about framing the walls on the floor because it was so much easier to do it that way. They would have no problem raising the walls to the vertical. Joe decided they should lay down the plate, and from there frame the walls vertically, stud by stud. They could follow the plans closely and put in the windows and doors exactly with all the necessary headers and reinforcing studs. The day quickly came when he watched Brad nail down the double plate at the top.

Joe walked down towards the water, then suddenly turned to stare at the cabin-in-progress. He folded his arms across his chest and checked all the angles. He lined up one stud with another to check the squareness. He envisioned the canoe under the roof covered porch. There would be a sleeping loft at the other end of the cabin. He could see the chimney rising above the imaginary roof line. He had decided against a fireplace as impractical. He would use a kitchen range. It would provide heat, a place to cook, and storage for hot water. It would really make the cabin cozy. "Boyhowdie!" he said out loud.

Joe got the proper pitch for the roof from Sven. Joe wanted to be responsible for using the stair gauge clamps on the framing square to mark the bird mouth on each rafter. While he was at it, Sven suggested, he could mark the plumb cut on the end of the rafter to which the fascia board would be nailed. Ordinarily that would be done later with a strike line, but to save hand sawing at the site, any slight error would still be worth it. Richard, Peter, and Gerald joined him for three nights after work to make all the cuts needed on the thirty-six rafters.

That Saturday, all eight of them were there to put up the roof beam and the rafters.

It was the middle of August, and finally, to Joe, the cabin began to look, as a cabin should.

Joe got an extra-special deal on planking to cover the roof. It was less than half the cost of plywood, and although it would not go up as quickly as plywood, he was already quite behind on expenses so that had to be his first consideration. The others, as usual, offered to pitch in, but Joe would not hear of it. The cabin was a promise he made to and for himself, and now with the plankowners it meant more to him than ever.

Joe decided to stop working with Sven the last week of work before Labor Day to complete the roof with planking. He let the others know it was a last gasp play to close in the cabin as Sven suggested, and he would welcome all the help he could get. His plan was to put down felt and cover the roof with asphalt shingles. Sven, not one to push for his way, took time during a lunch break with Joe to say, "Joe! You have every reason to be very proud of this cabin. It's really very neat! You know, when I get out of the service, that's the first thing I'm going to build for myself."

Joe interrupted him. "Why would you build another cabin when this one is as much yours as anyone else?"

"I suppose. Only thing I would do different, though? I'm going to put cedar shakes on mine."

Joe hitched forward taking the bait, "Cedar shakes?"

"Yup," Sven said. "Black cedar shakes from the swamps of Georgia. With a six-twelve pitch I'll make a rough guess you'll need at least 16-square. They might take a bit longer to put up, but they are more fun. My guess is you'll be going for the long haul. I'd say cedar shakes—take your time and put them up right on 40-pound felt, maybe double it—should last 35 years easily, 50 with a push."

"Wow ..." Joe said quietly. "But asphalt shingles are guaranteed for 35 years, the good ones."

Sven chewed a bit looking up at the cabin. "Would you like to see a pretty girl all dressed up wearing a very practical, useful, cheap farmer's hat? I look at that cabin and all I see is one thing: cedar shakes! Course, it's just one person's opinion, and only one-eighth my cabin ..."

The cedar shakes did take longer than Joe expected even with the enthusiastic help of the plankowners. It was beginning to look so much wonderful as a cabin, they would scoot up to the site at lunchtime, and if the light held out, after supper. Joe was overjoyed at the look when they all completed the job.

Now they could store the rest of the materials they needed under cover. He used his birthday money to pay for the plywood to cover the outside, the outside plate, boards for the fascia, and the clapboards.

With school starting, they would have only weekends to work on the cabin. Depending on how favorable the Indian Summer they might just get up to putting in the windows and doors provided Joe had the money to pay for them. If not, they would cover the openings with plastic. They would start putting on the clapboards hopefully getting up a good distance on all four sides before the cold weather closed them out. What was left after that were the fascia boards and the lattice work from the ground up all around the cabin and the front porch.

In the meantime, he spread the word around that he was looking for a Garland kitchen range. He wasn't going to be satisfied with just any old stove. The one he was looking for had spaces for baking, heating water, warming. He would have to be satisfied with a cement block chimney although he had his heart set on fieldstone, which would really set off the cabin.

On overnights, Joe and anyone who cared to continued to use the lean-to. They all were determined not to sleep in the cabin until it was totally completed. The cabin would remain unfinished for all the rest of its days if it was used prematurely. That's just the way things worked out, his dad said and when his dad spoke, he listened.

The tradition was to tie a broom to the chimney when the house was closed in, Sven said, but in this case, they could nail one to the peak.

By the Fourth of July the following summer, the cabin was totally completed. Every nail had been driven, all boards were in place, the loft and stairs were built, the range and chimney were in, and the decision about painting it or not was left hanging. That meant the celebration jamboree would have to wait until all eight could take their places by the fire pit.

The one thing they all agreed upon was the installation in the place of honor above the front door on the inside of the cabin. With great ceremony, when all eight of them were at the cabinsite, Brad presented the Indian lance to Joe, who accepted it for all of them.

Not one of them doubted the owner of the lance made frequent visits to the Spirits Cabin.

In the meantime, life had gone on and continued to go on.

CHAPTER 10

THE CRISIS between Joe and Maddy came to a head a week before the following spring break in April.

Joe, a junior, was five months from 17; and Maddy, a freshman, was four months from 15.

Joe had been troubled with thoughts of Maddy throughout his English class. It wasn't the first time they had exchanged telepathic signals, but to Joe these indicated agitation. The two of them usually met in the library. As soon as he got out of class, he spotted Maddy at the far end of the room, her arms full of books, a cardigan sweater thrown over her shoulders. Both were quite aware they had to be extremely careful not to be seen together. When the semester began Joe's father spoke to him alone out in the yard. There, Mr. Caruso told Joe he had a brief meeting with Mr. Malloy in his office. The point was simple and direct. Joe was to stay away from Maddy totally. Should Mr. Caruso not impress this on his son, Mr. Malloy might find reason to transfer Mr. Caruso to the Fairbanks, Alaska, office. Mrs. Malloy simply told Maddy that if she didn't stay away from Joe, she would be sent far away to a private parochial school where being incommunicado would be the least of her problems. Joe and Maddy knew the threats were very serious. If they were going to challenge their parents, they would have to be more discreet than if their lives depended on it. They were as careful as lovers could be. They always made it a point to smile at each other when they met, but this time hers was missing. She nodded her head signaling they should meet at the far end near the windows that were hidden by the stacks. Joe followed her, his brow furrowed.

Maddy put her books on the wide sill, turned to cross her arms, and glared at Joe.

Joe was taken aback. Since the first time they met when classes started, they had a tease going between them.

"Maddy!" Joe called that first day when he spotted her in the hallway near the lockers.

She turned. She had recognized the voice, but when she saw him her face broke wide with a grin. "Joker! Hi!" Maddy waited until he got close to her. "So? Did you get laid yet?"

Joe held up a hand. "Wait! I have a question for you first."

"OK," she said.

"So? Did you get laid yet?" he asked.

The smile completely faded from her face. She stared first in one eye, then the other. "I understand what you mean. I apologize. I was trying to be flip. I shouldn't have."

"Look! Maddy." He took her by the arm and guided her towards the wall, out of the line of traffic. "You're a little angry with me because you think I'm getting away with something you are not. Listen, things are going to work out as they should. You're going to start a wonderful experience here so don't shut too many doors too quickly. You'll have a better time if the kids don't think you're tied down to me or anyone else. It avoids getting razzed, too. So, we're going to cool it, OK? And not because we have to but because it's best for both of us."

To Maddy he was solicitous, did seem concerned, and in a crazy way made sense. "Nokay," she said, but they agreed to work within their disagreement.

They exchanged locker numbers and combinations so they could leave messages in them for one another. More often than not, their ESP let them know a meeting was needed.

With Maddy standing before him, the rockets red glare in her eyes, she remained silent. He avoided her eyes by staring out the window and focusing on a volleyball game. Finally, staring at her books, he asked, "Well, did you get laid yet?" They had asked the question of each other a hundred times, and each time they broke out in a smile.

Maddy had said, there was something solid in their being able to joke about the matter.

But, this time, Joe knew the tease had hit a nerve when the air about him crackled and Maddy figuratively levitated at least seven inches from the floor.

She remained silent. It was obvious to him she wouldn't say a word until he looked her in the eyes. When he did, she said, "Well! I guess I don't have to ask you!"

Joe exhaled heavily. "What are you talking about?"

"Brandy Salvato!" she said holding her ground.

"You know what you're talking about, but that's cryptic to me," he said.

"Don't say you don't know her!" Maddy said.

"Yes, I know her," he said matter-of-factly. "Spit it out, Maddy. What's troubling you?"

"I heard you were on her special list last weekend," Maddy said.

Brandy Salvato was not struggling too hard to make the grade as a nymphomaniac. She was a junior who hung around with seniors. On Friday nights, and Friday nights only, she would select three, and only three, seniors, on whom she would shower her favors. One hitch was one of the seniors had to know how to drive, and the other hitch they had to have a car.

Brandy and the chosen three would cross over the New York border to a local bar with a motel on its property. The owner of the bar agreed with the adage that if the seniors were old enough to die for the country, they were old enough to buy a bottle of beer.

The four would arrive at the bar and order drinks. With each passing minute they got hornier and hornier anticipating the bliss awaiting them. Brandy egged them on first with innuendo, and then blatant suggestiveness. Innocently enough, her fingers would brush them seductively to check the level of their penal blood pressure. Finally, Brandy would tug at one of the guys and they would leave. However long it took, when that lucky guy returned, the next one tap danced over to the room. Finally, the third senior—usually a first timer—would go over, and eventually return with Brandy. The first go-around usually went very, very quickly.

Again, the four of them would sit and order drinks. They would remain there until either Brandy decided she had wasted enough of her life boozing, or until the seniors achieved the proper state of arousal which Brandy—as usual—liked to check personally. After the three had revisited the room, any one of them could see Brandy again on an as-needed basis.

The clock limited the soiree, however. Brandy wouldn't ever dream of missing her parents' midnight curfew.

"Yes, Brandy asked me if I wanted to join the party last weekend," Joe said. "It's not the first time she asked me, and it won't be the last time I refuse."

"Joe! Marilyn said her boyfriend was so positive it was you! Half the girls in my gym class heard her say it," Maddy said sheepishly. "I almost died when I heard it, Joe. I almost damn near died. I did."

"I'll be a son-of-a-bitch," Joe said. "Look! Are we square on this?"

"Yes, of course!" Maddy said. "There is something else."

"Yes, I know there is, Maddy." Joe said patting her arm. "We'll get to that later. First I need the name of Marilyn's boyfriend."

"Don't be silly! Joe!" Maddy implored. "Just let it go. We're none the worse."

Joe knew the seniors sneaked around the back of the gym for a smoke before they boarded the busses. Donald Hyderdun, captain of the wrestling team, had come around the corner, his head buried into his cupped hands as he lit up. He looked over to see Joe leaning against the wall. A half-dozen smokers stood a short distance away.

"Hi! Don!" Joe said.

"Hi!" Donald said. "Do I know you?"

"You should," Joe said. "You had me fucking Brandy Salvatto last Friday. What I do? Four? Five times? Do you remember? I don't because I wasn't there. I'm Joe Caruso."

"Hey! Look! If I said that, that's what I heard!" Donald said.

"You're an asshole, Donald," Joe said. He moved away from the wall. "You were with Brandy last Friday. When Marilyn confronted you about it, you lied to her. You replaced yourself with me because you were told Brandy had asked me."

"No reason for you to be pissed!" Donald said defensively. "Some guys brag about being on Brandy's list."

"I'm no whoremaster. I don't like to be lied about. What I especially didn't like? You were having a damn good time telling everyone in school about it." Joe took a deep breath, and looked away from the arrogant smile on Donald's face. Joe turned back, his left fist finding the fourth button down on Donald's shirt lifting him off the grass and making him blow like a prodded calf. Joe's right hand mashed the lit cigarette he was smoking into his lips, nose, and cheek, decking him. Joe looked down at him. "That should help you practice keeping your mouth shut."

Five minutes later, Joe got on the same bus with Maddy sitting scrunched in the far corner. Joe sat beside her.

"Your hand ..." Maddy said speaking softly, her lips barely moving, her eyes on his swollen fist.

"Punctuation marks," he answered.

"You know what I'm going to say," she said turning to look at him, nodding.

"Yes," he answered.

"Why don't we say it?" she asked. "I want us to make love. Do you?"

"Good thing we're sitting down. I don't want to talk about this where I can fall down," he said. "To answer your question, do you think I'm crazy? Of course I do. That's all I think about. I fantasize all sorts of things."

She hitched closer to him. "I do, too, and I don't even know what it's all about except for this avalanche of a feeling I have inside me!"

They laughed.

"I never could, you know, with you, until you were of age. As they say, 'Be one-eight, or it's no date.'" He shrugged. "Your mother laid that on me as you know. She saw the smoldering heat between us, even as kids. She knew. She told me right out, 'Don't be with my Maddy if you can't respect her.' As I told you, I promised her I would look out for you."

"Shit!" Maddy said.

"I know," he said dejectedly. They sat quietly for a long moment. "I have to tell you, in spite of my promise, I could never go skinny dipping with you at the lake again."

"Me, too," she said. "It's a good thing it was too cold to swim when I came out to help you with the clapboards last September. Besides, I don't know if I could come right out and say during confession," she said lowering her voice in mock seriousness, "'I'm enjoying sexual intercourse.'"

He touched her with his elbow. "I wonder how many Our Fathers and Hail Mary's you get for that?" They're laughter hidden behind their hands. "There was something else. I don't know if we should get into it."

She leaned forward, her clasped hands pressed hard between her legs. She deliberately took deep breaths. Finally, she spoke, quietly, seriously. "Today, Joe, I felt as if I had been electrocuted. I'm not trying to be overly dramatic. When I heard you could be that way with someone else, I died. I still have some of that shaky feeling inside of me. You know what I mean? As if all the air had been taken out of my world. I don't want to live without you, Joe. I don't want to live not knowing you are all mine. I'm not trying to put anything on you, Joe. I wouldn't have said anything if I didn't think ..."

"I love you, too, Maddy." He took her hand. "I got pissed at Donald not because of what he said about me, but all the pain, the hurt, the anger he caused in you. You won't ever have to worry about anything like that ever again, Maddy. I promise."

"Then you are going to do something about it?" she asked.

He squeezed her hand tightly. "Next week during spring break."

Early the next morning, Joe went to see Sven. He found him in his shop packing up his tools. "How soon?" Joe asked.

"Three weeks." He continued to put tools in a numbered box, adding to the inventory sheet as he went along. "They're going to make me a Chief in the Seabees, so how could I refuse?"

"I need to borrow your car one day next week. I have to tell you, I plan to drive to Maryland and back." Joe looked at him, shrugged and tossed his head.

"Any day you say, Joe." Sven put his back to the bench, folded his arms and crossed his legs at his ankles. "You may have a problem. Gas. I gave away all my coupons. I don't think you can buy enough on the black market for that kind of a trip. If you don't mind, I'm not even going to ask you why you're making the trip. What about bus? Train?"

"Damn! Didn't give a thought to the gas. I'll let you know about the car, if that's all right." Joe put his hands on his hips and scuffed at the floor. "How do we stand on our accounts?"

"We cashed out clean with that last box of nails you took," Sven said looking away.

Joe looked at him askance. "I'm not so sure that's right, Sven, but thank you. And thank you again for everything you did for the cabin. I couldn't have built it without you especially along with the other six plankowners. Count on me to help you build yours..."

Joe went out to the cabin to consider his options. He had been lectured enough times by his parents that there were more solutions than there were problems. Joe agreed problems were pretty commonplace, coming up with solutions was the hard part. He was confronted with several problems. The first was getting to Maryland and back. He was pretty sure the bus trip could be done in one day, and the same with using the train. The second problem was to explain Maddy's and his absence for almost eighteen hours. Anyone with half a brain could think about and know what they were up to. As far as he was concerned, there was no third problem because he was totally positive it was absolutely the right thing to do. A slight problem was getting a wedding ring.

"You are a genius!" Maddy told him when they met that evening. "How did you ever come up with such a brilliant solution to all those problems?"

The Civics Class sponsored two-day excursion of the Nation's Capital came up with an itinerary that seemed to have been made with Joe and Maddy in mind.

When Joe was reminded of the trip, he knew immediately it was the answer. There was no difficulty at all in getting permission from their parents, after all, it was educational, it was under the aegis of the school, and there were plenty of chaperons. When they were asked if the other was going, each answered they weren't sure but they thought so. Now, they could be away from home for an extended period of time with approval of their parents.

The schedule the first day was quite rigidly constructed with no possibility of free time. The bus took them from one critical landmark to the next where they toured the White House, the Capitol where they met with the Senators and Representatives of Massachusetts, and finally the Washington and Jefferson monuments. The next day the tour included the Library of Congress, the Declaration of Independence, the National Gallery of Art, a quick tour of Mt. Vernon, and a stop at the Pentagon before ending at the Smithsonian Institute. There, they were allowed to roam freely with instructions if they missed the bus they were to make their way back to the motel for dinner, after which they would head back home.

Joe and Maddy, although remaining apart for the trip, walked in one door of the Smithsonian and out another. They stopped two cabs before they found a driver who knew a close-by Justice of the Peace. In the cab, Joe put on a thin mustache he borrowed from the school drama department and put a pipe in his mouth to make himself look older. Maddy applied make-up freely and changed her hair style to add a year or two, and loosened her skirt to give good reason to the marriage.

At the Justice of the Peace, Joe invited the cab driver to leave the meter running and come in to witness the ceremony. Joe introduced him to the JP as their uncle which he thought would speed up the procedure and minimize scrutiny. To Joe's surprise, the first question from the JP had nothing to do with their ages, but rather which branch of the service Joe was entering. Then, Joe realized from the aroma in the air, that they had barged smack into the middle of the JP's cocktail hour, heavy on the gin and vermouth, which was added in whispers.

"Navy!" Joe said, "Navy! What do you think?"

"Best there is! Young fellow," the JP said. "Best there is! Go give 'em what for!"

Maddy asked the JP's wife the reason she was crying.

"It's a crazy business to be in. Can you believe I always cry at weddings?" she answered. "You grab every bit of happiness you can, young lady!"

The JP started to ask for documents but got only as far as Maddy's social security card, then got so involved in the extra money Joe was handing him that the ceremony with "takes" and "I do's" was all over before they knew it. The JP's wife poured ginger ale and olives into three glasses so the drinks to toast the bride and groom would look the same if not include all the imported botanicals in the gin theirs contained.

As he dropped them off at the hotel with a fat tip in his hand, the taxi driver insisted he was only joking when he suggested they name their first born after him feeling Mustafa Caruso was not as mellifluous as he thought.

Standing on the sidewalk, Maddy took Joe's hand. "I feel so girly and giggly and all that. Are we really married?" she asked. "Am I really Mrs. Joseph Caruso?"

"This is not sandbox stuff, Mrs. Caruso," he said. "We have really done it, and I really love you."

"Oh! Joe! I have always loved you, even when I didn't know you." She reached for his hand. "I especially love you, but I understand why you did this."

He looked down at their clasped hands. "I want to kiss you, too, but we can't take a chance. We've really got to cool it. Maddy, no one, no one must ever know. No Best Friend secret or anything like that."

"Yes, I know," Maddy said. "There's only one person I trust who should know. I need to put the marriage license someplace safe. My instinct says someone else should know, in case of what I don't know ..."

As they parted to enter the motel dining room separately to join their classmates, Joe raised his hand with his thumb and index finger forming a circle. He mouthed the words, "Wedding ring!" As he pointed to the signing, he said, "You know, until you are 18 it doesn't mean any extra privileges."

Maddy smiled benignly at him and pointed to the circle she made, and said, "It also means no Brandy Salvatos."

CHAPTER 11

MADDY sat to have tea first thing with Mrs. Kowalchuk as part of the ritual that took place before the house cleaning began.

First, ostensibly the tete a tete was to organize the cleaning schedule so it would dovetail with what had been done and what had not been done the previous Saturday morning.

"We'll change my bedding because I can help with that. Then, if you will be so kind, do my bathroom. I'd like the living room dusted, and all the rooms vacuumed," Mrs. K. would explain. "While you're busy doing that I'll get back to doing the wash ..."

"Oh! I can get that started for you, Mrs. Kowalski," Maddy said.

"No, thank you," the elderly woman said, "I can't do very much because I've become more and more frail, but laundry—dropping it in the machine!—I can do."

Second, plainly, Mrs. Kowalchuck enjoyed Maddy's company. Living alone required an adjustment but it didn't mean she did not miss friendly companionship. Maddy was youthful and spirited. Her maturity went far beyond her years. Mrs. Kowalchuk found she was able to discuss with her the war, politics, current events. Once in a rare while they would be have several cups of tea then Mrs. Kowalchuck would exclaim, "Oh! Dear! I've taken half the morning settling the world's problems and not a single one of mine!"

Third, Maddy was usually aware of the latest gentle gossip in town. Whenever Mrs. Kowalski went to the beauty shop to have her hair and nails done, she usually caught up on the more serious rumors of people, politics, or polemics.

This day, however, they never got to the idle chit-chat. Mrs. Kowalchuk stopped right after she mentioned the laundry, and said, "What's troubling you, Maddy?" Maddy was more surprised at her perspicacity than the dogmatism of the question. "Did anything happen on your trip to Washington, D.C.?"

"I'm fine! Mrs. Kowalchuk. Perhaps distracted with school things and thoughts of the summer," Maddy said attempting an off-handed reply.

"What shows in your voice and on your face is business far more serious, young lady. I may not be wiser than you, but I am a little older," Mrs. Kowalchuck said. "I'm here to listen if you wish; I'm here not to listen if you wish. So? If you had a good time in the Capitol and all's well, let's get our day started!"

For the first time since Maddy starting helping the elderly woman they changed the bed linen without a word between them. As they heaped the bed with shams and pillows, Maddy said, "There that does it!" She collected the sheets and pillow slips and left the room to take them to the laundry. She returned to the bathroom to find Mrs. Kowalchuk barring the doorway.

"My lips are sealed! I will die with our secret! What is wrong?" Mrs. Kowalchuk said.

"You are such a sweet person, Mrs. Kowalchuk. Thank you for being concerned. There is nothing. Nothing," Maddy said.

"Fine!" the elderly woman said the rising inflection dismissing the subject while walking away. It was no more than ten minutes later when she reappeared in the doorway, and announced, "It's time for a break. Tea in the kitchen, now!" She disappeared not allowing Maddy time for a rebuttal.

"I really don't need a break, Mrs. Kowalchuk. I'd rather get the work done," Maddy said.

"Sit!" the elderly woman commanded. "You're on my clock. Do you want to tell me something? ... in strict confidence?"

Without looking up at her, Maddy answered, "No."

"Then, I want to tell you about my daughter."

"Your daughter?" Maddy said, "I didn't know ..."

"Why should you know?" Mrs. Kowalchuk asked. "Just listen."

Sonia Kowalchuck at the time of the story was about two years older than Maddy. Her parents doted on her. Her father proclaimed more than once that he was ready to throw himself in front of a train for her. She was a raving beauty: blond hair, blue eyes, buxom, exciting. Often her photograph was compared to the movie idols of the time. She was very respectful of her parents, helped her mother in the house, did not go out on school nights, and was very popular with both boys and girls. Then, one day, Mrs. Kowalchuk and Sonia were doing up the dinner dishes when the innocuous words coming out of her daughter's mouth made her skin crawl.

"Sonia? What is troubling you?" Mrs. Kowalchuk asked.

"Final exams coming up, Mom!" Sonia answered. "I should have them down pat, but you know? You get worried. You hope you studied the right things. I'm sure I'll do okay. Thanks for being so concerned. You and dad are the best, Mom," she said. "I'll be just fine. I didn't mean to bring you any gray hairs!"

"So?" Mrs. Kowalchuk told Maddy, "I took her at her word. She was always ... what's the word? Forthright? Yes, straight with me. I let it go. Like a fool! I let her sway me! And though my skin crawled when I was in her presence, I let it go. I ignored all the signs. I should have known! I should have been insistent!"

"For god's sakes! Mrs. Kowalchuk," Maddy said, "what happened?"

"I could tell you how good Catholics behave, the moral discipline, the forgiveness of sins. I can tell you the ivory tower of the Pope in Rome is far too removed from the reality of the innocent in Catamount, Massachusetts. What do they know in sunny Italy of how devastating the burden of shame can be," Mrs. Kowalchuk's face turned stone cold. "Sonia died of septicemia and hemorrhage from a botched abortion in a motel room across the border in New York State. She was left there to die alone. They found her the next morning."

She drank some tea.

Very gently she placed the cup on the saucer. "My Stanley was never the same. From that moment he went downhill very fast. He lost all caring, including for me." She looked up. "Maddy, let me do for you what I couldn't do for my daughter. Are you 'in trouble'?"

"No," Maddy answered.

"Maddy! I will not tell your parents. I want to help you do what you want to do. I do not believe in abortion, but I will help you find competent medical help—in this country, in Canada, in Europe to see that you have the procedure done safely, if that's what you want or need. Or, if you want to put the child up for adoption, we will tell your parents you must accompany me back to Poland for a last visit. We will find a hospital, and a social agency to find a good home for your baby! Or we'll find someone to take care of your baby until you are ready to take the child yourself. Whatever you want, I will help you do! Please! Give me the chance to redeem myself in the eyes of God that I didn't have for my daughter, Sonia! Do you understand what I'm asking?"

"Oh! Mrs. Kowalchuk! How I would love to ease your heart about Sonia! Young or old we are responsible only to ourselves for important decisions we make. Sonia chose to not include you for her own good reasons. She took a chance to do this on her own. I will tell you what happened in Washington to let you know your instincts are correct."

"Tell me?" she said.

"No one else knows ... You're going to think I'm a foolish romantic, Mrs. Kowalchuk, but Joe and I got married when we were in Washington." Maddy rolled her eyes and shrugged her shoulders.

"... because?" Mrs. Kowalchuk started.

"No! Not because!" Maddy said. "I'm not pregnant."

"Then for what reason?" she asked. "A lark? I hope not. Marriage is a serious thing."

"I know."

"A real, honest-to-goodness marriage?" the elderly woman asked.

"Yes. I'll show you," Maddy said.

"Then why?" Mrs. Kowalchuk asked staring hard at her.

Maddy pushed the teacup away, put her arms flat on the table, and leaned forward and spoke in a very confidential way. "Because Joe and I are deeply in love with each other. We know it like the sun will come up tomorrow. We wanted to share each other's hearts for as long as we could. There are forces that wish to keep us apart. This was the only way we knew we would be with each other. With the war on ... and all ... For each other we did the right thing." Maddy raised her eyebrows and shrugged in finality.

Mrs. Kowalchuk toyed with her spoon. She tapped the table. "Maddy, I know I do not have to reassure you, but I will. I will never reveal your secret. Also, I have no right to ask, but you will understand why I ask with the question, and you do not have to answer. Is the marriage consummated? Do you know what I mean?"

"Yes, I know. No, it was not," Maddy said smiling. "Joe and I did not have sex. You know, since I had the accident with my bike, and Joe 'saved' me? Well, my mother laid a trip on him that he was my 'protector.' You know, I think somehow my Mom knew what was between us even before we knew it. She wanted to protect me as much as she could. The result was Joe took it to heart. We—Joe and I—both agreed we will not make love until I am eighteen, no matter what. It's just something sacred between us. If I told my girlfriends they'd laugh at me. They'd think I was crazy. Do you think I'm crazy?"

Mrs. Kowalchuk reached over and patted her hand. "My Stanley and I were exactly the same. The difference? He wasn't made my protector. I was sixteen, and he was nineteen, and we had a heck of a good time! I think I got pregnant the first night!" She laughed out loud. "My Stanley used to say Sonia came into this world with the Stars and Stripes playing with Fourth of July fireworks!" She laughed again. Then grew quiet. "I don't know if I should say this. I don't want to appear as a know-it-all. I'm just an old lady who wants to give you what she can for your happiness. Okay?" Maddy nodded. "Love is for happiness, sex is for oneself. Love is to build a lifetime, sex is selfish. Nature, understanding the need for sex, provided also for the future and gave to her universe the honeymoon. The purpose of the honeymoon is so a couple can learn and adjust to being intimate, that's how babies are made. More importantly, to me, is so a couple can learn to do for each other. During a honeymoon, the couple learns how to give pleasure to one another. Once they understand how critical that can be involving a very personal thing like sex, they realize it is just as important to everything else they must do in their lives together."

Eyes wide open, enthusiastically, Maddy interrupted. "It is like a partnership where each one does what must be done for the good of the partnership!"

"And neither one keeps score!" the elderly woman said. "Couples who do that do for each other, are considerate, and respect one another are together for ages."

Maddy rubbed the table nervously. "Mrs. Kowalchuk, I don't want to ask anyone else, but ... there's something I'd like to know ..."

"Real personal?" Mrs. Kowalchuk asked. "Like hygiene?"

It was Maddy's turn to burst out into laughter, joined very quickly by the old woman.

"I love you, Mrs. Kowalchuk! You are my very dearest and best friend!" Maddy exclaimed. "It seems I should know so much more than I do. I feel so lacking! As if the world is so far ahead of me, and I'm so far behind! I want you to tell me about life!"

Mrs. Kowalchuk sat back turning her face to the ceiling and raising both hands in supplication. "*O, moja droga, slodka, kochana niewinnosci, pozwol mi opowiedziec di!*"

"What did you say? What did you say?" Maddy implored.

"I said, 'Oh! My dear, sweet, precious, innocent one, let me tell you!' I always revert to my native tongue when my heart is touched and moved deeply. Maddy, you are such a special person. In Poland we reserve a command for those such as you: *Nie umieray!* Never die! Yes, never die, Maddy. You are as a golden angel! How I wish I had the answer of life for you. It would mean I have it for myself. You must give me time to think of my answer. I can tell you this: Do not listen if someone wants to tell you what you will encounter as you live. Life is like a beautiful flower unfolding. As each petal opens, so does each day in your life. You should discover what it holds by yourself. It is a process of discovery. It is this enlightenment that brings a full and complete life. It is seeing a movie, not a re-run. Don't see what people tell you to see. First, see it for yourself. Be your own person. It is your enlightenment. Then check to see if you have missed anything worthwhile." They sat silently for a long moment. It was obvious Mrs. Kowalchuk was in deep thought. "Ah! Yes! As my father told me, and his father told him, and so on, let me pass on old Polish words to the young person moving on to the world. It says like this: Because the devil never sleeps, one must at all times be as smart as one can be. Because there are many adversaries and challenges in life, for example a terrible hurt, emotional pain—such as I felt when I lost my Stanley—one must be as brave as one can be always. We will always regret it when we do not face all situations forcefully. Then, because all of us walk close to the valley of tears, we must never miss a moment to enjoy life and be as happy as we can be. There! Three things: head, heart, and soul. Every day: be thoughtful, be brave, be happy. At this party—your life—be sure to bring your own good times with you."

"Oh! I will, Mrs. Kowalchuk! I want so much from life! I want to rush right into it. I want to have as much of it as I can. Joe and I just didn't want to waste time. Here," Maddy said reaching into her purse, "I carry this with me because I don't know where to leave it. I'm afraid someone will find it." She spread out her marriage certificate on the table between them so the older woman could read it.

"I didn't disbelieve you," Mrs. Kowalchuck said, "but there's no doubt you're 'hitched!' as they say!" She drummed the table rapidly. "Let me think a moment ..." She turned back to Maddy. "I have it! I must be just like you. When we know something is right, it's right! No need to fool around. Come with me and bring your certificate." The older woman led Maddy into the living room. She went to one end of the paneled room, pushed a panel in, and slid it over. It revealed a wall safe. "My Stanley was clever with things like this. The springs keep the panel in place and the safe out of sight. I want you to write down the numbers I give you, and then I want you to open the safe."

"Mrs. Kowalchuk! You are giving me a very big responsibility!" Maddy said.

"Nonsense," the elderly woman said. "You will have a safe place to keep your certificate. You will have the combination, and I will give you a key to my home as well so you may enter as you please. Should anything happen to me, you are free to do what you will. I will never change my mind."

"That is such a big trust, Mrs. Kowalchuk!"

She looked at her, raising her eyebrows. "And didn't you just give me a big trust?"

With the safe open, Mrs. Kowalchuk showed Maddy several packs of bills. "This is money. It can cause problems when you don't have it. Borrow as much as you want. Return it when you can. Also, important documents: marriage, birth, citizenship, deeds, jewelry, heirlooms. Would you like to add your marriage certificate?"

"I think it would be great! It will certainly put us at ease! I don't know why you're so good to me, Mrs. Kowalchuk."

"Because you're a big troublemaker. Does that answer your question?" she asked as she closed the safe, spun the knob, and moved the panel back in place. "Half the morning's gone and you have yet to start getting my home in order!"

CHAPTER 12

T A P S

A Military Bugle Call
Revised 1862 by General Dan Butterfield
and his Bugler

Day is done
Gone the sun
From the Lakes
From the hills
From the skies.
All is well,
Safely rest
God is nigh.

Fading light
Dims the sight
And a star
Gems the sky
Gleaming bright
From afar,
Drawing nigh
Fall the night.

Thanks and praise,
For our days,
'Neath the sun,
'Neath the stars,
'Neath the sky
As we go,
This we know,
God is nigh.

WHEN NEWS of the first serviceman from Catamount to be killed arrived in the Western Union office Ted Peterson read the telegram then walked it down to the Town Hall. There he handed it to Arturo Daigno, the town clerk, and after whispering to a clerk, left.

Arturo stared at the yellow envelope with his name in the window for a long time. The clerks in the office slipped out quietly.

Finally, Arturo slid the unopened message into his back pocket, left the office, and got into his car. He drove to Monument Mountain, a short distance north of town. He parked at the base, took his trumpet, and hiked to the summit. He went a bit past the Indian Monument, a huge mass of stones piled one on top of the other where a sachem was buried, they said, and stood in the gentle wind facing south. He put the trumpet to his lips and played all three verses of "*Taps.*"

In town, it was as if a megaphone directed the notes to fill the air on every street, in every lane. It just so happened it was precisely noontime when the first brittle bits of the haunting melody were heard. Not a second step was taken. Traffic froze. In the cold December air, drivers rolled down their windows of their stopped cars. In homes and buildings the sound caused everyone to cock their heads. Men and women put their hands over their hearts. Veterans stood at attention and saluted.

Although no one was told, everyone knew.

Catamount had lost one of its sons.

As the last note slipped into the air, Arturo sat down, the trumpet across his lap, took the envelope out of his pocket, held his forehead in his hands and cried.

Arturo returned to the Town Hall, walked into his office. He announced to the empty room although the staff was within hearing, "I have lost my nephew at Pearl Harbor. I will miss him like blazes." He printed his nephew's name and salient dates on a three-by-five card, which he glued to the wall outside his office door. Back in the office he said, "We have work to do!"

There was no formal proclamation that made it a Catamount tradition for the remainder of the war. Ted would call Arturo and let him know he was about to deliver a telegram, or the relatives would inform him, and ask if he would be kind enough to play "Taps." Whatever the time, day or night, or the weather, Arturo would climb the mountain, stand on the peak, and hail a fallen hero.

The war ended.

Arturo made the trip 27 times.

CHAPTER 13

WHEN RICHARD THOMPSON got off the train in Catamount he was spotted right away by Rosalie Apuzzo. She screamed, "Richard! Richard!" She raced toward him.

"Rosalie! Sweetheart!" he shouted as he dropped his bag, ran to her, and gathered her up in his arms.

They were still kissing when the train pulled out, and the station emptied.

He had been Maddy's eighth grade home room teacher some four years ago. He was a reservist and was one of the first to be recalled into the Army just when the drums of war sounded in Europe. She told him she was in love with him and would marry him as soon as she was 18 years old. He was not a native son of Catamount, but Rosalie Apuzzo, his fiancé, was.

During the time they were apart, she went to business school and trained to be a legal secretary. She worked for a local attorney. When she returned to the office this day after taking an extra long lunch break, she found the message from Richard. He would be arriving at the Catamount train station early afternoon. She got to the station as the train pulled up to a stop.

"I called from Grand Central Station. I couldn't reach you! I couldn't reach you!" Dick said as he retrieved his bag. "I figured we'd waste less time if I just came right up ..."

"I never take long lunch breaks, just today! I just got your message! Oh! Sweetheart! Am I happy to see you!" she said.

He took her by the arm. "Let's decide. I've got less than 36 hours. I've got to be on the 4:30 train to New York tomorrow afternoon. Things are so bad over there I barely got emergency leave for my mom's funeral. It's back to the Philippines for me, sweetheart. If you want to get married we'll use up a lot of time getting a ring, a license, hunting up a preacher, getting our friends together, arranging for a brunch tomorrow morning. Then we could have a four hour honeymoon. Or, we can just be together. Which shall it be? Your call."

Rosalie pulled him toward the cab stand. "Naturally, what girl wouldn't choose marriage to the man she loved?"

They slipped into the cab. Rosalie hitched up on the seat to get close to the driver. "Get us to the closest hotel-motel-cabin as fast as you can!" She looked at Richard. "We'll save the wedding for when you come back."

At some time during the 36 hours they spent together in the motel room, Richard tipped the owner $20.00 for bringing them a hot pizza and three bottles of wine. The pizza was still in the room—intact—but the bottles were empty.

While Richard was getting dressed, Rosalie wrote him a note, which started out: My one and only darling Richard— Don't you fucking dare get yourself killed and not come back to me and your son, because that's what we made today as an expression of our love! Yours forever Rose."

Chapter 14

RICHARD THOMPSON

The banzai attack broke out from the canebreak just off to the right of Sgt. Richard Thompson. He had been snatched out of the rear echelon as a replacement heavy, water-cooled machine gunner. The corporal next to him swore as he fought to load an ammunition belt.

"Fuck do I know! I'm a cook!" the corporal said.

Richard reached up, pushed his hand away, pounded his fist on the first shells to straighten them out and slammed down the cover. By that time the screaming Japanese has gained almost ten yards with guns and bayonets aimed at the American line.

Richard didn't take time to breathe as he methodically swept the blur of men on the charging enemy line. Uniforms melted away before him to be filled immediately with even louder shouting charging troops. The thickest groups were almost in front of him.

Richard picked an arc from two to three o'clock. He held the gun to fire just above crotch level, the widest, biggest target. A bullet to the pelvis would drop a man like a falling block of cement and in the least disable him. It seemed every bullet he fired found a mark, if not at the front of the line, one further in the rear.

The carnage for a moment stopped the advance. "Belt!" he screamed. With no action, he glanced over to find that the corporal had caught a bad one. He was thrown backwards, his face a mess. He looked up to see Japancsc soldiers less than ten yards in front of him. He pulled out his Colt .45 caliber, and fired as fast as he could pull the trigger.

Five of the enemy had fallen when he shot another off to his left. He barely caught movement to his right and saw the grimacing face of a Japanese soldier about to get him with his bayonet. Richard twisted his body to have the bayonet slice from side to side through his shirt. His pistol slipped from his hand. He grabbed the barrel of the rifle with one hand and twisted off the bayonet with the other. He swung the blade in a short arc and cut the man's throat back to his spine. Without hesitation, he turned the gun toward the Japanese on his left. The bullet stopped him where he stood.

Richard reached down to the ground for his .45. He fired it until it was empty. With the enemy no longer before him, Richard snapped open the machine gun and loaded another belt and put a fresh clip into the pistol. Off to the left, the Japanese were coming through the canebreak in two's and three's. He set his sights, and swept the area slowly, methodically. When he looked back to his right, he saw there was more work to be done. He fired with his left hand, and guided the belt with his right. The chattering machine gun cyclic made a steady dik-dik-dik-dik-dik in his ears, but it could not hide the yelling and screaming of dying men. It seemed three different movies were being shown on the same screen. The gruesome work was on automatic. The hordes seemed so stupid to run madly to their death. Where one fell, another took his place. Richard was hard-set and grim doing his work but amazed to find himself singing the Andrews Sisters' *"Boogie-Woogie Bugle Boy of Company B"* in time with the dik-dik-dik-dik.

He was totally surprised to find he was pushed backwards with a bayonet that was shoved into him just below his first rib and hit the inside of his wingbone. As calmly as if he was licking an ice cream cone, he picked up his pistol and shot the Japanese soldier right in the mouth. Unfortunately, he had been picked out by the Japanese officers watching the action as the kingpin who had stopped their frontal attack cold. In effect, he was chosen to be put out of business no matter how many soldiers got killed doing it. He knew the solder standing next to the man he killed wanted the honor of putting him out of commission. Now as the enemy's dead friend fell he jostled the one with the gun pointed right at his nose and the bullet went into his upper left leg. He would have shown surprise at his miss if Richard's shot didn't go through his chin, through the roof of his mouth, smack through the middle of his brain and out his helmet. Richard registered the look of surprise on the man's face.

Richard was brought back to the infirmary. Three days later, April 9, 1942, Richard insisted he was ready to return to the duty line. There was no need, he was told. At that moment Gen. Edward King was meeting with Maj. Gen. Kameichiro Nagano. After several hours of negotiations, the remaining weary, starving and emaciated American and Filipino defenders on the battle-swept Bataan peninsula were surrendered.

Richard sought out his captain. "I'd rather not surrender. I'd like to join up with the guerrillas."

"*That is the easy way. Earn the otter on your shoulder. You will be needed more by your brother soldiers on what you all face.*"

Friday, April 10, 1942. 6:30 am Marching - Camp O'Donnell 60/70 miles. In second group of 100 Americans/Philoes. Pocket search—hide Rosalie's letter in jockey shorts. Record diary on. Full canteen water, helmet, extra socks. Philo has Jap money. Butt to back, falls to knees. Jap Officer decapitates. Captain post tied—30 bayonet wounds. 11:00 am straggling. Helper/helpee both shot. Stay in middle. Count steps. Stops to poop. Shot. Stops to sip black grunge water. Shot. Fall gets bayonet. 1:00-2 standing burning sun. Give away helmet. Share water. Left behinders shot. Hunger. Hunger pangs. Night in field stop. Slip away to cistern to fill canteens. Chewing grass. Read Rosalie. Son?

Sat April 11 daylight maggotty rice ball. Change socks. Straggly groups. Knotted handkerchief wet on head. Shootings/bayonetting continue. Pants pooping. Yuk. Sun standing. Hunger pangs. Water sharing. Run for water puddle gets bayonet. My bandages bleeding. Sun standing. Decapitations practice. I become invisible. Helps buddy up...both bayonetted. Addled marcher screams at guard. Sliced. Grungy rice ball enough to make hunger pangs. Field sleep. Canteens fill. Socks change. Read Rosalie.

Sun April 12. Mouth buttoned. Center of group. Counting slow steps. Arbitrary casualties. Officer uses sword every hour on hour. I mark him. Sun burning. Collapse/bayonet. Crawling rice ball. Sleep stop. Slither in the nude to sword officer. Razor to throat. Creep/drag him to poop trench. Push him deep. Cover with dirt. Cistern water slip away fill canteens wash away blood, wash socks. Read Rosalie.

Mon April 13. Running out of space on Rosalie's letter. The usual. Hunger pangs. Wound pain. Standing in sun gets many. Hummed Andrews Sister. Best help is water I get. How will anyone know if I'm dead or alive? Read Rosalie.

Tues April 14. Brutal savage bastards never tire of killing. Hope slipping.

Wed April 15. Physical and guard toll is staggering on marchers. Crushed onto cattle train. We poop, pee, die upright. Soon in camp. I will escape join guerrillas. Rosalie. Rosalie. Rosalie.

CHAPTER 15

BRAD MC EVILY found the war to be his springboard to freedom. He had a taste of what the adult world offered, and he couldn't get enough of it. It was precipitated by the one night he spent with Brandy Salvatto. The experience turned him into a flaming jackrabbit. Before that, he knew he was onto something when he would visit his current crush while she was baby-sitting. They would be on the couch for hours sucking tongues-—swapping spits, as it was called—and giving each other hickeys by sucking hard at each other's necks creating huge, ugly black and blue discolorations. In the heat of the moment, he would feel her breasts, but that was as far as she would let it would go. He was dying to touch her in more private parts. Then, after the first extended encounter, Brad ran home, his testicles inflamed and aching—a condition known as blue balls—the result of a too-long turgescent penis without the relief of an orgasm. Much to his dismay, he found masturbating added to his pain; then, while gently cradling his sack and not jerking his penis back and forth too hard, he worked through it only to find matters seemed worse, not better. His vocabulary grew with the definition of a "cock tease." He swore that night he would never again be brought to that state without some promise of relief.

After Brandy, he ached for more sexual experiences. The problem was moving out of the house. Brad could be out from under his oppressive father, and nagging mother and be able to support himself only one way: if he joined the Marines. He let everyone give him credit for being a brave and patriotic American. In his heart, he knew what he was after.

Following basic training, his mind was focused on finding sex on and off the base. He asked a college professor in a restaurant if he could have her autograph because she looked like a movie star. She was a plain jane, but she ate it up. In a motel room, after the third go-around and he looking for more, she called him a satyr. When he asked her what it meant, she told him. It was the term for excessive or abnormal sexual craving. He had to agree. He loved to fuck, and lived for it, and was she ready for just one more ta-hime?

When Brad saw the outline of Saipan that mid-June day, the first question he asked his sergeant was if he thought there were any native girls on the island. Girls were not to be his main concern, he was told, but bushido was. It was the fanatical code that required Japanese soldiers to fight to the death. Snipers in palm tree tops had been cleared out near the airfield. It gave the gyrenes a false sense of security because, at night, the snipers took to their perches again.

Brad was snuggled down against the exposed shallow roots of a palm tree. He had an uneasy night with dreams of a scalding hot shower. He struggled to a sitting position and yawned. There was none of this nonsense in Catamount, but when he got back there, would he impress the ladies with his suave gyrene manner! He barely moved in the uneasy light, he so blended in with the immediate landscape. He opened a can of ham and eggs, his favorite ration, and ate slowly and deliberately. When he finished, he was still hungry. He was offered another tin. The sniper's bullet blasted his helmet off of his head. He dropped the can and spoon.

Brad slid downward to hide himself. He remained with his hands on his lap, his nose flared, and breathing in deliberate hard spurts. His jaw was clamped tightly. "Yo! Sarge! I need a scoped rifle!" he called out.

The sergeant pointed to his rear holding up his thumb and forefinger indicating a short distance.

Brad returned to the upturned roots. He dug into the earth carefully. When he had made a hole just large enough to poke the sniper rifle through he dug in the shovel to make a solid rest. He looked through the scope to scour the treetops.

He returned to the start of his arc and squeezed off a shot. Methodically, he went from treetop to treetop firing a shot at each stop.

The sergeant showed him a fist in approbation, then signaled his men to move forward. They were stopped after only a few yards with heavy machine gun fire from three sources.

Time to earn my wolverine, Brad said to himself. He loaded his vest with hand grenades. He checked his sidearm. He crawled through the undergrowth to within 15 yards of a chattering machine gun. He tossed two grenades and watched the nest fly up in the air. He used his pistol on two Japanese that only seemed dazed. Then, he headed for the next machine gun.

Alerted, the enemy was prepared for him. One bullet drew a red line from his temple to just past his ear, another in the thigh of his left leg.

By that time, he had two more grenades flying through the air. It silenced the machine gun and every soldier around it.

Taking giant steps towards the third machine gun a bullet caught his left arm just as he let the grenade go. It fell short but close enough to distract the machine gunner. Brad jumped to the rim of the nest. He used his pistol to shoot the five men surrounding the weapon.

Now able to advance, the sergeant asked Brad if he was able to get himself back to get medical attention. Of course he was, Brad told him. He tore off his tee shirt to wrap his left arm, and took a position at the front of the line with the sniper rifle.

CHAPTER 16

SVEN JOHNSON

SVEN JOHNSON spent three months jockeying a bulldozer until he was able to have it waltz sideways. He had a helluva wonderful time training with the Naval Construction Battalion, also known as the SeaBees. He appreciated the instruction because it widened his horizons concerning heavy equipment construction. At home his business was restricted to what he alone could manage, and the tools he could use. Suddenly, he was moving yards and yards of earth and gravel and laying down roadways and an airfield. A realistic and practical man, he knew the war would not last forever. He also knew the country would be on the move. He could go on building custom homes and commercial buildings in Catamount, and undoubtedly have a very satisfying and successful career. His eyes opened wide to bigger potential. He would pursue a substantially more immense goal. When he got out of the service, he would talk to the smartest people he knew and head for the land with the largest opportunities. At the moment, he was inclined to think airports were the thing. It was a burgeoning industry. Every city big or small needed one. And, here he was, going to help get one built on Iwo Jimo, a tiny island in the Volcano Island chain. It was 750 miles from Tokyo, halfway between Guam and Japan. Sven was filled with pride knowing he would be instrumental in cutting the B-29 flying time from Tinian, in the Marianas, to Iwo Jimo where they could make two trips in the place of one. He was determined to run his bulldozer every day as long as he could to have the B-29s touch down just as quickly as they could.

The problem was they wanted Sven and the CB's right there to start building the moment they could. In Sven's case it meant he would have to help take the strategically vital island. He was delighted to hear the rumor that it was to be a "piece of cake." Army air forces and the navy had bombed or shelled the island for seven months straight to soften the Japanese prior to invasion. "What the hell could be left to the island," Sven wondered.

What was left was a system of concrete fortifications, underground defenses, and a fiercely determined enemy.

Sven was put ashore on Iwo two weeks before the marines raised the American flag atop Mount Suribachi. "Give me a D-10, the largest bulldozer made, and I'll lay down an airfield before supper!" he bragged. But, the fighting was far from over. Sven was anxious to get "the lay of the land" where the airfield was to be built. Peering through binoculars he picked out activity above the far end of the field.

"What the hell are they doing?" he asked the officer next to him.

"Son of a bitch! They lining up howitzers so they can rake the landing field."

"I count maybe six?" Sven asked.

"More like a dozen! They don't want this strip finished! You can see all the craters they made at this end."

"Let's see if we can put the puma to work. Sergeant!" he called to the soldier down the line, "Can you make that Browning Automatic Rifle talk? I can use you!"

"Not me, friend! You can have it if you want!"

Sven jumped down and ran with the BAR and a fresh belt of ammo to the D-10 parked under camouflage on the other side of the ravaged strip. He fired it up, raised the blade and chose a more or less hidden trail to drive it up to the other end of the airfield. He cradled the BAR on oil pressure hoses to his right. He found he could swing it easily in an arc from ten o'clock to four o'clock. Especially moving at a fast speed, the large saplings and palm trees offered little resistance to the formidable monstrous machine.

As he got closer to the cannons he recognized the Pings! as bullets bouncing off of the huge blade he had in the

half-raised position. Judging his distance by checking the
other side of the landing field, he powered his way through
the jungle until he got to where he thought he would be in
a straight line with the cannon. He made a hard left.
Machine gun fire came from his right. He fired the BAR in
a short arc at where he guessed the nest might be. He
pushed the throttle forward. When he caught the first
howitzer just ahead of the wheels, he knew he was on
target. He adjusted his direction just a tad to the right.
Firing the BAR in bursts, he counted the jumps the D-10
took as it rolled over a cannon. Three ... four ... dut-dut-
dut-dut ... five ... six ... dut-dut-dut ... seven ... eight ...
empty BAR ... nine ...PING-ZING-ZING-PING! ... ten ...
eleven ...

Checking the field he saw he had bulldozed the entire
end held by the Japanese. He lowered the blade and shut
off the engine when he realized he caught a bullet in his
ass, his right leg above his knee, and in his left arm
muscle.

CHAPTER 17

PAUL MALLOY

PAUL MALLOY, the older of Maddy's twin brothers, was three weeks past his eighteenth birthday when he found himself in the Army on Bougainville. He hugged a Browning Automatic Rifle trying to make himself as small as he could be. He was huddled in a small indentation on the side of Hill 700. The stink of wet sour earth filled his nostrils. He tried to move his toes in his soaked socks. The rain alternated between coming down as a drizzle or plopping down in buckets. He rubbed his leg that was pushed up tight against himself to ward off the chicken skin. He used a knuckle to push off droplets on his nose. "How the fuck did I get here?" he said aloud.

Paul found the fellow next to him staring at him with wide open eyes. He was shivering. "Just got here myself. I'm a replacement. Where are we? I'm Clarence."

"The island? Bougainville, Philippines, part of the Solomon Islands chain."

"I'm fucking going to die on a place I don't even know how to spell."

"You're not going to die unless you want to. Just don't be stupid."

"Christ! I gotta poop."

"Not here you don't. Get it in your handkerchief, tie up the four corners and fling it to hell out of here. Preferably toward the Japs, over the ridge."

The package went sailing ten feet over the top and was immediately blasted with sniper's bullets.

A sergeant ran up and dropped on a knee between them. "Malloy, the report is the Japs are setting up for an attack. They're sneaking through the concertina wire on the other side of the ridge. Get your BAR up there and see what's going on and stop that crap." He pointed to Clarence, "You go with him."

Paul looked at the soldier. "You any good with that?" He pointed to the man's rifle.

"Yeah." He nodded. "I kin bark a squirrel."

"Let's go see if I've earned my dog." Paul crawled inch by inch toward the ridge. The mud and the incline made the slippery going a challenge. He put a hand out to grab a root. A sniper's bullet missed it by inches.

"See where it came from? The tree top to the right above the ridge maybe a hundred feet away?" The soldier nodded. "Now nail the son-of-a-bitch," Paul said. He took off his helmet, held it off the ground with his bayonet, and inched it to where he had exposed his hand. A bullet sent it spinning. Paul heard Clarence shoot. He watched the sniper fall from the tree to dangle from a rope, dropping his rifle.

Paul kicked Clarence with his toe. "Next liberty I'm on I'm treating you to an Around the World Hooker."

"Thanks. Never been. I'm just a shit-kicker from Georgia. Your first action."

"How did you know?" Paul asked.

"Your fucking shivering is making me quake," Clarence answered.

"I feel like I came out of a hot bath and got put in a freezer," Paul explained. He felt better when he spoke, so he continued. "The last time this happened to me I was in Los Angeles and had been picked up by a waitress. We went to a bar, had a few beers, then she took me to her dinky little apartment. I was nude in bed, shivering with excitement, waiting for her to get in beside me. I had never been laid before. She no sooner kissed me and touched my hard-on and I exploded! I couldn't help it. Man! Was I embarrassed. The fuck did I know? What to do until she started laughing. So, I laughed, too. I gotta tell you, no bullshit, I made up for it the rest of the night. God! Was she some piece. Sorry, but let's see what's going on over the ridge."

Over the ridge the enemy was attacking. Five Japanese had broken through the concertina wire.

Paul took off the safety and let the BAR do its work. "Clarence! I need ammo! More ammo!"

The BAR was silent only for a few moments until Paul reloaded. The "SPLAT!" of bullets meant for him hitting mud and trees resounded. "Clarence! The gun is too hot to shoot! I need another!"

In less than two minutes Clarence had replaced Paul's BAR with a fresh one.

The battle continued with wave after wave of Japanese assaulting the crest of Hill 700.

Clarence kept firing at a machine gun emplacement some thirty yards away, which kept their focus on him and not on Paul. During a lull, some two hours later, Paul estimated there were some thirty empty magazines and three other BAR's he used around him.

The sergeant dropped between them. "The captain says we've got them on the run. We're all going over the top together."

The sergeant personally led the assault, shouting defiance at the enemy and encouragement to his own men. Fifteen minutes later, the sergeant was seriously wounded in the chest. Paul spotted the Japanese machine gun nest. He dropped to one knee and killed all the men in the gun crew that was holding up his company.

His fire attracted another machine gun. Paul's gun was empty. Clarence's pin-point fire kept them distracted. Paul saw a light machine gun, its crew all killed. He disengaged the weapon from its mount, and firing as he held it in his arms killed a Japanese machine-gun crew that was murdering the charging Americans.

He saw Clarence fall, mortally wounded by a sniper in a tree almost dead ahead of them. Paul knelt beside him. "Hey! Buddy, you're going to be all right. We got a date, remember?"

The sniper put a bullet through Paul's right chest. Paul ducked down to put a fresh belt into his gun. He turned, sat up and emptied the BAR into the tree top until it fell to the ground to land on top of a dead sniper.

While waiting for a stretcher for Paul Malloy they were up to 167 enemy dead and counting when the counter attack came.

At the news that Paul Malloy was missing in action, Dorothea Malloy was sedated and kept in the hospital for six days. Maddy was by her side constantly. Dennis offered what comfort he could, but he moved about as if on remote control. Efforts to no avail were made through a senator and representative to have Peter brought home on emergency leave. There was difficulty locating him.

CHAPTER 18

PETER MALLOY

PETER MALLOY, the older of Maddy's twin brothers, was getting the lay of the land in the thick of the fighting on New Guinea. The news of his brother missing in action was in a stack of radio messages aboard a troop transport still anchored at Maui. Two weeks earlier, the day after they had arrived at the island Peter was standing at attention as the squads of men were given their assignments. The squads were dismissed and fell away. Peter remained at attention.

"Malloy! You're dismissed!" the sergeant said to him. Peter did not move. "Dismissed!" Still no reaction from Peter. "What's wrong with you soldier!"

Peter slowly turned his head to look the sergeant straight in the eyes. "My brother is reported MIA."

The sergeant stared hard at him. "How close were you?"

"My identical twin."

"Son, come with me. I'm taking you to the Chaplain."

Years earlier Peter had rejected the Boys Scouts, their uniforms, jamborees because of the boring sameness. Years later he hadn't changed, but pride compelled him to go through the motions of being a tough-ass Gyrene. Besides, now he wore the raven on his shoulder. Off-base, peer pressure took him to bars where beer and slug-fests were sought. He was shown how to whip off his belt and use it to cold-cock any living person standing before him. That wasn't his style either, so he dared, once, to slip away from his group to go to the U.S.O.

"Handsome fellow like you hiding yourself away in a dark corner!" the middle-aged lady said to him as she grabbed his hand, and pulled him toward the dance floor on which moving as a mass were uniformed men and smiling ladies.

She must have read his mind, he thought, because he had been watching enviously the other servicemen dancing. She swung around to meet him, putting her free arm around him, drawing him in close. He could feel her body push up against him. He liked the sensations it sent crackling inside his gut and catching him at his throat. "Ma'am! I've fallen in love with you, and I'd like us to get married as quickly as possible!" He realized what a dumb thought that was as the spicy fragrance of her perfume filled his lungs.

"Relax! This is supposed to be fun, not warfare!" she said as she pulled her head back to stare into his eyes.

She was as pretty as his third grade teacher whom he adored. She had come to life again and had rescued him from his watching post and breathed life into him. The music segued into another song. She held on just as tight and though he knew she was talking to him, and he responded he couldn't remember a thing because of his near-catatonic state.

At a break in the music, she led him to a cute blondie who looked like June Alyson. "Junie, it's my turn for coffee detail so I'll turn over this handsome devil to you. Be careful! I think the last woman that held him was his mother!"

Junie slipped lightly into his arms just brushing up against him now and then in just the right place to find himself aroused.

"No," she said.

"What do you mean?" he asked.

"Even if I wanted to take you home with me, I can't. We're not allowed to date outside of the club," she said.

"You mean, the elopement is off?" he replied.

"The orgasm has a greater purpose, it should not be solely a selfish objective," she said.

"I bought a wedding ring," he said.

"It's closing time. Goodbye! Good Luck! Be safe," she said.

"No! The evening's ending too quickly!" Peter said. "I want to dance some more. I know how to talk to you now. I promise I won't be shy ..."

"Shy? Shy?" he thought he heard her say, "It rhymes with die! Die!" It's a tease! A fucking tease! I'm just learning about the joy of life and living and it's going to be snatched away! No! No!

Outside, a Marine he didn't know guided him onto a bus for the ride back to the base. From that time on in his mind he kept pushing his rising hard-on into her then found she wasn't as soft as he thought. Instead she was hot and dry and turned out to be not flesh but the sand of this foreign island halfway around the world from Catamount. The grains under his hands flowed quickly as if in an hour glass as he remembered they did as a child on the dunes at Truro Beach, Cape Cod. "No!" he said to himself. "I can't die without having had a real good fuck!"

Here on New Guinea, he looked up at the sky, past the ridge of the wide impression in which he had flung himself. There was not a bit of a cloud in the pale blue sky he could see. Not even a bird. All he heard was the blasting drone of a shooting war exploding all about him. He did not recognize the metallic smell of fear fomenting inside the soldier laying just five feet from him. He stared at the man and knew he had to exert himself to keep from messing himself.

Peter stared at the sky with all his might as if it could bring him out of the dream stifling the uneasiness rustling about in his chest. If only he could have gone home with the blondie.

He took a deep breath, grabbed his flamethrower and yanked it towards the crest. The other member of the team saw him move and followed. He could hear the attacking Japanese shouting, "Chusuto!" and "Yaruzo!" followed by "Harimosu!" He had no idea what the words meant, but figured a pretty good interpretation would be, "Fuck you!" As he ran up the fire-swept hill he could see in his peripheral vision the blistering fire knock down his comrades. Peter, shaking wildly, made it to the cover of a large boulder several yards on the downward slope. He spotted the pillbox some fifteen yards away. He spoke softly to the raven until he understood what others were counting on him to do. Slithering forward inch by inch, he got to within ten yards of the pillbox. Three machine guns were inside chattering a cacophony.

Peter stood up in full view. Remaining cool, he aimed his flamethrower and let it go. He doused the emplacement with liquid fire killing everyone in the pillbox.

Peter threw himself onto the ground and headed for a second pillbox off to the right. In it were at least two large caliber machine guns lacing the ridge with a constant barrage of deadly firepower.

Pulling his equipment after him he crawled as quickly as he could toward the Japanese. He could see them intent on their deadly task when one of them—gaunt, drawn, dirty faced—turned and looked directly at him. Holding his stricken gaze, Peter got on one knee and released his inferno point blank into the pillbox. The screams overtook the sound of the firing machine guns.

A third pillbox was further on, but Peter was out of fuel. He race crawled on all fours to the ridge and fell over the top. He saw the blood on his blouse above his hip and knew he had caught a bullet in his side.

He beckoned the sergeant. "I know the location of the pillbox that's giving our boys hell. I need another flamethrower!"

"Alls we got here are bazookas. Take the one from the fellow holding the shells and have him go with you after them."

Peter took the weapon, again crawled over the crest. He caught another bullet in the muscle of his left leg. He kept going despite the bullets spattering about him until he reached a shallow depression. He turned to find the soldier that had followed him looked like a high school freshman— deadpanned and blank eyed.

"The pillbox is about twenty-five feet away. Load me up!"

The kid rapped Peter on the shoulder. "The enema for the enemy is ready!"

Peter looked back at him. Disgust on his face for the bad pun. Then smiled. He turned back to aiming the weapon at the pillbox. Taking deliberate care, he fired. The pillbox exploded.

"Load me up!" Peter shouted. "You stay here! I'm going after the further machine gun emplacement!"

He had gone no more than four yards when a sniper put one in his shoulder. The pain was crushing. He screamed at the top of his lungs, "I'll fix you, you fucking son of a bitch!"

"What do you want to do?" he envisioned the sergeant screaming waving them on, "Live forever?"

Then, it didn't matter anymore that she didn't want to take him home.

Peter got up on one knee, grabbed the bazooka, and fired it at the machine gun. The gun flew into the air, the crew killed.

Peter blacked out from the pain.

CHAPTER 19

SALVATORE CARUSO

SALVATORE CARUSO wrote to his younger brother, Joe: "Mindanao—On The Road To Tokyo." This is a godawful stinking place! I live on quinine to put down the malaria, and I pray a lot to keep down the runs. Half of my buddies are fighting with a load in their pants! I'm with the 189th Battalion. The weather is rainy, steamy, sweaty. What a rotten piece of real estate. For the last eight weeks we've been going out ten men to a squad. I'm surprised I've lasted this long. They give us all the ammo we want. I usually take six bandoleers, and load my trouser pockets with three grenades in each side. By the end of the day, I've used everything up if only just to cause a distraction. Every single leaf that moves gets the focus of our attention and two-dozen bullets. Two days ago my squad went out to find out what happened to a double squad that was sent out on patrol. We found them. Perhaps a dozen were buried up to their necks. Their heads were doused with fish oil. The oil attracted quite carnivorous Philippine ants. They were all dead, each and every one. We were surprised we didn't hear them screaming fifty miles away. Yesterday morning, the colonel sent out eight patrols to hunt for those murdering Jap bastards. We found them. Those we took alive or wounded, we held down and used our rifle butts to slowly hammer bayonets right between their eyes into their skulls. We would have killed them twice if we could have.

Moments after leaving the dead Japs to return to their line Sal's squad came under a sudden and heavy attack by a large force of Japanese.

At the height of the attack, Sal was approached by his lieutenant. "Sergeant! We're going to pivot on you! You've got to hold! Hold!"

Sal emptied clip after clip at the attackers. A Jap fell dead at his feet as another charged from the side. His rifle empty, Sal used it as a bat to smash a Jap in the face. The sudden pain in his chest told him he was just bayoneted. He had drawn his jungle knife, stuck it into the Japanese just below his navel and ran it up to his sternum, getting the man.

Sal pulled out the bayonet, then lunged for the Japanese officer's pistol. He snatched it, used it to kill the officer and three other attackers.

He reached for a grenade stuff in his pocket. He used two of them to blast holes in the line of attacking men.

A Browning Automatic Machine gunner dropped down beside him. His intense fire with Sal's grenades stopped the charge. Sal's squad, now much smaller, returned to their lines carrying Sal on a stretcher.

Because of his wounds, Sal was loaded onto a Navy landing craft and sent to Cebu Island.

Two weeks later, a report filed at headquarters said: The Japanese have killed every single officer and soldier of the 189th on Mindanao.

CHAPTER 20

GERALD MALLOY

With his rifle propped between his knees as he sat on the floor of a cold, dank building. Gerald asked the corporal next to him where they were.

"If you're not home, they're all shitholes. Melmedy, I think. Belgium. Today's the 10th with Christmas just 15 days away. Why does anyone do this?"

"I'd like to meet the man or woman who invented war. I'd ask, 'Why?'" He blew his nose and sneezed twice. "We got chased out of our position with anti-tank guns and tank destroyers how in hell can we defend this broken-down factory?" He stood up and peeked out the window for long moments. "Christ! There are three Tiger Tanks coming up the road single file towards us. They'll put us through the grinder. Let me have the bazooka."

The Captain stepped forward. "Hold it, Malloy. Enemy infantrymen have taken up a position in that little house a short distance from the road they're using. Besides, we only have one rocket here. The others were left in that building across the street. Trying to get to them will get you blown to pieces."

"I understand, Captain. I'm going to circle around the hill and drop down behind the first Tiger Tank. I'll put this rocket in its backside, and that should pretty much block the road. I'll get more rockets, and we can do business with the other tanks stuck behind the first one."

"You can't get to the rockets! You'll be caught in a murderous crossfire! Besides, we need all the help we can to defend this position, Malloy. I can't order you to go, and I won't order you to stay."

"I need to please my owl. Let's see what we can do."

The corporal said, "What the fuck's an owl got to do with this? You'll need someone to load the bazooka. Let's go."

The moment Gerald and the corporal stepped out of the factory and started running for the house across the street they were met with intense fire from enemy tanks and the infantrymen in the house. Disregarding the small-arms, machinegun, and artillery fire, the two of them made it into the building.

They found the cache of rockets. The corporal grabbed two, Gerald one.

Once again they faced the withering fire. They ran to take refuge behind a hillock. They could hear the heavy metallic clanking of the formidable tanks grinding their way up the hill below them.

Laying flat in the snow, Gerald crawled until he got a view of the road. Just below the first Tiger Tank was passing. He rolled closer to the corporal. "Stay here. The first tank is a good twenty feet ahead of the other. As soon as it passes, I'll drop down, fire the rocket, and get back up here." The corporal nodded.

Gerald split the distance between the two tanks. He slid down to the road. As cool as the snow on his face, he aimed the rocket launcher at the back of the tank, and squeezed it off.

The explosion stopped the tank in its tracks.

The crew in the second tank were startled into inaction. They did not fire their machine guns until Gerard had disappeared up the slope.

There the corporal loaded a rocket into the bazooka and rapped Gerald to let him know it was ready.

Confident now, Gerald stood up until he had a good view of the second tank trying to push the first tank off the road. He put the rocket right in the middle of the tank, blasting the track. That would keep them away from the factory building.

Moving back into the open space, Gerard saw three Germans in the doorway of the house they occupied. He used his rifle to kill all three.

He emerged from cover and advanced alone to within 50 yards of the house. With the bazooka loaded again,

Gerard, covered by friendly fire, stood erect, and put the rocket right through the open doorway and knocked down one whole wall.

While in this forward position, he saw a small group of American soldiers who had been pinned down for hours by fire from the house and a nearby tank. Realizing that they could not escape until the enemy tank and infantry guns had been silenced, Gerard remembered there were antitank grenades in the vehicle that was left across the street.

With the corporal giving him covering fire, he grabbed an armful of antitank grenades. Despite the heavy enemy fire, he launched the grenades at the enemy. They were not as effective as he thought they would be. Looking around he noticed the half-track. He realized he was pressing his luck because it was in full view of the Germans. Disregarding his perilous position he climbed onto the half-track and fired its machinegun at the house. It did not seem to have much effect. Determined now more than ever to free the trapped soldiers, he saw another option. The crew of a machine gun had been killed a short distance away. With bullets firing around him, he ran over to it and manned the machinegun. Under his covering fire the soldiers were able to run to the safety of the factory building. Because of the loss of the tank and the heavy infantry casualties, the Germans were made to leave their positions and withdraw but not before the corporal and Captain were killed in ensuing action. It enabled the American soldiers to rescue Gerald who had three bullet wounds and had fallen over the machine gun. He was transported back to the battalion hospital.

Only a brief testimonial was made of Gerald's heroic performance that day, but it was enough to be noticed by the division commander.

The record of the Battalion would show that on December 17, 1944, there occurred the Malmedy massacre in which 80 American prisoners of war were murdered by members of *Kampfgruppe Peiper, 1ˢᵗ SS Panzer Division.*

CHAPTER 21

JOSEPH CARUSO

"GENERAL QUARTERS! GENERAL QUARTERS!" blared the destroyer's speakers throughout the ship. It was preceded by the metallic screech of the claxon horn, and the "Whoooo-weeeeeeee-you!" of the boatswain's whistle. Then, the command, "Now hear this! All hands! General Quarters! General Quarters! All hands, man your battle stations! All hands, man your battle stations!"

Joe Caruso responded in the early morning dark to the general quarters alarm by racing to his station on the engine telegraph in the destroyer's wheelhouse. The ship had been on alert for more than 36 hours. He tried to grab a minute's worth of shut-eye. The ship was one of a dozen on picket duty patrolling the defensive perimeter that guarded the aircraft carriers attacking Okinawa. Joe's destroyer was on the outermost edge that was the first to put up a barrage against the Japanese kamizaze suicide pilots that flew their bombers or guided their bombs right into their targets. They flew over by the scores. Although only a few hundred actually crashed into ships, the damage was immense. The planes they used were not always in peak condition, and at those times when the pilot felt he would be unable to reach a prime objective, such as a carrier, battleship, or cruiser, he would take on the first enemy ship in his sights. Others were directed to take out the destroyers in defensive stations on the picket lines protecting the aircraft carriers.

In the early morning light the enemy appeared, then came in range.

Joe could feel the deck vibrating beneath his feet with the "Whomp! Whomp! Whomp!" of the five-inch cannon.

Underneath the rhythmic, "Poom! Poom! Poom!" of the 40 mm. anti-aircraft gun when both its guns fired together. Then, it would suddenly go out of synchronization from: "Poom! Poom!" to the double blast of "Po-poom! Po-poom! "

"All engines ahead full!" the captain commanded. Joe immediately echoed, "All engines ahead full, Sir!" When the engine room responded making the bells ring on the engine telegraph and the arrows responding to the same command, Joe would announce, "All engines answer to full ahead, Sir!"

A short time later, the captain ordered, "All engines one-third ahead!"

"All engines answer to one-third ahead! Sir" Joe replied as he looked out of the starboard side of the wheelhouse to see the squadron of kamikaze move out of range. The ship wallowed waiting to chase the next specks on the horizon. Joe saw a Navy plane with a huge white star on its fuselage less than 75 yards away skim the surface of the water. Suddenly, the tail of the plane seemed to catch on a wave bringing the plane to an instantaneous halt. The wings slammed hard onto the water. Joe's astonished eyes watched as the pilot barely dragged himself out of the cockpit and rolled into the water.

"Sir! Sir!" Joe called out, "The pilot's alive! He's in the water!"

No one heard him, nor did anyone else seem either to spot the downed plane, or show any interest. Joe without further thought, kicked off his shoes, ran to the starboard bridge, and dove over the railing into the water.

Slowly and steadily he swam directly for the downed pilot.

It took a short time in the rough water to reach the pilot. Joe was grateful for all the training time he got as a kid swimming in the hard surf off of Nauset Beach on Cape Cod.

"Thanks!" the pilot muttered floating on his back, "Leg's broken."

"You'll be fine, Sir," Joe said his mouth close to the pilot's ear. "We'll have you aboard ship in a minute!" Joe grabbed him by the vest, and started pulling him toward the ship.

It took a much longer time to cover the distance, but as he got close to the destroyer, other seamen came into the water to help in the rescue.

A winch, spar, and collar that held the pilot under his arms was used to bring him aboard. He was taken directly down to the hospital station. Joe and the other three sailors were brought aboard in the same manner.

Three weeks later, late in the morning before the assembled officers and crew of the ship, Joe Caruso stood before the captain. "This is one of the rare and pleasant duties I have as captain of this ship," he said. "It gives me great pleasure and honor to award you, Quartermaster Third Class Joseph Caruso, the Silver Star for gallantry and courage in exposing yourself to danger for effecting the rescue of the downed pilot, and for maintaining the highest standards of the Navy."

Later that same afternoon, Joe stood before the same captain. "This is one of the more frequent and unpleasant duties I have as captain of this ship," he said, "to preside over a courts martial. No matter how heroic your action, the facts show that while in a battle zone with the enemy nearby, you willfully and knowingly, did abandon your post and your responsibilities to your ship, and to your duties. I hereby find that you, Quartermaster Third Class Joseph Caruso, be hereby demoted to seaman second class losing all pay and allowances ..."

For two days thereafter, his destroyer was under attack. In the system of warding off the enemy, the destroyers were the first picket line of defense forming a semi-circle at the outer extreme. They were the first to encounter the enemy planes. Those planes that got past them soon came upon the cruisers. Their guns could reach out to cause havoc to the human bombs. Then they had to get past the battleships to get at their objectives, the much-valued aircraft carriers, the Queens of the Day.

Whenever they appeared, the kamikaze were pursued and fought off. Late on the second day, a Japanese plane got through the barrage and aimed itself directly for Joe's wheelhouse. It held the control center. If that was knocked out, the ship was dead in the water.

"Hard starboard! Hard starboard! Emergency full speed! Emergency full speed!" the Captain shouted taking evasive maneuvers.

A shell tore off the plane's wing.

"Hard Starb ..." was as far as the helmsman got when the kamikaze blasted into the wheelhouse on the port side. Everyone on the bridge was doused with flaming gasoline from the plane. The crash instantly killed the captain and all officers and men near him. Then it blasted the signal station with all the signalmen, and the combat information center just behind the wheelhouse. It spewed flaming gas throughout the center structure, the officers' living quarters, and down to the main deck and into the main engine room where the bomb exploded. The blast tore off all the port superstructure and funnel, and left a gaping hole in the bottom of the ship.

CHAPTER 22

MADDY rotated in the forward seat to face Joe and allowed her body to settle into the bottom of the canoe. She rested her head against the seat thwart as she slipped the paddle alongside her.

They caught each other's eyes.

They stared.

Joe was resting on his paddle set crossways allowing the vespers that unexpectedly cut across the lake to take the canoe wherever they so wished. It was the rarest time of the year. Joe acknowledged it held no equal. The jet stream, the gibbous phase of the moon, the drenching rain two days prior with the hard frost the morning after made Nature overnight ejaculate the changing foliage. The lush roiling, rolling Catamount hills slopped with flaming yellows of the maples. The red rockets of the sugar maples, the hardwood hickories and oaks spewed rusty browns with the dead greens of the firs accenting the multichrome panorama against the robins' egg blue and immense splotches of bilious clouds. It was Indian summer.

"I don't know much, but I do know this, Maddy Malloy. I'm going to love you past eternity."

"You don't even know what time of day it is, Mr. Jokester." She tilted her face to the sun.

"You're going to get freckles. I may not know about today, but I go into the Navy tomorrow."

"I can guarantee you one thing, Mr. Smartass. You just look sideways at some chick and she's going to hasten you up with a perpetual dose of the clap."

"How could this innocent lady of my life know of such things?"

"My brothers. They said some whores will give you a blow job and fill your lungs with cockroach piss."

"If I use a rubber, can they do only one side?"

She covered her eyes with her hand. "Why did you have to go enlist?"

"My brother Sal, before he left, said the Marines 'Sempre Fi' meant on the verge of dying. Your brothers said all they get in the Army is shit on a shingle. At least, I know how to swim. Rather than get drafted, you know, I got my choice."

"I want to creep up there and kiss you."

"I can meet you half-way."

"Still no honeymoon for us?"

"You make it hard for me I'll hold it against you."

"Promise? It's our last night together."

"Don't say such things. We're going to have many nights together. Tonight we're going to go down to that very romantic restaurant in Connecticut. I'm going to try to get you drunk and then take advantage of you."

"Promise?"

"They have a cozy fireplace. I want to sit there with you and talk about our life together when I get back. We can have about ten or twelve kids, all boys, and one girl we'll call Maddy just for me. I will spoil her rotten. I'll teach her about staying away from rotten, selfish guys, how to rebuild a truck motor, and how to paint a house."

"How you going to do all that when you can't jump over a board down the middle of the bed?" She skooched up to a sitting position. She reached to touch his paddle. "I don't want to go to a restaurant. I want to be just with you. Nobody else around to dilute the intensity. I brought the fixings for barbecuing at the cabin."

"You think I'm easy. Couple hotdogs and I'll be seducible. Is there such a word?"

"Action, yes; word who cares? You'll look so darn cute in your sailor suit."

"Aye! Aye! Ma'am!"

By the time Joe had locked up the canoe under the cabin, Maddy had a slow fire going down to ashes. Foil wrapped sweet potatoes were buried in the coals, now at a perfect temperature for grilling sausages and shrimp. She opened jars of artichoke hearts, roasted red peppers, and hearts of palm. They used paper plates and chop sticks from the cache in the cabin. They took the empty bottles and trash with them when they left.

They took time with everything they did as if it would make the day last longer. They savored every morsel and made piti-pacchi tid-bits to feed each other.

The sun had long ago set by the time they had the carrot cake and the basket packed ready to carry out. The breeze had picked up tinged with the promise of another frost.

Joe and Maddy sat before the fire wrapped together in a huge Indian blanket.

"Stop kissing me or you're going to get sick," Maddy said.

"And you'll show no pity?"

"None. I warned you."

"What if I let you in on a secret? We are the onliest people in the world."

"Wouldn't change a thing. We promised each other. Not the world."

They sat for a long time with Joe's arm around Maddy, she tucked cozily against his body.

"Joe?"

"Mmmm."

"Joe, you know this is our safe place. Just ours. If either of us gets into trouble, we must make ourselves think of being here, like this. Side by each, you know? I can't imagine we would ever be separated. Because we will be, we must have a safety way, someplace to snuggle into in our thoughts to fight the enemy what ever it is. Do you know?"

"Yes. I think I knew that even before we got the land. I think that's the reason I worked so hard to complete it. I didn't know I was going into the service. It's ours at the right time. I'll meet you here in my dreams wherever I may be."

"I'll meet you here in my dreams wherever I may be."

Joe poured water on the embers. He held up the key to the cabin.

Maddy leaned over to tilt up their stone.

Joe put it on the flat rock. Maddy let their stone cover it.

Maddy slipped her hand out from under Joe's atop their stone. She pressed hard onto his. They looked deeply into each other's eyes. Maddy moved toward Joe and kissed him lightly. "Joe! Joe! Come back to me."

CHAPTER 23

ROSALIE APUZZO

EVEN THOUGH Rosalie heard the bell signaling she had reached the end of the carriage on the Royal typewriter she continued typing the legal brief on dead keys. She pounded away for another half-dozen words before she realized she was into a futile task. What actually made her stop was the chagrin she felt that came knowing she was being watched. With her hands hanging over the keyboard, she exhaled heavily then turned to the front of her desk.

"I didn't mean ..." the girl started. She looked twelve or thirteen, her hair caught up in a flouncy pony tail, wearing horn rimmed glasses, a sweater and a serious face. She shifted from one foot to the other.

"It's fine," Rosalie said. "Girl Scout cookies? War Savings Stamps?"

"Nothing like that," the girl answered. "I'm Julie McCree. Are you Rosalie Apuzzo? Mr. Mitchell's friend?" She tried hard to smile.

"Yes, I am ... I was," Rosalie caught herself. Shaking her head she asked, "What ... ?"

" ... Miss Apuzzo? ..."

"Rosalie."

"Thanks. Rosalie," Julie continued, "I'm not sure ... I mean ..."

"Did you know Mr. Mitchell?" Rosalie asked.

"Oh! Yes! Yes, I did," Julie said. "He was my seventh grade teacher before he left school to go to the war. He made me feel special. Then, this morning we had an assembly like we usually do, except today they had speeches about the war and what was happening and why there was fighting. Then, the principal spoke about Mr. Mitchell and how patriotic he was and how he enlisted. The assembly was for all the soldiers and sailors that Mr. Mitchell was missing in action. That was the first time I heard that. I was frozen in my seat, you know? It really took me by surprise, you know? How did you find out? Did they send you a telegram?"

"If we were married I would have gotten a telegram that he was missing," Rosalie said. "His mom and dad got the telegram. His dad called your principal from Ohio about ten days ago. Then, the principal notified the town clerk who called me. I was right here at my desk."

"Did you get frozen in your seat, too?" Julie asked.

"Frozen solid like a block of ice," Rosalie answered with a smile.

"You know, as soon as I heard I knew I had to come see you," Julie said.

"You knew about me?" Rosalie asked. "He told you about me?"

Julie nodded. "When we went out for recess we would talk. We would talk about a lot of things, and one time we were talking about special people in our lives. He told me about Rosalie Apuzzo—you—and how you made a difference in everything he did and how he looked at things. He said you made him a better teacher because he wanted you to be very, very proud of him in everything he did. He said you both cared very much for each other and one day soon you would both be married. He made a big joke about the idea that not only would you both be married but that you would be married to each other! But you didn't, did you, get married?"

Rosalie shook her head. "Nope, we didn't. We would have when he came home on leave, but we just ran out of time. Yes, he made me feel special, too. How did he make you feel special? Because you were able to talk with him at recess? You were lucky to be able to talk to him like that, you know?"

"I know!" Julie nodded. "It started because I used to be by myself a lot. You know, off to one side. I don't make friends easily. Mr. Mitchell noticed. At first, he would stop to talk to me about the weather, or about the girls doing double Dutch, and then walk on. Then, before I knew it, he had me talking about myself, the bad feelings I had, and how I thought no one liked me. He tried to make me see things differently. I didn't listen to him because I didn't think he meant it? Then, one day he said, 'If I didn't care for you, if I didn't think you were a good person, would I waste my time talking to you?' I heard that before, you know? But, Mr. Mitchell was so ... sincere? ... is that the right word? He was so sincere right then and there he made me feel important, special. You know? I didn't become Miss Popularity all of a sudden but I understood what he was trying to tell me. I knew in my heart it would work. It didn't right away, because, you know, because rather than be with the other kids, I wanted to spend the time with Mr. Mitchell. I knew everything would be all right because when he came into class in the morning, he would smile at everyone, but it seemed he always saved a special smile for me. Miss Apuzzo? He changed my world for me. He was wonderful. You know?"

"Yes, Julie, I know," Rosalie said. "He was an excellent teacher. He told me he knew he was going to be a teacher from the time he could talk. He would be very proud of you to know you remember him in such a nice way." Julie nodded. "Thank you for coming by, Julie. It is really very sweet of you. You make me feel better." Julie stood still. She stared blankly at her. Rosalie wrinkled her brow. "There's something else?"

Julie nodded her head rapidly for a long moment. "Miss Apuzzo ... Rosalie? I'd like to ask you for a picture of Mr. Mitchell ... if you have one to spare?"

Rosalie pulled back from the desk. She sat up very straight and coughed into her closed hand. "I have a couple in my wallet. I think I could spare one of those ..." Rosalie quickly turned away from Julie. She swallowed hard, lifting her chin to the air. She reached down for her purse on the floor leaning against the desk. She took out her wallet, went through several photos, and finally picked one out. She slid it out of the holder and held it out to Julie. "He liked this one ... because of the smile ..."

Julie took the photo in the palm of her hand, and covered her heart. "Oh! Thank you! He was just so really special ..."

Rosalie could not look at her face, and busied herself putting away her wallet and purse. When she looked up, she expected and wanted to see Julie heading for the door. Julie was right there, staring back at her. "Yes, Julie?"

"Rosalie, I told you I was a little different from the other kids. I didn't want to lose what Mr. Mitchell taught me to gain, so, I almost did in the assembly, but I couldn't. I don't know about these things, if I would look stupid, or something, you know?" She burst out in tears. She sobbed uncontrollably. Dry-eyed, Rosalie cradled her in her arms. She could feel the pain criss-crossing the young girl's body. Finally, she stopped. "I haven't another tear in my soul," the little girl said. She kissed Rosalie on both cheeks, then on her lips, turned away and left.

Rosalie returned to her work. Despite the days and nights of crying, she had not run out of her tears, and as they dripped, allowed them to let them to run and soak her skirt for the remainder of the afternoon.

It would be awhile before she heard of the Bataan Death March.

CHAPTER 24

Peter's father, Dennis, Maddy's father, decided not tell his mother, Dorothea, of the report of him being MIA. His father's quaking heart knew only too well the effect it would have on her. But, they might as well have spelled it out. She knew. She knew before she heard Arturo's notes. No one would dare utter the words to her. They watched her closely, apprehensively. Paul's news a mere three weeks earlier. No one could tell if she had made a seamless transition from one trauma to the other and was bearing the double blow.

"Tell me about Peter?" she would ask whoever was around.

The standard answer was to avoid a direct response. "His last letter said he was doing great! Just loved being a Marine!"

Dorothea died within nine months. They wondered how she knew Peter had been missing in action three weeks after his birthday. The supposition made a good case for a mother's ESP. Then, Arturo told Gerald that Dorothea had come to visit him at the town hall. He wondered about the reason. She had taken special pains to look at the list of names he put up on the wall outside his office. He put their names in the drawer with the cards that were for others reported "missing in action." Arturo felt Dorothea's name should have been right up there with them, except he didn't know what Peter's mother knew. It was very simple. She hated her mother. Dorothea had been Catholic, raised in a private Catholic school, and then to get back at her mother, rejected the church to marry Dennis. Her mother cursed her daughter, Dorothea, and prayed vengeance on her head for being a traitor and a disbeliever. Payback was a bitch. From the moment she learned Peter was MIA, Dorothea willed herself to death. It took eight months to do it.

CHAPTER 25

It was mid-January when Dennis Malloy, her father, informed Maddy he needed her to accompany him on a business trip. He did not say where they would be going or for how long. Maddy had an idea her dad was suffering over his family but really had no idea how badly. She knew exactly the trauma her heart felt with the devastation thrust upon the Malloy's, but she could only guess the pain going on within her father then multiplied it by a thousand. With news of the trip, she cringed at the thought of being out of Catamount for the holidays. There was comfort in seeing Mrs. Kowalchuk and her friends. She felt her stomach knot whenever Joe came to mind. Her body felt compressed and seemed she didn't breathe for hours on end. That all was bad enough. Being away would make everything worse. She wanted to say something to her dad. She shook it off. He was way far more in pain than she.

It did not take much for Maddy to know the loss of his wife and the news of three sons within such a short span of less than a year was much too much pain for him. She had suggested to him counseling. It was not a newly popular medical program. "I'm not crazy!" he would reply. She suggested he speak with the priest, who also happened to be a close friend. "I'm no bawling baby," he would reply. It did not take a professional to know his foundation had crumbled.

Maddy thought he had found an answer by drowning in work. She found he was suddenly occupied around-the-clock. He left the house very early and returned very late at night. He answered whenever she called the office to remind him to come home for dinner—which he never did anymore. "I had a sandwich brought in," was his answer to his need for sustenance.

In yonder days and times no matter what time he got home, he always took a moment to have a nightcap and discuss some aspect of the day or the world news, usually with his wife, and even with Maddy as first son was gone, then the other, and the third? When he lost his wife, he shut down everything in his world except work.

Maddy did not find his request to accompany him out of town unusual. He needed someone to tend to the details, like scheduling, breakfast, lunch, dinner, clothes cleaning, and transportation.

The first clue she got that something unusual was going on was that he had ordered a cab to take them to the airport. Usually he drove his own car and parked it at the airport.

The next clue was when they landed at Chicago's O'Hare Airport where they took another flight to Los Angeles. The biggest clue, the name on the tickets was not Malloy.

When they landed at Los Angeles airport, a cab took them to a home in Ojai.

Maddy and the cab driver brought the luggage into the living room of the nicely spacious home. Then, her father handed her keys and asked her to take the station wagon out of the garage, and asked if she would be kind enough to drive them to a restaurant. He had much information for her.

CHAPTER 26

MADDY

MADDY closed her finger in the book. Looking up, through half-closed eyes she fought the mid-morning California sun sparkling against the panorama of the sky, sea, and shore. She reclaimed a wisp of her hair that had been caught by a breeze and pulled across her forehead, laced into her eyelashes, and sealed her mouth. Sitting on a bench in the shade of palm and Brazilian pepper trees, she nodded to herself to confirm and acknowledge a decision of major significance.

Mr. Malloy, her father sat in a wheelchair a short distance away. As usual, he was immobile, as if he were poured concrete. He would stare at the water for hours at a time. Maddy walked into his line of sight when she thought he was ready to leave. If he nodded, she pushed his wheelchair to the station wagon, loaded him and the chair into it, and took him to the home he bought for them in Port Heuneme, a short distance away. He used the wheelchair only for the beach. It provided a well-cushioned, comfortable seat; it allowed them to park and loiter where others were not allowed; and it anchored his daughter to him.

Every single day for almost the past three years this was part of her daily routine. She made and served him a late breakfast on the patio. He read the paper and listened to the news on the radio. When he was ready, they would go to the seashore. When they returned home, Maddy made a late lunch. Then, while her father rested for several hours, she had her free time. She worked in her studio painting watercolors and doing pen and inks. Twice a week she used the time to work as a volunteer at a nearby hospital. Then, after she had prepared and served her dad dinner, he sat in the living room listening to the radio until he got tired and went to bed. When television came along, he let that occupy his time. One evening a week Maddy went out to play duplicate bridge.

The chasm between this life and the one she knew in Catamount was challenged constantly each night in her dreams. It seemed, one day, suddenly, the events in her small, sleepy-hollow New England town flew at her so fast she could scarcely catch her breath. Her total world as she knew it collapsed. She characterized it as devastating.

It began simply enough, and that only because she did not comprehend the full meaning, nor understood the dilemma of the world at war. When he first climbed Monument Mountain to play taps Arturo Daigno was the subject in almost every home in Catamount for almost the entire dinnertime. Each succeeding taps, the discussion about whose son was killed grew shorter and shorter as Daigno's list on the wall grew longer and longer.

For Maddy, the war became meaningful when Richard Thompson was reported missing in action on Battaan. Then, the war really became personalized when her brother, the younger twin, Paul, was sent to Bougainville. That pain and strangeness hardly settled in when less than three weeks later, her other brother, the twin, Peter, was MIA. Joe had been her consolation for Peter. Joe had taken her out to the cabin where they spent the entire afternoon just talking about her brothers and the million things they had done that made them a family.

Then, she had run out of tears for Paul. Again, Joe brought her out to the lake. Although the amount of time was shorter, it was just as intense. Overlooking the frozen water by the cabin, Maddy said to Joe: "Our family has been devastated. Annihilated. My heart and soul has been torn to shreds. How is one to endure such horrible pain? My father is desperate for his three sons, the dearest people to him. Yet, I am missing one more. He is moving away to go someplace to die. I may never know when he does because he does not also want me to suffer his loss. Joe? How can I tell him I need him and have him listen? I cannot tell him how grateful I am that I have you in my life

Joe because you are my anchor. I have no idea how I would live with the wind sucked out of me. What it is that tells me we should make love to replace the lives snatched from us? Peter. Paul. Gerard. Dad. Mom seems to wish not to be in the world anymore. I have yet to comprehend the calamity of it all. How do other people survive such things? Shall I come out here to the cabin to live? I would you know. In the face of all of this to feel a thorn, imagine, with something as picayune as the fact that I'm too young to get a driver's license! Do such mundane things bring us face to face with reality? A stupid driver's license, but there no privilege or permission needed to dance on the flaming coals of life's fire bed. How clearly I can think, so safe and secure here, with you, in this fortress, our cabin. Thank you, Joe. I will love you forever. Now you'd better get me back home. Kiss me, Joseph, kiss me, and hold me tight."

Maddy's family devastation was not yet complete. It was obvious eight months before she died that her mother, Dorothea, had lost her will to live. It was not something Maddy could see. It was not a matter of shriveling or wasting away. She did not withdraw to a darkened room. She performed as she normally would, eating, sleeping, shopping. What Maddy was able to feel was the diminishment of her will to live. It was almost palpable. It did not happen in chunks, or bits and pieces. It was as if her rheostat of life kept decreasing. With each sunrise there was a bit less. The days turned into months when one morning Dorothea asked Maddy not to go to school, but to linger with her at the breakfast table.

"Maddy, would you be so kind," she said, "I would so much enjoy a cup of tea."

Maddy, at the sink doing up the breakfast dishes, felt her words strike her back right between her shoulder blades. Maddy turned slowly. Her mother looked up into her face smiling, her eyes glistening as usual. "Coming right up, Mum."

"Thank you. I'll be in the living room, Maddy."

She was sitting in her favorite chair. She had several sips in a row. "Mmmm! Just what I needed." She turned and put the cup and saucer on the table next to her. She folded her hands on her lap, and looked up. "Thank you,

Maddy. My dear Maddy. You fill my heart." She turned to look out the window, closed her eyes, let her chin roll gently onto her chest and was gone.

She was no sooner buried when her father began behaving in a strange manner. He was always a work-a-holic, as they were called, but during this period he was at his task day and night, weekends as well.

Maddy noticed as his time became more twisted, his temper shortened, his demands unruly, his behavior near irrational. He wanted things done before he even thought of them. Maddy wondered the reason he was so driven.

The first real hint came when she learned Joe Caruso, Joe's father, was involuntarily given early retirement. The job he was promised would be his for the rest of his working life was gone.

That was just before Christmas. Early in January, after they had services for Salvatore, the telegram that Joe was missing in action was delivered. Late that afternoon, Tony found them both dressed, atop their bed, holding hands, unconscious from a heavy overdose of sleeping pills. They were buried two days later.

Early February, Maddy, a senior, was at home when the notes of Taps, as brittle as crystal cut through the freezing air. Who now?

Maddy focused on her graduation five months away. Mrs. Kowalchuk had already cleared the way for Maddy to attend her Alma Mater, Smith College.

Mr. Malloy did nothing to disabuse Maddy of the idea that he was not long for the world. The way he spoke and made plans, he gave the impression he would not last out the year. Maddy's emotions, already trampled to pieces, especially with the news of Joe's missing, left her totally uncaring of herself and susceptible to her father's needs.

CHAPTER 27

JOSEPH CARUSO (Continued)

IN THE DESTROYER'S wheelhouse, Joe found himself screaming. He was tucked away in the starboard corner of the wheelhouse two yards from the helmsman who was obliterated by the plexiglass covering the cockpit of the Japanese bomber. Joe saw the pilot's teeth jammed shut, his lips a taut circle below welded eyelids. Flaming gasoline doused Joe just as he instinctively turned and juked around to the right. In a split second he was a human torch. The flaming gas from the suicide plane caught him full on the left shoulder of his Mae West, flowed down his back, under his arm and swept down to his buttocks. There was a full-flame barbeque searing his T-shirt, shirt, and vest to his back. In a wild frenzy to escape the blowtorch, Joe grabbed his shirt collar, T-shirt and the top of the vest and yanked as if to pull himself away from the pain. The front of the shirt and t-shirt came flying out of the vest in flames. The back of his vest was one flaming red hot broiling coal scorching his hair under his helmet.

"Gotta get in the water!" he screamed to himself as he got up from the flaming deck. He found himself in the hatchway to the starboard wing standing over a man with a charred, blackened face, screaming and holding out his arms to him.

Reaching inside himself for all the strength and courage he had, Joe grabbed the glowing metal sheet covering the man and threw it aside. He caught the man under his armpits and pulled him upright. He struggled to the railing with the dead weight and managed to roll him up and off the ship. Joe let himself collapse onto the railing and slipped over the side. As he went under water, it felt as if his skin from heel to head was being stripped off of him.

The shock of the icy water almost made him pass out. He tried to hold the scream until he blasted back to the surface but couldn't and gulped thick oil and seawater. He came up spewing and coughing. He saw the man he had pushed overboard bobbing helplessly as the stricken vessel pulled away from them. Despite the excruciating pain, he dog paddled over to the wounded man who was sliding out of his Mae West. It had been burned off down to his chest. Tatters remained of the front of his shirt, his "T" shirt, his trousers, his underwear only from below his belly button.

"Fucking fuckers!" the man tried to say.

Biting his tongue, jamming his eyes shut Joe was determined not to acknowledge the pain. Joe tried to speak but gargled oil, and salt water. He spit and coughed. "Save strength. You be fine," Joe encouraged him. "Grab ... front ... my Mae West. Yours is ... gone.   Pull you ... to hunk of emergency ... raft."

"Who you?"

My name. Say it. "Joe Caruso. Joe Enzo Caruso."

"Joe Caruso! You GET Navy Cross for me." Then, "Jesus Christ Good Almighty! This hurts like fucking hell!" He tried to scream but sputtered and coughed.

"You'll be fine," Joe said. "I'll hold you to the raft. Who you?"

"Jay ... Jay the Man, Jay Weiner ... Oh!"

Joe focused on the jagged chunk of cork, gray tape wrapping, and netting awash in the roll of the gulping waves. The other half of the emergency raft bobbed crazily some distance away across the shiny black slick of greasy oil. The sun, low on the horizon, made reflective triads of the wind whipped water. A distant pale pastel strip marked the joining of the cloudless sky and massive sea. The heaving scend of the waves lifted the men high, the pressure pushing the breath from their chests, the wind-blown spume spattering their faces, to start them down the curved roller coaster chute to the coal-blue trough. Each rise brought the broken raft closer, each fall further away, although gain on it they did. After several painful exertions Joe managed to grab onto the elusive chunk of flotsam. That's when he realized he had left the skin on his hands brazed onto the baking hot door covering Jay.

"Not going to make it, kid," Jay gasped. He cried. He cried for a long while. "God! I hope I go fast! Can't stand all this fucking pain! I want to scream, but I can't anymore."

"Stop talking," Joe ordered trying to spit the sticky, salty oil from his mouth. "I'll hold you to the raft until I can get out of my what's-left-of-it Mae West and get it on you ..." He struggled to remove the vest so he could put it around the injured man

"You're crazy, kid." He fell silent. "God! I'm all cried out. Sorry for that. A wimp."

"Gotta way to go before you earn that title."

"Joe? Gotta listen. Lemme go ... I'm done ... I'll take you with me. Look! Do you know who I am?"

"No," Joe said looking at the oil and flame blackened burlesque face, "Your makeup is on kind of thick."

"Christ! Don't make ... laugh! It hurts!" he said. "I'm that bad, huh? You? You okay?"

"Like you, only it's my back," Joe answered. "Hurts like a son-of-a-bitch. Look, you hang on if I pass out ... Okay?"

"Man ... do me a favor. ... I don't want my wife ... to wait ... seven years while I'm MIA. ... I'll be KIA not MIA ... she'll get ... my insurance, and can ... get married again quickly. Understand?"

"What are you talking about?"

"You ... (gurgle) ... married?"

"Yes. ... married ..."

"No MIA! No MIA!"

"Fucking crazy thing to be worried about! You're not going to be missing in action, or killed in action. You'll be fine. Stay quiet," Joe ordered. "They know the ship was hit. They'll be here to pick us up. Hang on."

A while later, the man with his eyes closed asked, "You married?"

"Yes I'm still married," Joe answered. "Maddy. I'm married to Maddy."

"Yeah ... Mandy. ... One ... of us ... better fucking make it!" the man said. "Listen, you gotta remember my name: Jay Wienstein. Better still Jay Wienstein. How's that? Remember it so I will be KIA. My full name is Jay Edward Wienstein. Stupid fucking parents..."

"What's that for?"

"That makes my initials J.E.W."

Joe laughed. "That's the funniest thing I've ever heard."
Jay snickered.

"What's your crazy middle fucking name?"

"Enzo. E-n-z-o. 1927. Enzo, Italian, was the only
person to win five gold medals in Olympic competition in
the sport of fencing."

"Your name again?"

"Joseph Enzo Caruso, like the singer."

"Got it."

For a long while each was lost in his own thoughts as
the sky lost its color and the wind picked up holding the
waves higher.

"Jay? You believe in god?"

Joe instantly returned in his mind to standing with
Mandy in front of the ceremonial fire pit on the cabin site.
"Do I believe in god? He once was standing right in front of
me, nose to nose and I was too embarrassed to
acknowledge that fact. My joke was bad. I wish I could go
back there." He rubbed his fingertips with oil as if to soothe
them.

The silence was broken when the man said half under
his breath, "Holy Jesus Christ all fucking all mighty!" Joe
surmised his pain had grown intense. "Listen, Buddy," the
man said, "Take this Mae West off of me. You gotta let me
go."

"I can't do that. You'll drown," Joe said.

"Yeah. A nice, peaceful easy way to die," the man said.
"I don't want any more pain."

"It'll get better. We'll be picked up soon," Joe reassured
him. "You'll be fine. Try to relax. You know, in the Catholic
Church it's a mortal sin to commit suicide. Sounds funny
doesn't it. Then I got them figured out. It's based on faith.
You must have faith in God. Faith in God means you must
believe He is capable of anything ... anything. A man may
be dying of cancer, screaming in pain, asking his wife to
overdose him to end his misery. She can't do it, not
because she doesn't want to become a murderer, but if she
did, she denies God. She flat out says He doesn't exist. She
doesn't over dose her screaming husband because she
believes in God and believes, if He wanted to, He could

perform a miracle and save him. If she leaves her husband alone God can save him. If she doesn't God can never save him. Get it?"

"Cup of tea..."

"What?"

"Cup of tea. I'd like a cup of tea."

"First thing you get on the ship."

"Hey, Joe? Know what? Feel religious will you? It's time for a miracle."

"Do my best."

"Better be very soon. You haven't seen them," the man said tossing his head.

"What am I looking at?" Joe asked. The sinking hulk had disappeared long before, either it had sunk or had gone beyond the horizon. Then, he saw. Breaking the cadence of the waves, the shark fins were about fifty feet away, Joe estimated. Four? Seven of them? Nine dozen? He tried to count. It was hard to see. "What difference how many?" Joe said to himself clenching his teeth.

"Come on, man!" the man pleaded. "Let me go! I'll let myself sink below the surface and it'll be over nicely ..."

A pinpoint of the orb became discernible. Then, like magic, a bit more. A symphony orchestra would rumble a bit under and slowly come up to a crescendo as the sun blazed forth. Now, sir, was this the second? Or the first? Or the third arising? Best seat in the house for this show. Sir? Sir? Where did you go? Bet I know. Would a freezing cold beer in a freezing cold mug would stop whoever it is hammering a spike in the middle of my neck going right down to my tail bone and ... Kaleidoscope day night criss cross jumble jack cough sleep wretch die awake splash slap live ...

CHAPTER 28

Maddy recognized Mrs. Kowalchuk's pick-up truck parked outside with the motor running as she walked toward the homeward bound busses. She stopped. Frozen. She wriggled her shoulder to allow her purse strap to fall off of her shoulder. She let the bag land on the cement. She stooped to pick it up. Her hands were shaking. She found her breath hard to catch like when she raced with all her might on the track. There was no one else in all of the town of Catamount who could do this to her besides Mrs. Kowalchuk. No one else knew her secrets. The secret that made her choke and cough had to do with Joe. He was very much on her mind when during first period her flesh turned cold with the first few notes of Taps coming from atop Monument Mountain. Everyone in her classroom, in fact, the entire school, automatically got to their feet as if they heard the first notes of the *Star Spangled Banner*. They each stood silently while in their minds thoughts whizzed like racquet shots against a wall.

Hadn't there been enough casualties for this lazy country town? Before the last lingering note ended the chatter started. "Who?"

Maddy knew Mrs. Kowalchuk was there for her. But, it was a mistake, right? It was for something else or somebody else. Their secret would be out. Arturo Daigno would know immediately the reason Maddy Malloy got a telegram for Joe Caruso's widow addressed to Mrs. Joseph Malloy Caruso. She was the primary recipient. The secondary recipients of a telegram about Joe Caruso would go to his parents. She held her breath. "God forgive me for even thinking such a thing!"

Dear Mrs. Kowalchuk would never blow the horn to get her attention. It seemed she understood the scenario. It took everything in her, Maddy felt, to remain in the truck and wait for Maddy to go to her. She kept her gently wrinkled face dead forward. Maddy knew if she looked into her eyes her blood would freeze. She occupied herself with the purse and the books she was carrying. She remembered her mother telling her, "To every bad situation, put on a good face." She tried to swallow but she had no spit. Her mouth felt like a convection oven on high.

"Mrs. Kowalchuk! Am I lucky enough to have you come by to pick me up?"

She glanced sideways, nodded, and rolled her head for Maddy to get in.

"How are you, Mrs. Kowalchuk?"

She pulled out into traffic. "Better days are now memories. The rheumatism, you know." She looked right at Maddy. "You are a very smart lady. I could take you to the cabin because I know what it means to you and Joe, but too emotional for me. We're going to my house. They delivered a telegram for you at my home."

Maddy kept sipping air into her lungs until her hair was just about to touch the roof. It took the nearly twenty minutes to get to Mrs. Kowalchuk's home before Maddy finished exhaling.

"Come!" Mrs. Kowalchuk said as she led the way into the kitchen. She threw down her jacket and pulled out a chair at the table for Maddy. "Speak."

"I'd like to see the telegram."

The woman slid the telegram off the countertop and placed it in front of Maddy. "Tea coming up!"

Maddy didn't answer, intent on reading the telegram, the simple but formidable faded blue font decreeing the rest of her life. "No tea."

"Tea is the great equalizer. Tea it will be." Mrs. Kowalchuk did not say another word and did not look again at Maddy as she set about to complete her task.

As she was pouring the steaming brew from the teapot into Maddy's cup, she said, "It says, 'Missing in action.' That's all. 'Missing in action.' Joe is not dead."

"Maddy ..."

"Joe is not dead."

"Do not think for a moment I do not know about you and Joe. I know. It was mid-morning when I got the telegram. I heard the Taps. I was never more surprised to find that message in my hands. My husband had his connections. They remembered him still. I called a senator in Washington, D.C. I told him what I needed to have. It took all morning and until a half-hour before I came for you to get an answer. I love you, my child, I would never say or do anything to hurt you."

The facts were that Joe was on a destroyer that was on duty off of Okinawa. He was in the thick of battle inasmuch as his destroyer was assigned to the outer ring of the defense line protecting aircraft carriers. In this case the U.S.S. Bunker Hill. In this case the attackers were mericiless, throwing wave after wave of suicide bombers into the fray.

Witnesses report Joe's destroyer was hit by a Kamikaze that went dead on into the wheelhouse, where Joe was stationed. The plane, a heavy bomber destroyed everything in its path. The bomb went through decks, exploding in the boiler room. The ship went down in less than fourteen minutes.

It took many hours before a destroyer could be released to search for survivors. It rescued a total of 37 men. It searched the area for more than eight hours. Each and every man rescued was identified by his dog tag, worn around the neck. The rest of the crew was obliterated. There was absolutely no chance any other personnel from Joe's destroyer was alive. The term was "Missing In Action."

"Mrs. Kowalchuk, I love you with all my heart. You have only cared the best for Joe and me. What you have done this morning was the best you thought you could do for me. In my heart I know you are not asking me to betray my love for Joe and what I feel about him. I would know if anything happened to Joe. Despite what you say, I know he is alive. He is alive."

"Yes, of course, Maddy."

"I have an errand to run, and a place to go. May I borrow the truck?"

Maddy brought it to a stop in front of the steps of the Town Hall. She started toward the Town Clerk's office. Arthur Daigno was standing outside talking to a woman.

"Maddy … !" he started solicitously when he saw her.

Maddy walked past him and to the wall that held the names of the town's fallen heroes. She could not find Joe's card.

She turned to stand in front of Arthur Daigno. She reached down, picked up his hand. "Arthur! You didn't put up my Joe's name … ?"

"Maddy!" She turned. "I'm very sorry. I do want you to know you were the primary recipient of the telegram. Another one was delivered to his parents as secondary recipients, that was early this morning. I thought you should know. Also, he is listed as MIA. I've seen many a slip 'tween the cup and the lip. I keep them all in a special place. Every Sunday I bring the names to the Virgin Mary. You do know, she has her own special way of working."

Maddy barely broke a smile. She blinked her eyes rapidly absorbing the news. "Thank you, Arthur."

She drove directly to the Caruso's home.

"Ain't seen them much at all since he lost his job at the mill," the neighbor said. "Once in a while I'd see him out in his garden until they got news they lost Sal."

"Did they leave?" Maddy asked.

"Can't say. The car's in the garage."

"I've got an errand," Maddy said. "I'll be back later."

She parked directly in back of the cabin. She remained in the cab looking down at the dashboard. She wondered as Mrs. Kowalchuk did the reason she was not crying.

She searched inside herself. She knew a little bit about the meaning of the word "denial," the unwillingness to accept reality. No, it was not denial. She knew the reason she was not crying. There was no reason to do so. Joe was not dead. Wherever he was Joe was alive.

She would conjure the cabin spirits to help her in her quest.

She walked to the edge of the water and skimmed a stone.

She took out a cigarette. She walked to the fire pit. There were cold ashes in it when she first walked by. Now there was a gentle glow from ash covered coals in it sending up a curl of smoke. She took out an ember on a short stick and blew on it until it burst into flame. She lit her cigarette then turned to sit on the porch.

With the sun setting, she felt a chill. Then, there was warmth, as if a blanket had been wrapped around her. She felt the beat and hummed to it a chant. She closed her eyes and prayed there be another sign. It would strengthen her heart and steady her love.

She opened them slowly. Between Maddy and the firepit, perched on their stone was Mr. Raynard. He held the world in balance between them until the moon came up full.

Maddy wished she had brought a couple hot dogs.

She scolded herself for not returning to the Caruso's earlier when she found the house was still dark.

At the police station Chief Tony was just about to leave when Maddy stopped beside him and jumped out of the pick up.

"Maddy, I'm so sorry!" He held her shoulders and kissed her on both cheeks. "Joe, he was like a brother."

After a few minutes at the Caruso's the Chief knew what he was about. He put his shoulder to the door and took it in.

"Wait here," he said snapping on lights.

When he came back down the stairs, he took Maddy's elbow and guided her down to the cruiser. He held up one finger to her as he took out the radio microphone. Into it he said, "Mac, this is Tony. Get the doctor on duty at the hospital to come to Sal Caruso's home right away. Send the ambulance to Sal Caruso's home as well, red lights and siren. Also, I need a cruiser here right away."

He turned to Maddy. "It looks like your in-laws took sleeping pills. We may be in time to bring them around. An officer will be here in two minutes. Can you drive?" Maddy nodded. "I'll have him follow you home. ... Ah! ... Mrs. Kowalchuk's?" She nodded. "I will call you there to give you up-dates."

He went back to the microphone. "Call the Monterey police and ask them to send someone to Mo-Mo Caruso's house, his brother. Tell him we've taken both Caruso's to the hospital."

At home, Maddy found her father behind his desk in his office. "Did you have dinner, Dad?"

"Yes. Some of the lasagna you made last night."

"I got news Joe is missing in action."

Her father didn't look up, didn't change his expression. "Sorry."

"Dad? Mr. Caruso worked for you for twenty-five years. Why did you let him go?"

"I did him a favor. At least he'll get all his retirement benefits."

"It wasn't a week after he got the news about his son, Sal."

"We won't talk about his sons and I won't talk about losing your mother."

"They ought to change the name of this town from Catamount to Pain. There's enough of it around here to fill five skyfulls. Dad, Mr. and Mrs. Caruso are in the hospital from an overdose of sleeping pills. It doesn't look good. I hope they make it." She left the sub-text unsaid, "What good are all his retirement benefits now. I hope that was not the favor you intended."

"Too bad. You and I must make a business trip to Chicago."

"It will have to be after I know the Carusos are all right."

Maddy went to the kitchen, sat at the table and lit a cigarette. It was something she had never done before. It mattered little now. Her thoughts leaped ramparts, one higher than the next. For one, if Mrs. Kowalchuk had brought her the telegram at school when it came in the morning would she have saved the Caruso's by visiting them earlier?

Joe, you son-of-a-bitch, I know you're okay. Why don't you let me know where you are? As if the signs weren't enough? No! they weren't! I want to send you my energy. I want to send you my vibes. I want to do anything I can to keep you alive? You hardly made me a wife if I wasn't so god-damned stubborn and stupid we could have made love in the cabin that last night and I could be carrying our child, for all I know. All I have now is faith. God! You rotten bastard! You promised you'd come back to me. Don't you fucking dare break your promise! I wonder the reason Dad wants me to go to Chicago with him? Could it have anything to do with the rumor that's flying around town that an awful lot of people are going to be laid off? It started at Christmastime. No one in the world would be a big enough prick to do that, including my father.

Three days later Mo-Mo buried his brother and sister-in-law.

CHAPTER 29

JOE CARUSO (Continued)

What was it he felt, Joe wondered. Was it hot? Or was it cold? He dug into his mind. The fact was he wasn't feeling anything. No, there was something. He was as thirsty as a son-of-a-bitch. He had been spitting and digging out oil from his mouth for hours, it seemed. "I need to feel something," he said. "I know, you don't feel it so make yourself feel scared shitless. No? Funny. I can't do that. How about laughing? Tell yourself a joke. Ah! Yes! I feel something. Everytime a wave comes at me just right it lifts the skin off my back. Oh! Fuck! Fuck! Fuck! Does that hurt!"

"Hang on, fella. We'll be fine," Joe said to his companion.

"They don't even know we're here ... Only the sharks know."

He felt himself about to pass out. He looked at his companion. Mercifully, Joe thought, he was unconscious. At least, he was grateful the man's eyes were closed so he didn't have to see the terror swamping them. Perhaps they should both just drift off and slide beneath the surface. He had heard enough stories about what the merciless sharks could do to a man floating in the water. He had chicken skin from head to toe from the contrast of cold salt water and the heat of the burn on his back. Joe shivered uncontrollably. He was certain only it was not from fear. It did seem as if the sharks were doing a circle swim dance and moving closer.

With his arm thrown over the side of the broken raft, Joe wound the center webbing around his wrist to hold himself to the raft. He could feel the waves of unconsciousness washing over him. Joe fought the sensations then suddenly succumbed.

When he opened his eyes, he was startled to find dusk nearly gone. He blinked rapidly to clear his eyes so he could see in the settling light. The forms were not clear although close-by. He shook his head because he could not believe canoes paddled by Indians surrounded him. Beyond that perimeter, he could see the shark fins. On a breeze, over the sound of lapping waves, was the subtle, steady murmur of the fall and rise of their chant, "Uh-wah-wah-wah-wah-wah-wah-wah-wah! Uh-wah-wah-wah-wah-wah ... !" He acknowledged he was hallucinating. He smiled at the joke about the Fagowee Indian Tribe. For sure, the thought, they must be asking themselves, "What the fug are we doing out here?"

Then, he heard it. "Yipp-yipppp—yipp-yip!"

He couldn't see it but he knew the source. Mr. Raynard had come to visit.

Suddenly, he realized his companion was gone. He checked the surface of the sea. He let his head fall against the cork of the broken raft. He groaned. "The poor man," Joe thought, "he just drifted away." Joe looked around and heard the Indians in the circle of canoes keep a pulsing, steady beat as they dug their oars in the snarling water. He felt worm trails of ice throughout his body. Just by the way the baseball batter turned his body before he connected, Joe knew he was going to get a third base zinger. Joe exploded toward the baseline to snag the ball. It felt as if a grenade had gone off in his mitt as his chest crashed into the bag. Every muscle in his body tensed as he waited for the runner yanking for third base to slide. The cleats dug into his shoulder blades and raked him down to his hips. No matter, the son-of-a-bitch was ow ... was ... ouch! In the cabin at the fire ringed with stones he sat alongside seven braves. The smoke went straight up to the black of the sky through a hole in the roof. Braves stood behind each of them. On some silent, secret signal the standing braves would lift the blankets from their shoulders to shift them over to the person to the right. If any of the others felt the skin stripping off their back as Joe did, there was no indication. They remained as statues, only the fire reflecting from their blank eyes. Joe bit his tongue as hard as he could to keep from murmuring or Jesus Christ All Fucking Mighty! muttering a single sound. When the blankets were returned to their starting points the standing braves set four posts in holes already dug just beyond the perimeter of the seated braves. The brave next to Joe dropped his blanket, and lay on his back on the stretcher all ready prepared. The bottom was almost all open. The stretcher was brought over the fire and held in place with leather thongs that ran over the tops of the poles. There were seven knots on each of the thongs. Water was poured into a leather bag under the brave's head. As a drop of water fell, a brave around the fire held up a hand. As the last brave held up his hand, the stretcher was lowered to the next knot on the four thongs. The count continued. The water dripped. The hands went up. The stretcher was lowered. At the fourth knot the brave uttered a cry, "Gaaaaa-Yaaaawwwwwww-Gaaaa!" until he was hoarse. Only then was he removed from the fire. He was placed by the shore. If he dared, he could crawl into the cool of the water and further embarrass himself and his people. An elder filled his place at the fire. The next brave took his place on the stretcher. The ritual was repeated. Two braves made it to the fifth knot. Then, it was Joe's turn.

Each elder had something to say to Joe.

... This is the night the white buffalo in the sky sheds a white tear and is sacrificed.

... This is the night the bear with the broken white line down its side sheds a red tear.

... This is the night the bear tracks follow the horizon.

... This is the night the twin stars appear in the heavens to the north.

... This is the night the five heavenly steady-stars line up.

... This is the night of the double crescent moon.

... This is the night we must propitiate the gods so you must not fail to reach the seventh knot. We will gag you if we must, and burn you to a cinder, but succeed you will, so says the silver fox.

Joe responded. "Tell Raynard I do not need a gag. I will reach the seventh knot. I will not fail. You will have your champion so your gods will be paid. Then, you and I will owe each other nothing, and the cabin shall be ours.

Joe succumbed. He could not remember hallucinating, nights closing in, the sun rising two times.

"Sir? Sir?" the woman's voice said. "How nice you are awake. You are aboard a hospital ship. You've been lapsing in and out of consciousness for quite a while. We're trying to help you fight a pretty bad infection. You were badly burned, that's why you're in this funny frame of a bed—so we can turn you front to back."

The frame. Yes. It is called a dream catcher, are you familiar with a dream catcher?

-

CHAPTER 30

MADDY

Maddy's instincts went into overdrive. She hated to be feminist and say it was woman's intuition, but something was just not right. Her father knocked on her bedroom door when she was just about to retire.

"Maddy, things have moved faster than I expected. We are leaving for Chicago tomorrow morning at seven. Pack what you need for a two days. At least it's the weekend, you won't miss school. Thank you. You know I really appreciate it. Good night."

"Good night, Dad."

It was all sixes and sevens, as they say, referring to the numbered outer rings on the dart board. Not good numbers. The ten in the center was better. It all seemed so secret and mysterious even though he had alerted her earlier. She didn't expect the trip to be so soon. Because it was late, she wasn't able to call Mrs. Kowalchuk, or any of her friends. Her dad had always been a caring, giving father. He rarely—if ever—asked for personal favors. She loved him, and was an obedient child. What was the big deal?

The big deal was the next big hint during breakfast about something askew was when Maddy said she would be glad to drive them to the airport. Not necessary, her father said, a cab would come for them. That had never happened before. Maddy shrugged it off and gave it no further thought. She had just started a book by her favorite author and she could indulge herself for two days.

The mystery deepened after they landed at Chicago's O'Hare Airport. They didn't go out to grab a cab to go to a hotel, they went to another airline where her father picked up two tickets on a flight to Los Angeles Airport.

"Dad? Why are we going to California?"

"This is not the time, Maddy. For now, do as I say, please, and the very first chance we are alone I will explain everything. Everything."

"Dad! I have a right to know! The tickets aren't even in our names! I want to know what is happening."

"For now, you will have to be satisfied with one thing. What we are doing right now is a matter of life and death. Do you understand what that means? We could be victims of murder?"

"Who? Why? Where are we going?"

"Port Hueneme," her father said to the cab driver.

"You bet," the driver said. "Beautiful country. A straight shot right up the highway. I'll get you there in a hurry. Enjoy the ride."

The cab stopped under the porte cochere of a charming, two-story Mexican-style hacienda painted in a pastel coral. A lanai the length of the building faced the ocean. The garage was on one end with a high stone wall guarding the vista on the other.

Mr. Malloy took keys from his pocket to open the double wide doors to allow Maddy and the cab driver to bring in the luggage.

When the cabbie left, Mr. Malloy told Maddy they would tend to the luggage after they returned. He handed her a set of car keys. "There is a station wagon is in the garage. Bring it around to the front. You and I are going to a wonderful restaurant that has an ocean view deck where we can be very much alone so we can talk. When I'm done, you can ask me questions about anything at all, and I will answer you to the best of my ability. Fair enough?"

"Can you tell me this for now? Are we ever going back to Catamount?"

CHAPTER 31

SAN DIEGO NAVAL HOSPITAL
Patient Review Board – Intensive Care Unit
Nurse Kitty Dufresne stood. Her uniform was impeccable. Shirt buttoned all the way up front, collar in tight points, long sleeves folded back at the wrist and buttoned. Not a crease anywhere—skirt or shirt—because she did not allow herself to sit. White stockings, white shoes. Hair pulled back tightly to a bun. Atop her head sat as charming a nurses cap as was ever made—pointed corners rolled to form loops like a queen's crown down to a solid black band. It would fit a doll. A lapel watch claimed her left upper breast area. Few got close enough to get a hint of her distinctive Heaven Scent perfume. I-AM-PRO-FESS-ION-AL! the image declared.

"As secretary of the Intensive Care Unit the following is a report for procedures this day.

"Early afternoon we will admit to the Intensive Care Unit a patient who was not wearing dog tags. It is believed they were torn off of him when either he or someone else tried to tear off his clothing that was on fire. He was picked up wearing only the sleeves and a portion of his shirt and Mae West. He is known only as 'Jay.' In action on a destroyer off of Okinawa, the ship took a direct hit and was sunk by a Kamikaze. Wounds suffered by Jay were burns over sixty-per cent of his body from flaming aviation gasoline. He was rescued after six days barely hanging on to bits of a raft. 'Jay and jayviener' seemed to be the only words he uttered.

"A destroyer on the second perimeter found him and picked him up. He was hydrated, was left in what clothing had not been burned off. The report said he suffered burns from the nape of his neck to his buttocks when flaming gasoline poured in between him and his Mae West. The back of his shirt was burned off, the front was ripped off leaving the sleeves in place. His fingertips on both hands and a portion of the palms were burned. He was totally covered in thick oil, which was left in place after it was determined to be the best protocol not to cause further injury or infection, except his face was marginally cleaned. He was wrapped in sterilized sheets, and transferred to an aircraft carrier. He was flown to Tinian Island, from there to Hawaii, and has landed at San Diego Airport.

"He will be admitted here within the hour. Standard Intensive Care Service protocol will be initiated when the patient arrives. All patients in the ICU will have an admission biophysical assessment initiated within five minutes of admission and completed within one hour and daily progress notes from both ICU registrar and primary nurse. A baseline assessment is to be completed on each physiologic system at the beginning of each shift.

"To identify patient acuity requiring continuous non-interrupted nursing care and an assignment of ratio of one nurse to one patient. In this case, however, it has been determined that a two-to-one nursing assignment is made when a patient's nursing care needs require continuous nursing assessment resulting in ongoing documentation, monitoring intervention, procedures, therapies and evaluation.

"Need I say this case is heroic in the extreme. We may have to call the shots as they come to us. For example, the oil—a 50-50 call against causing or retarding infection—is acting as a barrier much as the skin is doing to prevent infection, which is our primary goal.

"The patient is young, robust. Personal assessment is after suffering the trauma of having the skin on his back burned off, being covered totally in oil, spending six days in the open sea surrounded by sharks, this man's heart is thumping like a base drum and even though I would give anyone else little or no chance of surviving, this sailor has a fighting chance to survive based strictly on his determination to live. Let's do what we can for him."

The first decision was that he would be put in reverse isolation known as an isolator, which was using a sterilized plastic tent with filtered air circulation. Nothing and nobody entered the tent that was not totally aseptic.

Jay's condition was charted on an hour-by-hour graph. There was no difficulty putting in a venous access port through which he received transfusions, antibiotics, protein, pain relievers, and medication to put him into an induced sedation. With two nurses tending his every need around the clock his body was meticulously cleaned until every bit of oil that was not on burned skin was removed.

Two doctors twice a day would examine Jay's back. A sterile cloth with a hole in it would be placed over an area where debridement was to take place. It was removal of the black and crusty burned skin until the healthy area was exposed. The major concerns were infection, keeping him hydrated, and sending Jay into shock. It was a slow, tedious procedure where the nurses were quick to relieve one another. Most of the time they had to be careful their emotions did not betray them.

Squares or rectangles of grafted or artificial skin would be placed over the cleaned areas. For a while, it was almost a game of one step forward, two steps back. Some grafts took easily. Some remained in place and seemed healthy then suddenly sloughed off. But, gradually, slowly, slowly the patient began to heal more and more. An outline of his back was hung inside the tent. The successful areas were painted green. The progress was gruesomely slow.

From the beginning, Jay was kept in a chemically induced sedated state. At times he would mumble unintelligible words. But, always for every nurses' shift, every nurse devoted a portion of her time after she went off the clock to read to him no matter what time of day or night.

The report to the Patient Review Board indicated a sense of positiveness in the patient's progress. None was more loudly received than the approbation when it was reported that the nurse to patient care was being reduced from four to two. By that time, sixty-per cent of the chart of his back was green. He would remain sedated as long as there was debridement—chemical or surgical—to be performed.

Although there were indications the patient had swallowed some amount of oil and sea water, bronchoscopies showed no signs of oil anywhere in the respiratory system.

The Patient Review Board indicated the fact that the patient was still alive after a month as something almost miraculous. With each additional report, a sense of pride in the hospital staff seemed to manifest itself in their posture and positiveness. Now, seventeen months later with the chart of the patient's back totally green for more than two months and about to be removed from his aseptic tent, everyone agreed it truly was a miracle.

As the routine settled in as usual and ordinary, everyone found the sailor, Jay, to be a genuine, likeable, personable young man. Even small victories were broadcast throughout the hospital like Progresso Soup Cans: He fed himself! Then, not surprisingly the rumor spread Jay was up for a medal. Jay heard of it from Louis, a male nurse, he got along with very nicely.

"Yeah. I think it's true, Jay," Louis said. "A Captain or Rear Admiral or something, will come here to honor you with a medal."

"What for? For surviving?"

"No. The story I got was that when you were found by that ship, you were talking a lot about the shipmate you were with that you tried to save. Did you do that?"

"Yes. I do remember. I threw him off the side of the ship and I followed. We hung around together for quite a bit and then I think I lost it. I was hurting a lot and kept thinking about the sharks all around ... Did they say if they found the other fellow?"

"They said it was a shot in a million that they happened to spot you. Anyway, they recorded your story, and it followed you here. Now, don't get me wrong, I'm not trying to take anything away from you, but you know? We need such things, medals and decorations, and heroes and such. As far as I'm concerned? Couldn't have happened to a nicer guy."

At a Board meeting while Jay was put back under sedation, Kitty reported a possible identification of the patient was made. From the ship's roster, which was sent to the Bureau of Naval Personnel by every ship before it left port to go on duty, it was determined one name that matched the name he repeated when he was first rescued and here while recuperating was Lieutenant Jay Edward Wienstein. There was a Lieutenant Jay Edward Wienstein serving aboard the destroyer. The Board cheered at the accomplishment.

The nurse coughed nervously. There was a problem. She turned professional and blurted out, "We are not sure that is correct, although it's the best we have at the moment based on haphazard information. The problem? Yes. The patient we call "Jay" may be Lt. Jay Edward Wienstein except ... he's not circumcised. She could not help it. She slipped into a chair.

The Captain and his entourage of officers crowded into the hospital room. Jay was standing as he preferred to keep any pressure off of his back. He was held up by a metal jungle gym with main braces under his arms, yet left them free to move them freely.

The four-striper carefully reached down for Jay's right hand to gingerly hold it as a passable hand shake. "It is my privilege and honor to know you, sir!" the officer said. He made sure everyone that could be squeezed into the room was there to watch his performance.

"In keeping with the highest of naval traditions ..." he started, "... in keeping with the honor of the Navy Cross, on behalf of the the President of the United States, Congress, the Secretary of the Navy, I wish to present to you, Lt. Jay Edward Wienstein ..."

Jay drew himself up and said, "I'm grateful for the thought, but I'm not Lt. Wienstein ..."

"What did you say?" the captain asked.

"Joe, that's what they call me. Joe Caruso, that's my name, Joseph Enzo Caruso. Lt. Wienstein was the fellow with me in the water."

CHAPTER 32

"Uncle Mo-Mo, this is your nephew, Joe, Joe Caruso ..."

"Joey! God Bless you! We got the report you were missing in action! God Bless! you are alive! How wonderful! Your Aunt Stella said she would make a novena and bring you home! Joey, we are so happy!"

"Uncle Mo-Mo, when I couldn't reach my father or mother, I called Captain Tony at the police station. He said I should talk to you before anybody else. What is it, Uncle? Where is Mom and Pop?"

"Joey! *Mi dispiace*, I'm very sorry, I would like to be sitting with you to give you this news. Your mother and father have passed away. Right after they got the news that you were missing in action your father lost his job. Something went wrong with union funds and pension and health funds were gone. After losing your brother, and then you, they had nothing left... ."

"Zio! What do you mean, 'losing my brother?'"

"Ah! *Caronia*! Guiseppe! *Tu non sa ... Dio mio!* You don't know Sal was reported missing in action. We still have no word ..."

"No. I heard nothing. I didn't know. The chief tells me Maddy has disappeared with her father?"

"Yes. Yes. I am so sorry. Our hearts go out to you and your parents. I don't like to tell you, but they died of broken hearts. I was named Administrator of the Estate. I arranged their funerals and the headstones. I sold the house and the car and all the furnishings. It has not all gone through Probate Court so I'm holding all the money in trust at the bank. When you come home I will turn everything over to you."

"Uncle Mo-Mo, I'm sorry to interrupt you but where is Maddy Malloy? I must know where she is. Do you know?"

"Who? Maddy Malloy? I don't know ... Wait! Aunt Stella says it's the mill owner's daughter. He left town and must have taken his daughter will him. No one knows where they went."

"Uncle, listen, you've got to find out where she is! Somebody must know where they are. Ask around. Ask everyone."

"Joey, *senti,* listen to me. Aunt Stella and I would do anything for you. We will start making calls to find out about Maddy. I promise."

"Uncle Mo-Mo, I want to thank you and Aunt Stella for taking care of everything. I should be released from the hospital in a very short time. I'll see you then. Uncle Mo-Mo, tell me, did you sell everything?"

"Everything? What do you mean 'everything,' Joey?"

"I bought a piece of property by the lake. I wasn't old enough to own it, so Pop put it in his name for me. Did you sell the land by the lake?"

CHAPTER 33

MADDY'S father spoke quietly to the maitre d'hote and slipped him a bill.

They were led to a secluded table in the far corner of the multi-chandeliered restaurant. There were no other tables nearby. The tables were covered with starched cloths and held glasses with ornately folded huge white napkins stuck in them. A harp and two violins playing quietly heightened the austere atmosphere of the room.

Mr. Malloy ordered a double V.S.O.P. cognac for himself and a cranberry cocktail for Maddy. He touched the silverware and nudged his water glass until the drinks arrived. He raised his drink. "To our new lives."

Maddy smoothed the napkin on her lap. She drank to his toast.

"Maddy, I am about to explain everything. You may interrupt me at any time you wish. Ask me anything and everything you wish. When we leave here I never want to speak about any of this ever again."

"Are we going back to Catamount?"

"Neither one of us can. Ever. I said it was a matter of life and death, and it is. There is no question my life would be in danger. I can't swear, but I believe they will try to get to me through you. We must remain incognito.

"My name now is George Johnson. You are Martha Johnson, my daughter. The Malloy's do not exist and must never be found.

"I tried to do things differently. You know what happened to your mother when we lost Peter, Gerard, and Paul. I am no different than your mother but not as strong-willed as she. All the rest of my days will be tortured. I will say I'm sorry to you once. After I'm gone, you will be free to do as you please. I do not want to be murdered or beaten to death, nor do I wish to see you harmed.

"I was warned by the union leaders that if I tried to close the mill I would be set upon and so would my family. I know they were sincere. I felt our lives were in danger if I did what I knew I was compelled to do. I had to close the mill. I wanted nothing more to do with it. I could find no buyer. It was the reason as you may have noticed I was so preoccupied day and night. As a result I made arrangements, all as secretly and surreptitiously as I could.

"At ten o'clock tomorrow morning the announcement will be made that the mill is closing and everyone is out of a job. All 267 employees are to take their personal belongings, pick up their final paychecks, and vacate the property by noontime, when the mill will be closed, the gates locked.

"If that is not enough to get them angry, they certainly will be when they learn their retirement and health benefits are lost as well. I was informed well over a year ago by a close union official who told me the officers including the chief accountant were cooking the books. If they knew I was closing the mill they would have left the country. This way there is a chance they may be caught. Maybe not.

"I know as well as anyone the mill closing will devastate Catamount. It will become a ghost town because there is no large industry within a 50-mile radius. That burden alone had become too much for me. Losing our boys and your mother left me a shell.

"Our home and all its furnishing, and the automobile are sold as of this morning. A "SOLD" sign will be put up in front as an effort to prevent anyone from setting fire to the place. Charge accounts have been established at several area stores so you may charge whatever you wish for clothing, personal items, and so on. Sorry if you have to live without some of your favorites.

"I regret to say I expect you to be by my side as the loyal daughter that you are. No, you will not be able to complete high school. We must keep as low a profile as we are able."

"Dad, I would like to visit the graves should they ever be recovered ..."

"I know. I would, too. I thought of it. I left a large enough sum of money with the florists on Main Street for them to bring flowers to the graves every year for at least the next ten years ... should they stay in business that long, which I doubt."

"Dad, I'm married. I married Joseph Caruso before he left for the service."

"I got news of that, even though I said nothing about it."

"Do you know he was reported as missing in action?"

"Oh! God forbid! Not another! I'm so sorry."

"For whatever you may have thought about Joe, he would not consummate the marriage because I wasn't over 18."

"More will power than I ever had. How definite is the missing in action?"

"I got the news from a dear friend who allowed me to use her address. That's where the telegram went."

"I know. Mrs. Kowalchuk. You cannot let her know where you are. If I knew about her, others will, too. Sorry. I do not expect I shall live much longer. I bought a station wagon because it's the easiest way to carry a wheelchair. It won't be much longer before I will need it. My arthritis has filled my lower back. When I go, you will never have to worry about being financially independent. You will be more than well-off. Maddy?"

She looked up to catch him full in the eyes.

"Dad, in your world, you have set things as nicely as you were able. I'm sorry about the mill. Unfortunately, I am a victim of your machinations. I am forced to do what you say. For me, I would tell you to keep all your money. For all of it I'd rather visit my mother's and brothers' graves. Joe is reported missing in action, but I know he's alive. When he comes home looking for me, exactly where will he find me?"

"I've taken care of all such emergencies. I have dealt with an attorney in Springfield. He's only fifty miles from Catamount. He will keep his finger on the pulse of Catamount and will be in touch with an attorney in

Chicago, who knows how to get in touch with me. That is the very best I could do for you. I warn you not to circumvent my plans if you value my life."

Exactly how to do that filled Maddy's thoughts hours on end. She knew her connection to Mrs. Kowalchuk was known in the town. Any form of communication with her would be hazardous. Not one of her classmates was isolated from the closing of the mill. It was a close-knit community and a whisper ran throughout the town like Taps atop Monument Mountain. She would have to come up with a plan.

In the meantime, hours ran into weeks, into months, into almost three years. They settled into a routine very quickly. Every morning Maddy would serve breakfast on the patio. Then, Maddy would drive Mr. Malloy, now Mr. Johnson, to one of the beaches. He would sit on a bench and read the paper completely, and then stare at the moving sea. Within a short time, just over a month, he took to the wheelchair. When he was ready for lunch, Maddy would drive him home and serve him lunch on the patio. He then would nap for several hours.

It was during this time Maddy had her own time. Several days were spent shopping for food and necessaries for the house. Then, becoming more proficient in her chores, she was able to use a good part of the afternoon in pursuing her own interests. Two afternoons she spent taking flute lessons. Two afternoon were involving with the Art League where she took lessons in pen and ink and watercolors. When she was able she went to a class in journaling. She always kept a notebook with her. It was always in her book bag when she took her dad to the beach along with a novel and bottled water for them both.

Although he frowned upon it—for fear of her being noticed—Maddy went to church on Sundays. She knew she had to have some place to send her prayers for Joe to someone who would listen to her plea. And she prayed for the repose of the souls of her mother and brothers, of course.

Living was life, and life had become a dull, boring routine, especially because she did not have one close friend to whom she could vent.

CHAPTER 34

AFTER two years Joe's progress continued to astound the hospital personnel. He had a round of doctors visit him every morning, even those with specialties in gynecology, pediatrics, oncology, psychiatry and such all barely related to his superhuman achievement. He became what was known as the "poster boy" of the hospital. That soon became 'the darling boy' as nurse after nurse found reason to go into his room to pat his bed smooth, fill his water glass, check the temperature, and even go so far as to check his pulse.

Debridement was a long gone activity replaced with special oils, lotions, massages, and physical therapy to reduce the tightening and pulling of all the scar tissue. His hands would receive soft tissue massage for hours at a time, until they because supple and easy for Joe to move and grasp objects.

Joe was kept in a private room where he enjoyed gourmet meals especially prepared by the chefs who visited him in his room to get his order. The women took off their aprons and toques with coiffures and make up befitting the cover of Gormet Magazine.

There were many luxuries for Joe. The hospital director pretty much knew about all of them and gave silent approval. Except for one treat for Joe that was super-special even he didn't know who was involved.

He remembered vaguely dreaming one night of caressing Maddy. In the morning he was embarrassed when a male nurse was called in to clean him up.

Then, in the early hours after midnight Joe would slowly awaken to find the restraining belts on the bed were secured around him. At first, he was mystified. He had not been informed of any procedures. He knew it was a woman, a nurse that was in the room with him. He started to say something when a hand covered his mouth very gently.

"Shhhhhh!" he heard.

He found himself gently massaged. His eyes snapped open. He never ever had been treated in such a manner before.

In less than three minutes it was all over. A pillow was placed over his face and the restraints removed. He heard a chair slide away from blocking the door. It opened, the person left.

The following evening he awoke to find just the pillow over his face. He didn't remove it until he heard the door click closed.

The early morning activity went on every now and then for the succeeding three months when he was discharged. Try as he might in the darkness he could not discern the visitor.

The morning of his discharge from the hospital, Joe was feted in the surgical theatre.

When he walked in wearing The Naval Cross and Silver Star on his uniform he was greeted with a standing ovation. Tissues came out all over the place to dry tears of joy.

The applause went on for almost a full five minutes as Joe held up his hand and called out, "Thank you! Thank you! Thank you!"

Finally he voice rose over the clapping and he said, "You want to keep me here because it's raining out, right?"

The director of the hospital and at least seven other doctors spoke on the overwhelming achievement of the human spirit and medical ingenuity. Joe was a testimonial to what could be called a terrestrial save. His case would be discussed and written about for use in treating other burn victims.

Joe spoke from his heart. He outlined how he found himself from his first cognizant moment to his now discharge. Applause rang out as he ticked off the specialists one by one who had devoted their entire selves to healing him.

Finally, he said he had one more person to thank. He asked Nurse Kitty Dufresne to come by his side. "The Intensive Care Unit saved my life. Nurse Kitty Dufresne is the Intensive Care Unit." The theatre exploded in applause, cat-calls, and whistles.

"Nurse Kitty Dufresne, you have gone far beyond the extreme in the call of duty. I owe you more than I can repay."

With that, Joe moved quickly to embrace Kitty. He held her tightly and kissed her wet and wildly. The audience at first gasped at the prim miss being manhandled, then cheered. Just before he released her, Joe whispered in her ear, "I'll never forget you. Thank you for being my night hawk."

As she stood by his side primping, she turned so only he would hear, and said, "T'was not I."

He grinned from ear to ear. "T'was then your perfume?"

CHAPTER 35

MADDY knocked on her father's bedroom door. When he replied she entered to find him in his wheelchair waiting. They chatted amicably as she wheeled him out to the lanai to the breakfast table.

"I have a surprise for you, Dad."

"Like I have no newspaper?"

"Here it comes now. Dad meet Oliver."

Oliver came through the doorway wearing a huge, toothy grin. He looked big enough to be a football quarterback. He carried the newspaper, which he placed in front of Maddy's father. "It will be my privilege and pleasure to serve you, Mr. Johnson," he said.

"Thank you," Maddy's father said as he took the paper and stared at Maddy.

"Oliver is working for you from now on, Dad. He is replacing me. There isn't anything I'm doing for you that he can't do better. Just toast and coffee for me this morning, Oliver. Mr. Johnson always has orange juice, and coffee. He will tell you what he would like, whether its eggs or cereal. I explained his routine. As I told you, Oliver, I'll call you every day for the first week or so to see how you're doing. I know you'll take good care of my dad."

"Yes, Maddy. I certainly will." Oliver left.

"What's going on?" her father asked.

"I told you, Dad, Oliver can do everything I've been doing and better. He can lift you in and out of the bathtub, if need be. You told me how it was going to be when you first brought me out here. After two-years and seven months, I am reclaiming my life. I love you dearly, but I would be sacrificing my life for nothing. You are worried for your own actions. I just need to live. You owe me for diverting my life. That will have to rest on your conscience. I never finished high school. I want to be free to attend college. I want to be able to visit the graves of my mother and brothers."

"How will you get travel money to get back home?"

"Father, if I had to, I would walk barefoot on sharpsided airport gravel to get to Catamount."

"You're going back to Catamount?"

"Yes. I have unfinished business there."

"They won't trace you back to me?"

"You're my father. Sorry you had to bring that up. I would never betray you. I'll take my chances with Catamount and any hate I find there for me. The town may not even exist anymore, Father. I have managed to sell some paintings and I sold my flute for my tickets. There's nothing you can give me except more hard times. Uncle Mo-Mo, your brother, clued me in. He is such a soft, lovely, and loving man, your opposite. He sat me down and told me the Italian aphorism. When one has a son, he carries on the family name. When one has a daughter, one forms a cane for their old age. I'm not being ungrateful, Dad; I just don't want to be a cane when someone else can do as well. I want my own life back. For taking these almost three years, I believe I am certainly entitled to it."

He looked into her eyes and held her stare. The coldness in them was replaced with hot ice. After a bit, he nodded imperceptibly. His eyes clouded over as the moments passed. He blinked several times. He waved his fingers. "No sense you hanging around." He turned from Maddy to stare out at the sea watching a kaleidoscope of waves, wind, and water.

Maddy got up. She suggested he get a doggie. Something should miss him when he was gone.

CHAPTER 36

BOATSWAIN'S Mate Second Class Joseph Caruso, USNR, was in uniform wearing two rows of decorations starting with the Navy Cross, the Silver Star, the Purple Heart, the Combat Action Ribbon, Pacific Theatre of War, and the American-European Theatre of War. He trotted up the incline carrying a leather suitcase up to the airport plaza. As he neared the top he saw Uncle Mo-Mo and Aunt Stella waving and shouting to him.

Stella was the first to grab him. She hugged him, squeezed him, tears rolling down her face as she called out, "Joey! My Joey! Joey! You're here!"

Mo-Mo got in on it grabbing Joe's face with two hands and kissing him full on the mouth, then on the cheeks, and trying the near impossible chore of hugging both Joe and Stella. Mo-Mo finally got a chance to get in a grab him around the waist and lifted him off the floor. "Joey! Joey! Benedire! Bendire! You're home safe and sound!"

The three of them drew some attention, but not as much as when a group of servicemen were passing by. The leader, a lieutenant junior grade with six enlisted men held out his hand and stopped the group. He caught Joe's eye. He pointed to the double row of ribbons. He pointed to them, pulled back. "'Ten-Hut!" he shouted. The group stood at attention, the crew joining him to salute Joe.

The officer pointed to the top row of ribbons. "I recognize the Navy Cross, and the Silver Star, Sir. May I shake your hand?"

"Thank you, sir," Joe answered.

"May I ask your name?"

"Boatswain's Mate Second Class Joseph Caruso, sir."

"It's a privilege and an honor to have met you, sir," the officer said as he shook Joe's hand. The others followed. "Godspeed, sir," the lieutenant said. Then they all departed.

"Joey! We didn't know! You're a hero! You have done honor to your family! We are so proud."

It was easy to see by this time Joe had become a little embarrassed with the heavy emotional display.

"Look!" Joey said, "I see a bar just off the walkway. We need to sit someplace so we can talk a bit. There is so much I need to know ..."

The waitress came over to take their order. Joe asked Stella, "What would you like?"

"What else?" Stella said, "Jack on the rocks!"

"Make it doubles all around," Joe said. His very next sentence was, "Mo-Mo tell me about Maddy Malloy. Anything at all on where she is?"

"Disappeared like grappa at a picnic. No word at all from or by anyone. Not even a hint. Gone. Just gone," Mo-Mo said.

"Somebody's got to know," Joe said. "What about the deed to the land on the lake."

Mo-Mo shrugged. "Joey, what can I tell you? I don't know. Your Aunt Stella and I went through every single piece of paper in the house. Your folks had a safe deposit box. Your father kept the key in a locked box under the floorboard in the closet that went up to the second floor. It was there, but nothing in the safe deposit box. I checked everywhere. Your Aunt Stella was with me. It is a mystery."

"That concerns me also," Joe said. "I first will try to locate Maddy. We were married when I left for the service ..."

The news brought another eruption of exclamations, wonderments, and cheers.

"Who knew? Who knew? We would have thrown a wedding for you! Why didn't you let us know?" Stella exclaimed and ordered another double round of Jacks.

"We were married in secret when we were on a field trip in Washington, D.C." Joe said.

"Mamma mia! How romantic! You're going to make me cry! So now where is your bride?" Aunt Stella said.

"You have to wait to hear about what happened at the mill!" Uncle Mo-Mo said.

"On the way home, Uncle, or we're going to have to find a hotel room for Aunt Stella!"

In essence, the mill was bought by a Canadian Company re-employing almost all the employees that had lost their jobs. Federal Investigators and insurance company executives were still trying to untangle the funds and health benefits that were covered by the federal law that spoke of underwriting.

Joe got to his father's attorney's office just as he was going out for lunch.

Joe offered to spring. The attorney wouldn't hear of it.

CHAPTER 37

JOE watched Attorney MacCormack use a wooden match to char the end of a large, hand rolled double wrapped cigar. He waved the flame out and lit another match to puff a glow as round as a nickel to the end of it. Smoke streamed from his mouth Joe catching the pungent, delicious aroma of expensive tobacco.

"I have to repeat, Joe, we're all so damn proud of you and delighted you are home safe. We all had some rough moments there. Congratulations on being a highly decorated war hero, I would be honored to do anything for you that I can. So, I am going to try to anticipate all your questions, but, of course, I'll try to answer any you may have."

He swiveled around to pick up a folder, which he opened on the desk. "Mr. Malloy and daughter, Maddy, were taken to the airport about three years ago, and have not been seen or heard of since. Mr. Malloy left with a serious cloud over his head. Financial difficulties with the mills raised all sorts of legal specters. You may have heard?"

"Yes, my uncle and aunt filled me in. I'm glad the mill is still running," Joe said.

"Catamount would have become a ghost town. We're all glad it was bought and still running. To get back to Maddy and Mr. Malloy. The IRS is still searching for him, which should answer any hope of you hiring private detectives to do the job. I do not know of any other means or methods of tracking down Maddy. There's no doubt if anyone hears anything of her, you would be the next to know."

Joe sat quietly. "I was very sad to learn Mrs. Kowalchuk passed. You said you were her attorney."

The attorney reached for another file folder. "Her Estate should be coming out of Probate Court very shortly. Of most interest to you will be that Mrs. Kowalchuk left her entire Estate to you: land, buildings thereon, contents, vehicles, clothing, jewelry. That will make you a very rich man, Joe. I have the contents of her safe at home in a security vault at the bank. In it, of special interest to you, we found yours and Maddy's marriage certificate, the telegram reporting you as missing in action, and documents sent to Maddy for claiming your National Service Life Insurance. You know the reason Maddy never filed for it."

"I wasn't aware you didn't ask for it, but if she didn't I know the reason. She didn't believe I wouldn't come back."

"I'm one tough bird, Joe, but that's enough to make me weep. You're right, of course. I don't think Maddy had time to think about leaving. Mrs. Kowalchuk was especially shocked Maddy didn't contact her."

Joe sat quietly. He touched the front of the desk. "I'm taken aback by Mrs. Kowalchuk's generosity. I liked her very much. We had become very good friends. She sold me a piece of land by the lake ..."

"Yes, I know," the attorney interrupted. "I'm not sure if you understand that now all the land around the lake is owned by you and Maddy ..."

"Oh! My God!" Joe said. He gripped the arms of his chair. "I'd swap it all for the piece of land she sold me."

"So I understand," the attorney said. "There would be no need. We understand how important to you was the deed to that property. Your uncle made that known when he finally brought it to the attention of your father's lawyer, who is a partner in this firm. You will find your father had the property transferred to you at the Register of Deeds and left the deed in the care of my partner. In effect, you and Maddy own every bit of land around Lake Eagle Talon."

"Oh! That's such great news! Mr. MacCormack! So great I could kiss you!"

"I hardly think that's necessary, but there is one more Estate you should know about."

"There is? Who's?"

"Sven Johnson."

"What happened to Sven? Sven was my dearest friend."

"He was reported missing in action from the Bataan Death March. Let us pray he in fact has survived. In the meantime, he legally left you everything he owns, but now that he'll be coming back, you'll just have to remain good friends."

"My Lord!" Joe got lost in his own thoughts. "Sven had a girl friend. He hadn't seen her for a while when I joined up. He said one day they would marry. Did they?"

"Since he's come back? Yes! They have a little daughter."

"And she does not share in his Estate?"

"As far as our records go, no. Nothing."

"Give me a second," Joe said. It took several minutes for him to sift his thoughts, and get them in order. "Mr. MacCormack, this is what I would like, and it must remain confidential between us. I do not want Sven's girlfriend to know he didn't think of her specifically. Estimate what Sven's Estate is worth. Then, use whatever cash is available from my parents' Estate, Mrs. Kowalchuk's, and Sven's to quote unquote buy Sven's property. His girlfriend and daughter should receive that money as if it was left to her. Can that be done for her when his will is settled?"

"That's extremely generous of you, Joe. Are you sure you would not like to sleep on it for a bit before it's finalized?"

"No. It's fine, Mr. MacCormack. If Sven had the time or thought of it, it is what he would have done. He was such a special friend, it is the least I can do. Make it look as if it was his intention from the start. Then again, if he's MIA, as I was and a few others who made it home, we can wait a while. We can wait a long damned while for Sven to show up. That's exactly what we should do. Let's hold everything in abeyance for a period of time in case Sven does make it home. Let's make that happen."

"Joe, we get some pretty nasty people and cases run through this office. I've been in practice for just over 35 years. One gets rather jaundiced by humanity when one learns what people are capable of doing. In all that time I have never had the privilege and honor to have anyone as decent and special as you come to me. I want you to call on me at any time for any reason for anything I am able to do for you, and I will not charge you for anything."

Joe told Attorney MacCormack he may wish to sleep on that statement because by the plans he came up with while sitting in his office there would be a lot of business for land titles and transfers because Joe intended to go into the home construction business. He planned to for a corporation with members and owners of the Spirits Cabin of Lake Eagle Talon and build them in all prices around the lake.

CHAPTER 38

MADDY crossed her arms in front of her and allowed the lapping waters to splash her toes that were dug into the sand. Her head bowed, she was pensive as she watched the spent sun's rays paint the surface and disappear into the lake. She was ecstatic at the thought of her reinvigorated world. She had the same feeling she got after she lost her favorite gold pussycat pin then discovered it way in the corner of her clothes closet. She had the same giddy feeling she got playing spin the bottle at her sixth birthday party and that near brain-dead kid she liked got up to kiss her. He barely brushed her cheek when she straightened him out by grabbing him and planting a long, hard one on his lips. What she sensed mostly was serenity, which enveloped her like the fragrance of a splash of heady perfume. The tranquility came of knowing she was empowered with control of her world. She had enough time to prepare for this moment. As a water person, there were endless hours the Pacific Ocean hummed its ending, neverending rolling and roiling tune by the shore, the waves coming in regularly at 26 to the minute. It infused her with the understanding of the need for such repose. At first it seemed much, much too long as the moments, the minutes, the hours, the days, the weeks, the years passed through her skin. The mantra she heard was patience, patience, patience. There will come with good reason a season to emerge from the chrysalis as her own woman with a magic path that shone beyond the pale. Holding her finger as a placemark in the book a wisp of hair tugged her into awareness that the time had come.

Within the day, the deed was done. Catamount and who knew what else awaited.

CHAPTER 39

Out of the lake stepped Joe. He wiped his face with both hands and pushed his hair back. The loin cloth dripped wet as he padded to the flat stone at the head of the fire pit with the blazing fire, and sat cross-legged.

Next was Sal. He flicked his arms as he raised them high and took his place beside Joe.

Richard took hard, splashing steps as he marched out of the water, and continued them until he got to his place next to Sal.

Paul shook himself like a hound and waited until he got to his place before shaking the water from his hair, sprinkling Joe, Sal, and Richard.

Peter burst from the water raising a geyser and whooped as he jumped and hopped to his place next to Paul.

Sven pulled water up to his chest with his last steps in the lake and strode purposefully to his place next to Peter.

Gerard did a backward flip emerging from the water and clapped all the way to his stone.

Brad ran out of the water with his hands cupped carrying water which he dropped on Joe's head just before he sat down.

TRANSLATION FROM THE MAHAGAWANY LANGUAGE:
JOE: I am proud to sit with you at council fire, my brothers.
BRAVES: As we are with you.
JOE: Our deeds have brought us here, each and every one. We have been true to our spirit guardians. When our enemies shut their eyes, in that blink we escaped.
BRAVES: Yes.

JOE: We will not be enlarged by what we have done.
BRAVES: No.
JOE: We all know the reason. We have left there the best of our brothers who deserve to be here by the fire more than us.
ALL: So say the spirits of Lake Eagle Talon.

CHAPTER 40

Joe felt always the thumping tom-tom of his heart. In deep and dark mysterious places where none else resided was always the perceptible echo of the calling sound. He was not to hear the abysmal beats of the lost and lonely. It was amazing, simply amazing that freezing nor frigid nor frozen sounds dulled the overtones of the true harmonic. As steady and reliable as the drip and tick of a metronome it was a steel-clad tether to the next drip and tick. It was the pull that drew him steadily through the black porridge of death until he slid on silk through to the jets to the neros, to the grays, to the goldens, to the yellows, to the white. Not for an abysmally imperceptible instance did he doubt his faith. The reason was rock solid. Because she never did either.

Maddy turned to look at him seated on the porch, his bare feet on the steps. She looked him right in the eyes because he was staring at her. She bent down to touch Mr. Raynard's wet nose.

Joe reached over to pet back the lynx's ears.

Joe moved down outside the fire circle with a fire nicely waving from the center.

Joe and Maddy met by McEvily's side. He was drinking a beer and moving a bit from side to side to an unheard beat. McEvily laughed and put his hand on Joe's shoulder as Maddy crowded against him putting her face in the hollow of his chest.

Peter Malloy saw them coming and put down his beer. He reached over to wrap his arms around his sister and then extended his hand to grab Joe's. Peter kissed her on the cheek and nodded in agreement about some wonderful philosophical point Joe made.

Sven saw them coming and hunched down to make a sorry attempt at a Russian dance finally falling on his back. The three of them laughed as Joe grabbed his hand and helped him up. Sven put one hand behind Maddy's and one behind Joe's and pulled them together until his forehead touched them both. He commented about the three of them making one good one, which caused them to burst out into laughter.

Paul Malloy got up and stood before them his hands on his hips. He pretended to be stern about the fact that if he knew where Maddy was going when she sneaked out of the house things may have turned out differently! Maddy grabbed his face with both of her hands and kissed him soundly.

Joe knew how shy and bashful Clarence would be when he introduced Maddy. He got up from his seat around the fire, brushed his hands against his trousers, and kept his face downwards. She reached over, gently raised his face until she could look into his eyes and catch his twinkle. She said something about him being the very best Japanese squirrel barker in the world, they broke out into laughter.

Jay got up immediately and with no hesitation put his arms around Maddy. As he held her against him, he reached out for Joe. They put their arms around each other as Joe told Maddy that Joe was so proud of being Jewish he wore cuff links that said: JEW. When Jay explained their laughter rolled out over the water.

Waiting for them to get to him, Salvatore was standing, a huge smile on his face. He kissed Maddy on both cheeks and hugged her tightly. He grabbed Joe and gave him a warm squeeze, rapping his back hard. He said something about Joe being the smartest one in the crowd by grabbing the prettiest girl in town. She kissed him on both cheeks. Joe kissed his cheek and squeezed back as hard as he could.

Maddy turned to find herself lifted off the ground and whirled in a circle as Gerard gave her a loud kiss on her cheek. "I love you, Sunshine!"

"I love you, too!"

Joe and Maddy let the smoke from the fire warm their hands as they passed the seated braves, women, and children wrapped in their colorful blankets.

They held hands before their stone and looked out over the gathering around the fire pit. Maddy looked up at Joe. He kissed her forehead.

They were home where they were supposed to be.

THE END

PAUL ARGENTINI is a Random House bestselling author and prize-winning playwright. He and lives in Florida. He has two grown daughters, Lisa and Mona.

www.ingramcontent.com/pod-product-compliance
Lightning Source LLC
Chambersburg PA
CBHW051816020726
47502CB00005B/1485